Arlen & Nancy Jenkins
208 Tharp Drive
Moraga, CA 94556

THE Alphabet Year

THE Alphabet Year

Kathryn H. Kidd

HATRACK RIVER
PUBLICATIONS

Cover art by Paul Mann
Cover and title design by James Fedor
This book was set in 16-point "Goudy," "Tekton," "ITC Zapf Chancery Medium Italic" and "ITC Avant Garde Gothic Book" from Adobe, using WordPerfect 5.1 and a Hewlett-Packard LaserJet III printer with a Hewlett-Packard Postscript cartridge. It was then reduced and printed as approximately 12-point type on pH-neutral paper.
Printed by Publisher's Press, Salt Lake City UT
Sole distributor of books from Hatrack River Publications is:
Publishers Wholesale
805 West 1700 South
Salt Lake City UT 84104

Printed in the United States of America

First printing August 1991
10 9 8 7 6 5 4 3 2 1

Library of Congress Catalog Card Number: 91-73625

ISBN 0-9624049-3-4

to Marla Jensen,
Annette Wheeler, and
Janece Ford —
who understood
this book
before I wrote it

Other Books by Kathryn H. Kidd

Paradise Vue
The Innkeeper's Daughter
(Young Disciples series)

Other Books from Hatrack River

Gert Fram, by Nancy Allen Black
You're a Rock, Sister Lewis,
by Susan Dean Smallwood

Forthcoming Books from Hatrack River

Rachel at the River (Young Disciples),
by Kathryn H. Kidd
Rachel at the Wedding (Young Disciples),
by Kathryn H. Kidd
Paradise Too, by Kathryn H. Kidd
Spite & Malice, by Kathryn H. Kidd
Helaman's House, by Orson Scott Card

Contents

Chapter 1

If Kate Carbine had indeed left her heart in San Francisco, it was now approximately 763 miles from where the rest of her body was sitting. Most of Kate was somewhere in Salt Lake City, Utah, driving the kids behind the U-Haul trailer that Martin was steering up the potholed streets toward their new home.

As Kate tried to concentrate on her driving, the children screamed and fought and whimpered in the back seat of the station wagon.

They weren't Kate's children, she knew. Oh, she had carried each one of them inside her for at least nine months (and she would have sworn it was more like fourteen). She remembered birthing them all, too. But sometime, maybe when Kate was asleep after the trauma of childbirth, each of her civilized offspring had been replaced by a barbarian — a child who whined and cried and asked questions and threw up on the sofa and did all the things they never told you about when you were innocently planning your temple wedding.

It must have come from Martin's side of the family.

Kate was almost in tears even before Martin turned the U-Haul onto the street where he had bought a house three weeks ago. When she actually saw the neighborhood, her eyes glazed so that she could barely see the road. Kate was sure she had moved to another planet.

Martin had promised he wouldn't buy a bungalow when he went on the house-hunting trip without Kate. That was Kate's only criterion — more important to her than shopping or schools. As soon as he got off the plane in Oakland, Kate knew from his face that he had let her down. When he didn't even have a picture of the new house to show her, she steeled herself to accept the worst. All he could say in his own defense was that he'd had a feeling this was the house they were supposed to buy. Martin never argued with his feelings, just in case they were inspirations. Once he had a feeling about the bungalow, Kate's misgivings didn't matter anymore.

Kate had never wanted to live in a bungalow. Even the name sounded squalid. It was abbreviated on the realtors' sheets, *bung*. And that's what the houses looked like — Bung the Circus Elephant, balanced precariously on his two front feet. Purple bricks. White trim. Tiny rooms with no closets. Bungalows were even worse than the split-levels that comprised most of Salt Lake City's recent architecture. At least split-levels had decent bathrooms.

Kate sighed. She knew she should have helped Martin pick out the house. She could hear his voice, with the pedantic tone that drove her crazy, reminding her, "There's a reason we're supposed to live in this house. We just have to find what that reason is."

Looking at the houses on Farley Avenue, Kate didn't care what the reason was. All she saw was that all the houses on the street looked alike. *All* of them looked like Bung the Circus Elephant. All of them were tiny, one-story structures with a basement. All were built in shades of purple brick and trimmed in coats of white paint that were in various stages of peeling. And Kate would have wagered that not a one of them had any storage space at all.

Finally, at the far end of the block, Martin eased the U-Haul against a curb and turned off the engine. Kate parked the station wagon behind him. Turning off her ignition, she crossed her arms over the steering wheel and warily looked from house to house, wondering which of them was her new home. She finally placed the house by the lawn, whose grass had sprouted a full nine inches before it died, unwatered, in the summer heat.

Martin bounded from the cab of the U-Haul. The spring in his step told Kate he was pretending things were all right. Martin thought he could make any problem disappear by pretending it didn't exist. His smile was as phony as NutraSweet. No, it *wasn't* a phony smile; Kate had to be honest. It was a hopeful smile. Martin hoped Kate would at least give the new neighborhood a chance.

"This is it!" he boomed, confirming Kate's worst fears.

"I hate it already." To Kate's surprise, the words didn't come from her. She looked in the rear-view mirror at Angela, her oldest child. Angela's face was an eight-year-old mirror of her own. Both Kate and Angela were tired and scared and miserable, and nothing Martin could say would comfort either one of them.

"*I* think it's neato." Sam, who was seven, thought everything was neato. "*Look* at all the purple houses!"

"I hate purple," Angela said.

"Well, I *like* purple," Sam said forcefully. "I bet the Bat Cave is purple."

"I don't want to live in the Bat Cave."

Kate couldn't argue with Angela. She didn't want to live in the Bat Cave, either.

"Which one is ours, Mom?" Sam asked, looking appraisingly at all the identical houses within view.

"The one with the grass," Kate said, trying to sound cheerful. Martin nodded, apparently pleased that Kate was making an effort.

"Neato!" Sam bounded from the car and waded through the dead lawn, looking for bugs in the former grass.

Only Jessie's opinion was left to be heard. When Sam had slammed the car door behind him and the rest of the family was silent, she spoke. Only, Jessie never spoke; she shouted. At three, her body was the smallest in the family, but her voice was the biggest. And she always waited until the world around her was quiet and her shouts would have the most effect.

"MOM!"

Kate turned around to Jessie, keeping her face neutral.

"DO I HAVE TO LIVE IN THIS HOUSE TILL I'M DEAD?"

Martin looked at his watch, biting his lower lip as if he were gauging the minute and the hour. "Not quite that long, Pumpkin," he said. Martin was always better with the children than Kate was.

"OKAY!" shouted Jessie, apparently satisfied. The car door slammed behind her, and she joined Sam in the grass. Suddenly, Jessie stomped on the sidewalk, landing on a moving object with both feet. Then she knelt to the pavement and inspected the spot she had made.

"WOW!" she said.

Sam ran over to see what made Jessie so excited. "Wow! Neato!"

Jessie stood, balancing herself on sturdy legs. Turning toward the car, she screamed, "MOM! THERE'S NEAT GRASSHOPPERS IN UTAH. IF YOU SQUASH 'EM, THE GUTS ARE BOOGER GREEN."

"That's gross," Angela said. Folding her arms in front of her, she slumped in the back seat of the station wagon.

"At least two of the family don't hate me." Martin said it quietly, and Kate felt immediately guilty.

"I like *you*, Daddy," Angela said, straightening up again. Martin's job had brought them to Utah, but Angela was only angry with Kate. Angela was always angry with Kate. She and Kate had been adversaries since the day she was born.

"*I* like you, too." Kate did like Martin. She knew it in spite of Utah. "You did the best you could, Martin. Eventually, we'll get used to it."

"There's a reason for all this," Martin said doggedly.

It was the worst thing he could have said. Kate smiled, a grim smile that wasn't a smile at all. "I know there's a reason," she said. "Maybe we'll find it soon. Then we can move home to California again."

Inside, the new house looked much as Kate expected it to look. The entrance had opened on to the living room, which extended into a dining room that was barely big enough for the dining room table. There were three bedrooms on the main floor, each no larger than her laundry room back in California. Kate thought there might be an advantage to that. She could turn off the light or turn on the television or get clothes from her dresser without ever getting out of bed. At least there wasn't much floor space to vacuum.

The whole family inspected the new house at their own pace. If Martin wanted to act as tour guide, he must have been sorely disappointed. Jessie and Sam skipped the entrance hall altogether and started in the living room. They stayed a room ahead of Martin and Kate and Angela throughout the house. In each room, the comments were the same.

"Neato!" Sam liked every room, and his cheerfulness bounced off empty walls.

"IS THIS ROOM MINE?" Jessie asked it about the living room and the dining room and the den, as well as each of the bedrooms. As far as she was concerned, only one room was important. It didn't matter *which* room was hers, Kate knew — only that *a* room was hers. Until the room assignments had been made, Jessie surveyed each room only enough to wonder if she would be sleeping there.

Angela's remarks were also predictable. Lagging behind Martin and even Kate, she only said, over and over, "I hate this house. I want to go back to California." Kate only realized when Martin gave her a look of disgust that she was nodding her head in agreement with each of Angela's complaints.

Finally, Angela found one room that was acceptable. It was the corner room in the rear of the house, next to the bathroom. It was also the master bedroom: Kate could tell because there were two tiny closets along the wall instead of just one. When she saw the room, Angela sat against a wall and folded her arms across her chest. "This room's mine," she announced, looking sullenly down at her folded arms.

To her surprise, Kate didn't get angry with Angela. She only shrugged. "I don't see that this room is much larger than the others," she said. "It just has two closets. If Dad says it's okay, you can have this room."

Angela looked questioningly at Martin, who nodded yes. Angela brightened long enough to give Kate a half smile of gratitude. Smiles were rare from Angela, and Kate leaned over and kissed her on the cheek.

Angela stayed on her new floor, still unready to stop sulking. Everyone else trooped down the stairs to see the basement, and Kate was pleased that the bedroom downstairs was just a little nicer than the one she had sacrificed for Angela. There was even a closet that was bigger than both of the ones in Angela's room. Kate smiled her first real smile of the day. She *liked* the basement. That was one feature of bungalows that California houses didn't have.

The thing about moving in on a Wednesday was that no men were available to help. In fact, the whole street looked deserted. Children were either off at school or down for their naps; mothers were either away at work or indoors cleaning house; fathers were at the office until nightfall. Kate hoped the Elders Quorum would miraculously appear out of nowhere, ready to unpack the U-Haul while she supervised. But Martin hadn't tracked down the new bishop, and no one knew the Carbines were members of the local ward. Minutes passed, and only an occasional passing car showed there were people living in Salt Lake City.

If Kate hadn't majored in physical therapy in college she would have had an excuse to sit back and let Martin do the work, but years of patterning hydrocephalic children had made her biceps as hard as granite. She suspected she was stronger than Martin, and she knew she had more stamina than he did. Wearily she blew her bangs out of her eyes and started hauling furniture and boxes.

"Dad, when are you going to unload the refrigerator?" Sam asked. Kate and Martin were sitting on the back of the U-Haul, drinking warm 7-Ups from the Coleman cooler. Between sips, Kate held the metal can to her forehead, pretending the aluminum was icy and cold.

"There's no food in the refrigerator," Kate said. "Maybe we'll get a pizza tonight."

"Neato, but when are you going to unload the refrigerator?"

Martin surveyed the contents of the U-Haul. "We'll unload it when we get to it," he said. "See? The sofa's in front of it, and the dishwasher and the love seat. The refrigerator's almost the last thing on the trailer."

"Bummer," Sam said, scowling at the U-Haul. He stood motionless for a moment, as if hoping the refrigerator would move on its own accord. When nothing moved, he shrugged and walked away.

A few minutes later, he was back. "Mom, how long can you breathe in a refrigerator?"

"Not very long," Kate said absently. "Refrigerators aren't made for people."

"I *know* that. I'm not dumb enough to get in a refrigerator." Sam sounded exasperated. That made Kate raise her eyebrows. Sam was her one child who was usually even-tempered. He trampled down the dead grass into an "S" at his feet. Kate watched him, listening to the dead grass crunch under Sam's neon tennis shoes.

Then, "Mom, if I was littler, could I live in a refrigerator?"

"How *much* littler?" she asked, playing the game.

"Dog-sized. Or cat-sized. Or frog-sized. If I was frog-sized, how long would I last?"

"Oh, I think you'd last for days and days. Frogs don't use much air at all."

"Neato." Sam rewarded Kate with a grin and skipped away.

Kate took another swig of soft drink, then another. Draining the can, she crushed it and tossed it on the U-Haul. She had never crushed a can in her life, but she thought that people who unloaded moving vans *should* crush aluminum cans and toss them aside. She felt like an athlete in a beer commercial, although she had drunk her 7-Up instead of just waving the can aloft. Martin watched her and braved a smile. He seemed relieved when she smiled back.

"Little kids ask crazy questions, don't they?" he asked, stretching a kink out of his neck.

She nodded. "He's been fixated on frogs lately. Ever since he found that frog in the yard last weekend, it's been *frog* this and *frog* that. He'd never seen a frog before that one."

Kate stood and surveyed the contents of the van, deciding what to move next. If she left the moving to Martin, he would relax in the shade of the U-Haul all afternoon and nothing would ever get unpacked.

Then Martin asked, "What did Sam *do* with the frog?"

Kate's breath caught in the back of her throat. Dimly she remembered telling Sam *of course* he couldn't take the frog across the country with him to Utah. She had assumed he had let the frog go. Suddenly, she knew he hadn't.

"I think we'd better unpack the van. Fast." But Martin was moving before the words were out of her mouth. Out came the love seat and the sofa and the dishwasher. Out came the brass headboard and the queen-sized mattress and box springs. Out came box after box after box. Everything was hastily dumped on the lawn instead of being taken inside the house. After each load they were back in the van, picking up another heap of household items to be quickly jettisoned on the grass.

Finally they reached the refrigerator.

"It's still taped shut," Martin called jubilantly as Kate shoved the last carton aside and returned to the back of the U-Haul.

Kate bent over and inspected the refrigerator door. The light was so dim that she confirmed her suspicions by running her fingers over the area. Just as she thought — there were places where her fingertips stuck to the enamel paint. "No," she said finally. "It's been taped *again.* Feel it? There are sticky marks where the tape used to be."

"Do you want me to open it?" This was Martin talking, the same Martin who had fainted in the delivery room when Angela was born.

"I'll do it." Kate knew she sounded like a martyr, but she felt like a martyr. As soon as the words left her mouth, Martin trotted to the glove compartment and retrieved a flashlight so Kate could see to do the job.

Kate didn't find the frog immediately, but the smell almost knocked her flat on the floor of the U-Haul. Sam must have hidden the frog soon after the refrigerator was loaded on Monday. Yes; Monday was the day Kate had taken the kids to McDonald's for lunch. The remnants of a McDonald's hamburger sat on the middle shelf of the refrigerator, rotting. There was also a jar cap that had probably held water before it sloshed out as the U-Haul rumbled toward Salt Lake City. Judging by the stench, Sam's frog had died roughly thirteen seconds after Sam had shut the refrigerator door and had been busily decomposing ever since.

Then Kate saw the frog. It had expired on the uppermost shelf, and its carcass drooped through the metal bars. The floor of the refrigerator was wet with urine. Frogs peed when they were scared, and they had immense bladders. Kate suspected that Sam's frog had been the Urine King of San Francisco.

"I'm sorry. I have to throw up." Martin sounded apologetic, but Kate couldn't help thinking he was already ten paces away from the source of the smell. He stopped long enough to pick up a box before he jumped down from the U-Haul. Then he disappeared inside the house.

Sighing, Kate returned to the mess in the refrigerator. She was still wondering who was going to clean it out when Sam appeared. As if he knew what had happened in the U-Haul, he stayed outside the van. When he spoke, his voice sounded little and far away.

"Grover's dead, isn't he?"

Kate shut the refrigerator door and left the U-Haul to kneel beside Sam on the grass. "I'm afraid so," she said. "Grover's been dead for several days."

"I *left* food for him. Water, too." Sam sounded almost angry at Grover; he hadn't expected the frog to die. "You *said* there was enough air in there." Sam sounded angry with Kate, too.

"This is August, Sam. Maybe the heat killed him."

"I don't care. He shouldn't have died."

"You shouldn't have put him in the refrigerator," Kate said.

"I had to. You wouldn't let me bring him in the car."

Before Kate could defend herself, he added, "Grover stinks. I didn't know he'd stink that much. I've never smelled anything that stinked as much as Grover." Under the mournful expression, Kate detected a glimmer of pride.

"Tell you what," she said. "If you'll help me find the Lysol in one of these boxes, I'll clean up Grover and your Dad will take you all out for ice cream. Is that okay?"

"I'd rather have Grover," Sam said.

"I promise you — you don't want Grover the way he is now. Go get some ice cream with your Dad. When you come back, we'll have a froggie funeral."

"Neato." Sam ran off to find the Lysol. Already, the pain of Grover's death was dimming.

Cleaning the refrigerator after Martin and the children had gone for ice cream, Kate suspected that the smell of Grover would linger long after the memory of him was gone.

Chapter 2

Kate smelled like a dirty clothes hamper. She could detect it on herself, and that meant anyone within a ten-foot radius could smell it, too. Cleaning frog urine from the refrigerator didn't help matters a bit. Now Kate reeked of dirty clothes and sweat and dead frog and Lysol. She sat on the front porch of the new house, leaning on a box and feeling sorry for herself as she aired herself out in the summer heat. One of the things Kate hated most about bungalows was the ubiquitous front porch, built in an era when people had nothing better to do than sit on a porch and watch the world go by. Kate didn't have *time* for porches. They made her feel guilty and resentful. She tried to ignore the existence of the porch, even as she sat on it feeling sorry for herself.

For about the dozenth time, Kate wondered if she could ever love any man enough to live in Utah with him. Looking at the parched lawns and the sunbaked trees, she suspected the answer was no.

After a few minutes of brooding in the relentless sunlight, she was relieved when a shadow passed between her and the sun. Then the shadow cleared its throat.

"You look delighted to be here," the shadow said. Kate looked up to see a woman bearing a pitcher of lemonade. Kate didn't know whether she was happier to see a friendly face or a cold drink, but she felt herself starting to smile.

"I'm just delighted as I can be," she said. "My daughter wants to move back to California, and there's a dead frog in our refrigerator."

"*That* explains the smell," the shadow said, and Kate cringed. "Don't be embarrassed; I know exactly how that frog got there. I have two sons, myself." Sitting on the porch step next to Kate, she poured lemonade into two plastic cups.

"Mary Shelley Stevenson's the name," she said, giving a cup of lemonade to Kate. "People call me 'Fangs'."

"Fangs?" As casually as she could do it, Kate took a sidelong glance at the visitor's canine teeth. They didn't look long or vicious. In fact, her teeth were only remarkable because they were as white as the teeth in toothpaste ads. She must spend twenty minutes a day polishing those teeth, Kate thought. Fangs they weren't.

"It's the Dracula connection."

Kate looked down at her toes, wondering if she should say anything. Finally she took a deep breath and plunged in. "Mary Shelley wrote *Frankenstein*," she said.

"You know that, and *I* know that, but people still call me Fangs. I picked up the name in third grade and never got rid of it. I don't mind."

"Just the same, I'll call you Shelley."

"Thanks for the effort, but you might as well call me Fangs. Everyone does it — even my husband. *Even* in bed. Heck, I think of myself as Fangs. I'd forget to answer to anything else."

Kate drained the cup of lemonade in one gulp. It was real lemonade, squeezed from real lemons and sweetened with real sugar. Kate hadn't tasted real lemonade in so many years that she considered the making of real lemonade a lost art. She was sorry when it was gone. "Fangs it is, then," she said, looking longingly at the empty cup. "I'm Kate Carbine. Thanks for the lemonade."

"It's my pleasure, really." Fangs took Kate's empty cup and filled it again. "I'm just glad to see another Mormon on the block. This neighborhood is overrun with Gentiles. Now that you're here, there are three Mormon families on this end of the street."

"How did you know we were Mormons?" This time, Kate sipped the lemonade. She didn't know when she'd taste real lemonade again, and she wanted to savor every drop.

"You have the Mormon look," said Fangs.

Kate glimpsed into a mirror that was propped against the porch. Her reflection was more than ordinary; it was nondescript. She could have been a Catholic or a Baptist or a Jew. She looked like a million other women in America, with absolutely no distinctive characteristics.

"What's the Mormon look?" she asked.

"Look at us. It's 97 degrees out here, and it won't be much cooler inside even after you get the swamp cooler running. Yet neither of is wearing shorts. We're in jeans with shirtsleeves down to our elbows. *That's* the Mormon look."

"Oh," Kate said. "Then the Mormon woman is sweaty."

"In August? — precisely. Now, how can I help you unpack?"

"You can visit with me while I work, if you don't mind. I haven't talked to an adult in two days."

Kate lifted her elbow off the box next to her and inspected the jumble of items inside. They were the contents of her kitchen drawers. She hefted the carton and carried it to the kitchen. Fangs kept pace with her, lemonade in hand. A rivulet of sweat stung Kate's left eye, and when she put the box on a counter she wiped her forehead with the back of her arm. Fangs didn't seem to be sweating at all.

"You said there were three Mormon families," she said, wiping out a cupboard as Fangs unloaded spatulas and measuring cups and slotted spoons onto a counter.

Fangs nodded. "The others are Gus and Lissa Chrousos. That's short for Melissa, but nobody ever calls her that. No kids. She's been trying to get pregnant for seven years. Gus has been driving home for nooners every month since the day they got married."

"That's sad," said Kate, only half sincerely. In retrospect, Kate didn't know if she would have tried that hard to have children.

"Oh, I guess so. Gus seems to like the nooners, though, and Lissa has a cat."

Kate dropped a Pyrex measuring cup and tensed to hear it shatter on the floor, but it only bounced. She picked it up and dusted it off before putting it in a cabinet.

"It's not just any cat," Fangs continued. "It's a show cat named Fido. That's the Cajun spelling: *P-H-I-D-E-A-U-X*. Be sure not to misspell it if you send him a birthday card."

"Why would I send a cat a birthday card?"

"Phideaux has birthday parties, that's why. Phideaux only looks like a cat. That's Lissa's child, and don't you forget it. She talks about Phideaux just like he's a person. It's Phideaux this, Phideaux that. She hasn't said Phideaux *says* this or that — yet. Personally, I think the day will come."

Kate picked up a box of salt and absently put it in the cupboard next to the glass measuring cup. Her hand brushed the cup handle, and it toppled off the shelf and onto the floor. This time, it did shatter.

"Damn!" said Kate. Then, wincing in embarrassment, she amended, "Rats!"

"Looks more like a *damn* to me," Fangs said. "I'll clean it up." Before Kate could protest, Fangs knelt and picked up the pieces, dropping shards of glass in the unbroken bottom of the measuring cup. Then she used the side of her hand as a broom to pick up the tiny glass chips. Not a sliver lodged in her flesh. If Kate had used her own hand for a broom, she would have looked like a Pyrex porcupine.

She watched as Fangs neatly put the broken measuring cup in the empty moving box. Fangs reminded Kate of the women who demonstrated food processors in department stores, smiling at the audience as they sliced celery stalks into neat little wedges. Invariably, Kate splattered celery slivers all over her kitchen ceiling and dribbled juice all over the floor. Kate didn't know what she could possibly say to interest someone as poised as Fangs, so she blew the hair from her eyes and worked. Finally, just to make conversation, she asked, "Which house is yours?"

"Does it matter? They all look alike."

Kate's smile broadened. "I think I'm going to like you," she said.

"In that case, we're next-door neighbors. The house outside your kitchen window is mine. Lissa Chrousos lives across the street and two doors down from me — the house with the blue Volvo in the driveway. By the way, the people living on the other side of you are human hairballs. Barking dogs. Rock music. You're going to *love* living here."

"Oh," Kate said in a small voice. Tears of self-pity filled her eyes, and she turned her head away so Fangs wouldn't see her cry. Looking out the window, Kate studied Fangs's house. She blinked once. Then she blinked again. Then she said, "There's a naked child doing somersaults in your front yard."

Fangs didn't raise an eyebrow. "Blond? Three years old? Male?"

"Conspicuously male," Kate agreed.

"It's my son, Boffo. His real name's Benjamin, but everyone calls him Boffo — for obvious reasons. I can't keep clothes on that kid for longer than two minutes. He's a real thrill in Sacrament Meeting."

Kate paused, trying to think of something positive to say about a naked three-year-old. Finally she said, "At least it saves on laundry."

"Not so you'd notice," Fangs said. "My other son wears clothes all the time."

The front door opened and slammed, and a clatter of feet stampeded through the house. Martin and the kids had returned from the ice cream parlor.

"MOM! MOM!"

"I'm in the kitchen, Jessie." The racket grew louder as Jessie's feet followed Kate's voice.

"MOM, THERE'S A BOY OUTSIDE, AND HE'S NAKED! I CAN SEE HIS WEENIE."

"That's Boffo Stevenson. This is his mommy, Sister Stevenson."

"Call me Fangs, Jessie," Fangs said. "'Sister Stevenson' makes me feel over the hill." She spoke to Jessie the same way she spoke to Kate — adult to adult. It had never occurred to Kate to talk to her children the same way she talked to people.

"Okay," Jessie said. Her curiosity satisfied, she wandered off. Only after she left did Kate realize that Jessie hadn't yelled her response. Jessie *always* yelled. Maybe the sight of Boffo Stevenson's weenie had shocked the yells right out of her.

"That's my three-year-old, Jessie," Kate said. "The other two are Angela, who's eight, and Sam, who's seven."

"Jessie was a surprise, I take it." Fangs was so casual that Kate never thought she was prying. Kate only nodded in agreement.

"Jessie was a shock. I had just gone back to work when I learned I was pregnant. The day that kid starts first grade, I'm getting a job." Then Kate realized how that must sound. Fangs obviously stayed home with her own children, or she wouldn't be here now. She added quickly, "I hope that doesn't offend you. I didn't *mean* it to offend you."

"Why should it offend me?" Fangs asked. "I'd kill to get a babysitter co-op going so I could spend some time with adults."

Kate's eyes brightened. "Do you mean that?" she asked. "You're not just making me feel better?"

"Lady, I don't say *anything* just to make people feel better. At least, not about co-ops. I've been trying to get a co-op started for two years. No takers. Boffo's a handful."

"I'll co-op with you." Kate tried not to sound too anxious, but she failed miserably. She sounded as desperate as Angela did, whenever she pleaded to get her ears pierced.

Fangs didn't even consider the offer. "Nope. Won't work," she said, shaking her head. "I have two kids that aren't in school. You only have one. It wouldn't be fair."

"It would be fair to *me*. To have two free days a week, I'd babysit Attila's Huns on the other two days."

"I'll think about it," Fangs said, in a tone that told Kate she probably wouldn't think about it. Fangs *was* just being polite. Kate should never have gotten her hopes up.

*

Fangs deserted Kate soon after refusing to co-op with her, leaving Kate to hope she hadn't offended half of the only two Mormon families on her end of the block. But she reappeared promptly at six, bearing dinner. Kate grinned when she answered the door. She didn't know if she was happier to see the food or the person who made it.

Fangs carried the bowls and dishes to the kitchen on a tray. Only when she entered the house did Kate see she was followed by a little boy who toted a loaf of French bread like a submachine gun. Kate and Jessie and Sam followed the procession to the kitchen as if they were the visitors and Fangs was the host.

Kate assumed the boy belonged to Fangs, even though she didn't recognize the child with his clothes on. Jessie recognized him, though. "MY NAME'S JESSIE," she yelled, peering into Boffo's face to inspect him up close. "YOU'RE BUFFO AND I SAW YOUR WEENIE."

"Yep," said Boffo, as if that was the whole reason he had been naked. "I brought a flower for your dead frog. Can I see him?"

"WHERE'S THE FLOWER?"

"It's in my pocket." He slammed the loaf of bread on a kitchen counter and rooted through the pockets of his shorts until he finally produced a crumpled marigold. He handed it to Jessie, clutching it by the mangled blossom as he passed it into her hand. "Here. *Now* can I see the frog?"

"It's my frog," said Sam. "Besides — we already buried him. We had a funeral and everything."

"That's okay," said Boffo. "We can dig him up."

Before Kate could protest, three pairs of feet dashed out the back door. She thought about calling them back, but she didn't want to look like an ogre. Not in front of Boffo, and especially not in front of Fangs.

"And you thought you'd gotten rid of the odor," Fangs said.

"On the contrary. I'll be smelling that frog for a long time. I guess it won't hurt if they dig him up. He can't be any rottener than he was this afternoon."

Two minutes later, Fangs and Kate and Martin watched from the back door as Sam disinterred Grover for Boffo's inspection. He unwrapped the frog from Martin's donated handkerchief and showed the corpse to Boffo, who shook his head in disgust and delight.

Kate knew she should have been revolted at the scene, but she was more interested in Boffo. Somewhere between the kitchen and Grover's grave, Boffo had lost his t-shirt and his shorts. Before Grover was planted again, Boffo's underwear was gone. Kate didn't see him take his underwear off; it just *was* off. Boffo shed his clothes like vinyl repels water.

She was a little concerned that Jessie would stare at Boffo. Jessie wasn't used to naked people; none of the Carbines wandered around unless they were somewhat clothed. But Jessie, having seen Boffo in the altogether, was already used to his nakedness. The putrefaction of Grover was far more important.

Chapter 3

Kate awoke to the sound of dogs barking. They were big dogs with resonant barks that could carry for blocks, but they were close enough that Kate thought they were in bed with her. These were the dogs Fangs had told her about. These were the dogs from hell.

Sighing, Kate looked at the digital display of the alarm clock. It was 7:23 — 6:23 A.M. California time. She had hoped to sleep in, but the dogs were as insistent as alarm clocks. Sighing, she got out of bed. Then she tripped over a box and landed on her fanny on the edge of the dresser.

Looking through the gloom of the basement bedroom, Kate saw that she was surrounded by boxes. Her household possessions had bred like rabbits in the night. There were entire litters of moving boxes that she knew hadn't been there when she went to bed. Cleverly, the new boxes had disguised themselves with labels just like the ones that Kate had written on her cartons in California. "Martin's flannel shirts," one box proclaimed. "Kate's sweaters," said another. The words appeared to be in Kate's own handwriting, but the penmanship didn't fool her. There were at least twice as many boxes as there used to be. Kate knew that if she didn't get the boxes all unpacked today, they'd replicate themselves again as soon as she went to sleep.

"Awake already?" Martin's voice was thick with slumber.

"The dogs woke me," Kate said. "Didn't they waken you?"

"What dogs?" Martin had the annoying talent of being able to ignore anything that was unpleasant. With Kate, the unpleasantness was magnified a hundred times. The dogs next door sounded like a whole kennel, but Martin didn't know they were there.

Kate sighed again, feeling sorry for herself. Then, realizing that self-pity wouldn't make the day any easier, she brightened. "Are you awake for the morning?" she asked.

"I am if you want me to be."

"Good. I hear the kids running around upstairs. At least, Sam and Jessie are. Angela will sleep till noon. If you control them today, I'll unpack the boxes. You can take them to the zoo or the movies, or wherever they want to go. They can even stay here, as long as they don't cause trouble."

"You're a gem," Martin said, smiling. "You always give me the easy job."

Kate only shook her head. She wouldn't tell Martin that she had kept the easy job for herself. Household possessions didn't have to be fed, and they almost never argued with one another.

She sent Martin and Jessie and Sam down the hill to buy breakfast and milk at the supermarket. They came back with a whole sackful of jelly doughnuts. The idea of jelly doughnuts made Kate cringe. Jelly doughnuts were disaster in a paper bag. They meant baths and laundry and sticky floors. Jelly doughnuts were invented by someone who hated children, as a means of revenge against their parents. Kate hated jelly doughnuts.

"THE GROCERY STORE DOESN'T GOT A FRONT DOOR," Jessie announced. "ALL THE AIR CONDITIONING LEAKS OUT IN THE SKY."

She reached out to Kate, handing her the bag of jelly doughnuts. Then, her attention distracted by something only Jessie knew, she let go before Kate grasped the sack. The bag fell to the floor with a heavy thud, and Kate saw red spots oozing through the white paper.

"Neato!" said Sam. "It looks like blood 'n' guts. I want a squished one."

"*I* WANT A SQUISHED ONE!" Jessie cried. She and Sam, like their father, turned any trial into adventure.

"Looks like we'll all have squished ones," Martin said philosophically. He picked up the paper sack and distributed leaky jelly doughnuts to Jessie and Kate and Sam. Then he licked his fingers before dipping back into the bag for a doughnut for himself.

"*I* don't want a squished one," Angela said. "And I wish those dogs would shut up." Kate turned around and saw Angela, who was standing in the doorway of the kitchen in her nightgown. She looked like Kate felt — groggy and sullen and miserable. Her hair was matted with sleep, and her eyelids were caked together. Kate wondered if the reason she didn't like Angela very much was that Angela was so much like she was. Immediately she dismissed the thought; it was too early in the morning to contemplate ideas that were so unpleasant.

"I *like* squished ones," Kate said, defying her natural inclination so she wouldn't sound so much like Angela. "They look like blood 'n' guts." She took a big bite of jelly doughnut, and a pocket of crimson jelly spurted onto her blouse. Kate didn't even swear. She scooped up the jelly with her index finger and sucked it from her skin. Angela rolled her eyes in disgust.

An hour later, Kate watched Martin and the children pull away in the station wagon, off to the mall or the canyon or parts unknown. Jessie waved until she was out of sight.

When the station wagon finally turned the corner, Kate felt pangs of loneliness. The boxes would keep; she should have gone exploring with her family. It would have improved her mood.

Then she thought of the remnants of Fangs's dinner. The dishes were still in the sink. If she washed the dishes, Kate would have an excuse to return them. Then she could postpone the unpacking of the boxes for just a little while.

Balancing the clean dishes on her arms, she waded through the tall grass to Fangs's manicured lawn. She saw a flash of bare skin disappear around the side of the house — Boffo in motion. Already there were two reliable features in the new neighborhood: Dogs barked, and Boffo roamed the street in his nakedness. Despite the annoyance of the dogs, the continuity was comforting.

Fangs answered the door before Kate knocked. She was fully dressed. Kate noticed that Fangs wore shoes in her own house. Her makeup was on, and her hair was in place. Worse, the house was spotless. Looking inside, Kate could see vacuum tracks on the carpet.

"Are you expecting company?" she asked before Fangs had even said hello.

"No. It's just a normal day around here. We've been awake since six. Come on in."

She took an armload of dishes from Kate and carried them to the kitchen. Kate followed her, hoping she didn't have any dirt on her shoes. Fangs's whole house — at least the part that Kate could see — was clean enough to pass military inspection. Even the kitchen had been remodeled. There was more counter space in Fangs's kitchen than Kate had ever seen in one tiny room. The appliances were new, and the cupboards were shiny. Kate felt herself starting to salivate. She tried to swallow her jealousy.

Fangs put the dishes away, dispensing them from the top of her arm as though she were dealing blackjack. Every cupboard she opened was neatly organized. Then she perked up her ears. "Do you hear anything?" she asked.

Kate shook her head. "Just the sound of ocean waves." The whole house sounded like the seashore. Until Fangs told her to listen, she hadn't noticed the banging of waves on the beach.

"Not that," Fangs said. "That's the tape I use to drown out the dogs and the rock band. Sometimes, when I'm lucky, it drowns out the telephone, too. I thought I heard a fly."

Kate shrugged. "It must be gone. I don't hear anything but the waves. They make your house feel cool and peaceful."

"I don't know about the peaceful part," Fangs said. "I could have *sworn* I heard a fly." Furrowing her brows, she listened for another moment. "I hate flies."

"Everyone hates flies."

"Not so," Fangs said. "Everyone detests flies — I'll agree to that —, but I *hate* them. They're loathsome creatures. I won't have a fly in my house."

As if in defiance, a fly buzzed across the room and landed on the window above the kitchen sink. Fangs's upper lip curled. Without taking her eyes off the fly, she opened a drawer that was full of neatly folded plastic sacks, the ones that were designed to hold vegetables in the supermarket. She unfolded the sack and drew it over her right hand like a huge glove. The outstretched hand with its plastic sack made a surface that was at least ten inches wide.

Kate watched as Fangs's hand approached the fly on the window. Kate waited for the fly to bolt and head across the kitchen to land in a safer place, the way it always did whenever she used a fly-swatter. But the fly, obviously puzzled by the transparent membrane of plastic, hesitated a moment too long. Trapped under Fangs's hand, it stood helpless until Fangs pinched it between two fingers, crushing the life out of it. Then, as primly as a surgeon putting on surgical gloves, Fangs turned the plastic bag inside out. The fly was now in the bag, dead. With a smile of satisfaction, Fangs crumpled the plastic bag and threw the bag and the fly in the garbage. Her skin had never touched the insect.

"That's my own invention," she said, smiling in triumph. "I don't know why, but it works every time. I keep thinking I should send the idea to the Mensa magazine fly-killing contest, but I figure if those bozos are as smart as they keep telling everyone else they are, they can kill flies on their own."

But Kate's eyes were glued to the trash can. Finally she said, "You hear their bodies squash? You feel them crunch between your fingers?"

"Absolutely," Fangs said. "Do you know how many diseases flies carry? I *hate* flies. Do you want some lemonade?"

The fly forgotten, Fangs opened the refrigerator and produced some freshly squeezed lemonade. Kate realized that Fangs hadn't made a treat especially for her yesterday; Fangs had freshly squeezed lemonade around her own house all the time. Kate felt like a sham of a mother. The more she learned about Fangs, the worse she looked in comparison.

"We have to talk," Fangs said, as she led Kate to the living room sofa. "Were you serious about having a babysitting co-op?"

"Absolutely." Having said the one word, Kate held her peace. She didn't want to scare Fangs off with her enthusiasm, the way she had yesterday.

"And you don't mind that I'd have two children in the co-op, while you only have one?"

"Not a bit," Kate said. She wondered if the other Stevenson child was as crazy as Boffo — or worse. "Not a bit," she repeated, even louder and more firmly than she had before.

Fangs took a long sip of lemonade. She drank delicately through her straw. Finally she said, "You haven't met R.J. He isn't like Boffo, you know."

As if he had been summoned, Boffo threw open the front door and stood there for a moment, au naturel. A red towel was draped haphazardly over his arm; the rest of him was bare. After a moment's hesitation, he slammed the door behind him and ran toward Fangs.

"Mom, my Superman cape keeps coming off. Fix it — okay?"

Fangs put her lemonade down and tied two ends of the red towel around Boffo's neck. Kate watched the procedure, trying not to let her eyes wander to the obvious destination. She'd seen the plumbing; Sam was built roughly the same way as Boffo. She just wasn't used to seeing *all* of a person, his skin worn as casually as blue jeans.

Fangs patted Boffo on the bottom and he flew off, arms akimbo. He stopped only long enough to open the door and slam it heartily behind him. "I'm Superman!" he screamed from outside the door, as he faced the world in his red towel cape.

"As I was saying," Fangs said, "R.J. is different. He's not as, well, *bois*terous as Boffo and Jessie."

Kate smiled. "Frankly, I'd like a quiet one in the group."

"Then it's settled. As soon as school starts, we'll begin. You'll take them two days a week, I'll take them two days a week, and the fifth day we'll have off. Does that sound good to you?"

Kate's smile broadened. "It sounds perfect. I didn't think I'd have another day off until Jessie started kindergarten. With two days off a week, I won't know what to do with myself."

The tape of ocean waves banging against a shore ended abruptly, leaving the house in momentary silence. With a momentary click and a whir, the stereo changed tracks and the tape started playing again. Fangs stared absently at the stereo until the sound of ocean waves returned. Then she nodded approvingly.

"What *are* you going to do with yourself?" she asked abruptly.

Kate knitted her eyebrows, thinking. What she really wanted to do was get a job, but if she told the truth she would sound like a worse mother than she already was. Finally she said, "I really don't know. For the first little while, at least, I think I won't do anything at all. Bubble baths, maybe, and there's a whole stack of books I want to read."

"All that inactivity would drive me crazy," Fangs said, and Kate reddened in embarrassment. Bubble baths *did* sound boring.

"Then what do *you* want to do?" Kate asked.

Fangs shrugged. Then, as if it were the most obvious answer in the world, she said, "I want to start working again. If I could spend some time with adults, I think my sanity might return. I could set up a limited practice, say, two days a week."

"'Limited practice'? You sound like Melvin Belli."

"Marcus Welby is more like it," Fangs said.

"You're a *doctor?*" Kate asked.

"Last time I checked, that's what Welby did for a living. Why are you so surprised?"

"You're a mother. You're a gourmet cook. Your house is spotless. That's more than I'm doing, and I'm not a doctor."

"What are you?"

"I'm a physical therapist — but I'm a rotten mother and a worse cook, and I keep a filthy house."

"We can't all be perfect," Fangs said. Kate hoped she was kidding.

"Besides," Kate persisted, "you live in a bungalow. Doctors don't live in bungalows. Doctors live in mansions, way up on the hill. Is your husband a plumber?"

"Orthopedic surgeon."

"Then why do you live in a bungalow?"

Fangs raised her eyebrows. "Are you kidding? You should have seen the student loans. *And* we have a cabin. Rob likes to go to Europe, too — with the kids. He went to Italy on his mission, and he likes to visit his old haunts. We'll be living here till Boffo's in college. I don't mind. I don't have time for a bigger house."

"What's your specialty?" Kate asked, still getting used to the idea of Fangs as a doctor.

"Obstetrics — I'm the plumber in the family. It's not like riding a bicycle, either. The technology's always changing. If I don't keep a finger in it, I'll fall behind. That's why I'm so desperate for a co-op. All it would take is a couple of days a week."

Kate had never heard of babies waiting to be born until a doctor's work day — especially if the doctor only worked two days a week. Nevertheless, she held her tongue. The idea of having two days free for herself sounded awfully appealing, and she didn't want to shoot it down before it had even taken flight.

"Then we'll do it," she said. "I should be unpacked and ready to loaf by the time school starts. Speaking of unpacking, I have to go home. Every time I leave the room, my moving cartons multiply."

She stood to go, and Fangs followed her to the door. But standing on the front step, Kate had one more question for Fangs.

"Do you have a church job?" she asked hopefully. Fangs was a better mother and a better cook than she was. She was also apparently smarter than Kate, who had wanted to be a doctor but had been intimidated by the chemistry courses in med school. Kate almost wished that Fangs were only semi-active in church, so Kate could have one edge on her new friend.

"Oh, yeah." Fangs bent over and picked up an imaginary piece of lint from the carpet. "I'm Relief Society president." Seeing Kate's look of shock she added, "Don't be impressed. There are only a hundred and ninety-seven women in the ward. It's not a big job here at all."

Chapter 4

By Friday morning, Kate's moving cartons had stopped reproducing. The boxes that were going to be unpacked had already been unpacked. The decision to stop didn't come because all the boxes were empty — it came because all the drawers, shelves and cupboards were full. The rest of the boxes were haphazardly stacked in a corner of the basement. Invariably, the items that Kate needed most in the world would be hidden away in those boxes, as inaccessible to her as the gold in Fort Knox. But at least there was a basement to put them in.

With no more boxes to occupy her time, she turned to the yard. She mowed the dead lawn, which was so dry that grass stalks flew from the blade of the lawn mower like missiles. Kate felt as if she were mowing a cornfield after the harvest. She thought she'd be better served by hiring a farmer to plow it all under.

By mid-afternoon, everything was done. Martin was at work, visiting his new office for an hour or so before he officially started his new job on Monday. Angela was barricaded in her bedroom, reading, her need for privacy so great that she shut the door and deprived herself of the refrigerated air of the swamp cooler. Jessie and Sam were, well, somewhere. There was time for a quick nap before dinner.

Kate settled into a wing-back chair and stretched her feet out on the ottoman. She was more than half asleep when she heard a strangled mewling sound. She opened her eyes and saw Sam and

Jessie, headed up the sidewalk together. Sam was carrying a bear-skin rug — it must have been a *polar* bear, because its pelt was so white. As Kate drifted off, she thought she had never seen a polar bear as white as Sam's.

She dreamed she was in Alaska, riding in a dog-sled race. She never seemed to get ahead; her cries of *Mush!* fell on deaf ears. The team ahead of her flew above the snow, as effortlessly as if they had wings. Then Kate realized that the woman driving the leading team wasn't screaming *Mush!*. She was urging on her dogs with a strange Eskimo word: *Phideaux!*, *Phideaux!*. Whatever the word meant, it got much better results than *Mush!*.

Kate thought she'd have an even chance of winning the race if her own family would support her, but Martin was away at work, and Angela was abroad in Switzerland. Jessie and Sam were off on the sidelines, feeding Snickers bars to a polar bear. It wasn't fair.

She even heard Jessie's and Sam's conversation. Suddenly the dog race evaporated. Kate found herself floating above Sam and Jessie, eavesdropping on her Eskimo children.

"I'VE NEVER SEEN A CARTOON CAT BEFORE."

"Me neither. I wonder when his face'll get round again."

"HE DOESN'T LIKE SNICKERS. WHAT DO CATS EAT?"

"We could dig up the frog. Or Mom could buy some cat food."

Phideaux! Phideaux!

Slowly, Kate awoke. She wondered why Jessie was talking about a cartoon cat. The television hadn't been on all day. More curious than tired, she stretched and lumbered into Sam's room.

Sam must have had trouble carrying the cat home. It was at least a twenty-pounder. It was so fat that it did look like a polar bear, and its fur was as fluffy as a bearskin rug. The cat's pelt was as white as a radish, and its Persian face was so flat that it looked just like a cat in a cartoon, right after a mouse had smacked its head with a frying pan. Persians always looked constipated, but this kitty needed a whole box of Ex-Lax. Kate had never seen such an annoyed expression on an animal.

Jessie looked up from the cat, her face as excited as Christmas morning. "CAN WE KEEP HIM, MOM? HE FOLLOWED US HOME."

"I saw him following you," Kate said, suppressing a yawn. "Sam practically had to drag him here."

"He *would* have followed us," Sam said, "but he didn't know the way. Isn't he neato? Can we keep him?"

"*Phideaux! Phideaux!*"

The cat wailed.

There could only be one Phideaux on the block. The cries had to be coming from Lissa Chrousos, the third Mormon on this end of Farley Street. Kate tugged Phideaux's torpid body from Sam's grasp. "Listen!" she said. "Do you hear anyone calling a cat? I think this kitty already has a home — don't you?"

She hefted Phideaux to her shoulder. He weighed nearly as much as a Toyota, and that was dead weight; Phideaux was no more willing to cooperate than a sack of cement. Kate was impressed that Sam had mustered the stamina to carry his treasure home.

She went to the door, with Jessie and Sam trailing forlornly behind her. Sam had bits of Snickers bar stuck to his fingers, and he pushed his fingertips in Phideaux's face as he followed Kate. If Kate had been the cat, she would have bitten Sam. Phideaux was too lazy to make the effort.

Kate looked outside to see the blondest and fluffiest person she had ever beheld. Lissa Chrousos. Kate couldn't have found anyone blonder and fluffier if she'd read a "Playboy" magazine from cover to cover. Lissa's eyes were big and round, and she peered under every shrub and behind every tree as she walked down the street. Her eyes on the ground, she didn't even see Kate standing in the doorway with the cat.

Lissa stopped. "*Phideaux! Phideaux!*" she called plaintively. She searched forlornly before she started walking again.

Kate opened the door, keenly aware that both Sam and Jessie were trying to pull her back. She cleared her throat. "Excuse me," she said. "I think I have something of yours."

Lissa's head whipped around, and the first thing she saw was Phideaux. A ten million-dollar check from Ed McMahon had never been greeted with so much joy. She ran with her legs together, as if she were trying to hold up a pair of pantyhose that had rolled down to her knees. She leaped up the steps of the bungalow and snatched the inert cat from Kate's shoulder.

"I'm here!" she cried. "I've saved you." Phideaux seemed unimpressed. In fact, he looked no happier to see his mistress than he had looked when he was in the clutches of Jessie and Sam. If Lissa had received her ten million-dollar check from Ed McMahon, Phideaux wasn't even on Ed's mailing list.

"Where did you find him?" Lissa said, almost crying from gratitude and relief.

"I don't think *found* is the right word. I'm afraid my children catnapped him. I'm Kate Carbine. Sorry about the trauma. I think Sam and Jessie have some apologizing to do."

She looked pointedly at Sam, who mumbled a half-hearted, "I'm sorry."

Jessie was more to the point. "I'M SORRY WE STOLED YOUR CAT," she yelled. "CAN WE KEEP HIM?"

"I don't think so," Lissa said. "Phideaux wants to live with me. But you can visit him whenever you want. Here. Why don't you pet him, too."

Altogether, considering the scare she had suffered, Lissa was more civilized than she had reason to be. As Kate watched her children pet Phideaux, she studied the cat and its owner. Occasionally, Lissa blinked as languidly as a goldfish in a bowl. Then Kate stopped short. Do fish blink? she wondered. If they don't, why does this woman look so much like a goldfish?

Submitting to Sam and Jessie's sticky fingers, Phideaux looked singularly unimpressed.

Finally Lissa looked up from the children and the cat. "I'm Lissa Chrousos," she said. "I'm one of the few Mormons on this end of the block. I should have brought you dinner or something, but it's been a hectic week. Phideaux has a cat show this weekend — don't you, sweetheart? — and it's taken every bit of my concentration."

"What does a cat show involve?" Kate asked politely.

"Well, nothing. Phideaux just has to be clean and fluffy, but he's always clean and fluffy."

"I can imagine." In that respect, Phideaux was just like his owner. Lissa had the body and the personality to make a great Playmate of the Month. (Turn-ons: Romantic dinners, snowfalls, and fuzzy white kittens.) Too bad she was a Mormon.

Lissa sighed. "Still, a cat show makes me so nervous for Phideaux that I can't even function. He'd be so disappointed if he lost."

"I can imagine," Kate said again. She hoped sarcasm didn't show in her voice. Kate didn't think a nuclear holocaust would disappoint Lissa's cat.

Lissa and Kate stood uneasily on the front step for a moment. Kate didn't know what to say next, and Lissa looked just as uncomfortable. Finally, Lissa said, "I've got an idea. Phideaux has to get home for his nap. Why don't you walk over with me and visit?"

Kate thought that Phideaux's nap was already in progress, but she nodded yes.

Jessie tugged on Kate's sleeve. "CAN I GO? I WANT TO SEE THE CATHOUSE."

"That's *cat's house*, Jessie," Kate said. "*Not* cathouse. Why don't you stay here with Sam?"

"I wanna come too," Sam said, not cooperating.

Lissa only smiled. "Why don't you all come? I have Orange Fanta in the refrigerator. You children can play with Phideaux while your mommy and I get to know each other."

Everyone trooped up the street to Lissa's house. Kate was chagrined to see that Sam and Jessie led the way. They were well aware where Phideaux belonged. It was time to trot out the family home evening lesson on stealing. Next time, Sam's and Jessie's theft might not be quite so apparent.

"We're here!" Lissa chirped, though Jessie and Sam were already halfway up the front steps.

Kate nudged her children from Lissa's path. "Step aside," she said. "Sister Chrousos has to open the door."

Lissa looked pointedly at Sam and then Jessie. "Which one of you is Sam?"

"I am, of course." Sam rolled his eyes in disgust. "Jessie's a *girl's* name."

"That was silly of me," Lissa said. "Sam, why don't you open the door. Phideaux seems to be asleep. We don't want to disturb him."

Sam puffed out his chest importantly. He pulled open the screen door and then threw open the wooden door behind it. Then he strode into the house and held the wooden door open, just like a doorman. And doormanlike, Sam had concentrated on the door that would have stayed open on its own, letting the screen door slam in Lissa's face. As she pulled open the screen door again, Kate wondered if Sam expected a tip.

Inside, Lissa's house was as white as Phideaux. The only splashes of color were the paintings on the walls and the artwork along the baseboards. Baseboards? As discreetly as she could, Kate peered at the wall near the baseboards. Sure enough, the room was ringed with artwork, each one carefully stuck about ten inches above the floor. There were lions and tigers. There were birds. There was a squirrel. There were fish. There were also cartoons. Looking along the wall at the other side of the living room, Kate found a "Far Side" cartoon featuring cats in aprons.

"You've seen our art gallery," Lissa said.

"It's hard to miss," Kate admitted. "I've never seen pictures at toenail height before."

Lissa nodded. Her eyes glistened wetly. "They're for Phideaux, you know."

Kate had suspected as much, but until Lissa said the pictures had been hung there for the cat, she hoped there was another explanation. "Does Phideaux ever look at those pictures?" she asked.

"I've never seen him, but cats are nocturnal. He does most of his padding around after we're asleep. And of course, I'd never spy on him."

"Of course," Kate murmured. That was the moment she decided that Lissa was crackers.

Lissa deposited Phideaux on the dining room table, as carefully as she would have set a Ming vase on the mantelpiece.

"Excuse me, Phideaux," she said, as if waiting for the cat to answer. "I want to show your ribbons to the nice lady."

Phideaux remained in the exact position he had been placed. His head was thrown back uncomfortably, but he made no effort to improve his position. Phideaux's eyes slid shut, and he started to snore. No purrs here. Purring took too much energy for Phideaux.

Phideaux's ribbons and trophies were at cat height, too. Lissa knelt on the white carpet and picked up some framed ribbons. She held them up for Kate's admiration. Kate feigned interest, but she was far more fascinated with the artwork that rimmed the baseboards of Lissa's house. She wished she were a child again; Jessie and Sam had fallen to their stomachs and were wriggling around on the floor, from picture to picture. Phideaux's art gallery could keep them entertained for hours.

After Kate had paid proper obeisance to Phideaux's trophies, Lissa led her to the kitchen. She poured four Orange Fantas into glass — not plastic — glasses. Kate fervently hoped that Jessie and Sam could keep hold of their soft drinks. She suspected that Orange Fanta could permanently redecorate a white carpet.

All of a sudden, from the dining room, Kate heard a loud, "HI!" She turned around to see Jessie, her nose a scant three inches from Phideaux's flat face. Kate braced for the outstretched paw that could claw grooves into Jessie's skin, knowing she was too far away to prevent Phideaux's attack. Phideaux's eyes scudded open and he slowly got to his feet. In an economy of movement, the cat turned around in place, turning his backside to Jessie. Then, without further ado, he ponderously settled down on the table and immediately started snoring again. Kate hadn't realized that Phideaux was capable of such a raw display of energy.

"That was a close call," she observed to Lissa. "I thought he was going to attack her."

Lissa looked shocked. "Biting and scratching are *animal* reactions. Phideaux is non-violent. He's been declawed, you know."

"Has he been detoothed?"

"Why in the world would I want to pull his teeth?"

Lissa had a point. From what Kate had seen of Phideaux, Phideaux was too lazy to chew his own food. Even the Jessies of the world were safe from him.

Over Lissa's protests, Kate led Jessie and Sam to the front step to drink their soft drinks. Closing the door behind her, Kate joined Lissa on the Arctic-white sofa and concentrated on not spilling her own Orange Fanta.

Visiting with Lissa was like entertaining a wild bird. Lissa didn't stay in one place for longer than thirty seconds without hopping up to do something or another. Once she remembered a phone call she had to make. A minute after she returned, she hopped up again to thaw a steak for Phideaux's dinner. Then the soft drinks needed replenishing. After that, she decided Jessie and Sam might need more Orange Fanta, too.

Kate managed to keep herself busy. Whenever Lissa left the room, Kate would secretly experiment on Phideaux. She pulled his leg away from his body, and it stayed there; Phideaux didn't even retract the muscles. Next she took another leg and folded it in an awkward position under Phideaux's body. There it stayed. Once, in a moment of inspiration, Kate opened Phideaux's mouth and put one of his front paws between his teeth. Phideaux kept it there. When Lissa returned, her beloved cat was apparently sucking its thumb as it slumbered.

Phideaux didn't even know he was being tortured. No matter what Kate did to the cat, he remained comatose. Kate had seen doorstops that were more animated than Phideaux. He reminded her of a Gumby toy: No matter how he was contorted, he'd stay in the position he was placed in. No amount of comfort was worth the small amount of energy he would have to expend to regain a more natural state.

Finally, Kate tired of the game. The next time Lissa settled down for a few moments, Kate asked her, "What do you know about R.J. Stevenson?"

Lissa sniffed. "For one thing, it drives me crazy when people give their kids initials instead of names," she said. "If parents can't bother to find a name for a kid, they shouldn't *have* kids."

"Doesn't R.J. stand for anything?"

"It sure does. It stands for 'Reuben James', just like the ship in the folk song. I say, if they're going to name a kid after a ship, they should name him *Titanic* or *Bismarck* or *Lusitania*."

Kate nodded, relieved to see that Lissa had opinions that weren't Phideaux-related. Then she asked, "If you had a son, what would you name him?"

"Something classical. Leonardo, or Marcus Aurelius. I'd name a girl Saxon."

Kate thought it was just as well Lissa hadn't reproduced. "But what about R.J.?" she asked. "What kind of kid is he?"

"As far as I can tell, he's perfect. He doesn't even get his clothes dirty."

"At least he *wears* clothes."

"That's a step," Lissa agreed. "Why do you want to know about R.J.?"

"I've never seen him," Kate said. "I've only seen Boffo. Fangs and I are going to do a baby-sitting co-op. Fangs seemed a little reluctant to put me in a co-op with R.J."

Lissa shrugged. "Fangs has always been like that. The way she talks about R.J., you'd think *he* was the kid who went around naked. Like I say, R.J. is as close to perfect as a kid can get. I'd like to have a whole houseful of R.J.s — but at *my* house, they'd have *real* names."

"Like Leonardo."

Lissa nodded benignly. "Say — do you think I could get in on the co-op?"

Kate ran her finger around the rim of her empty glass. The Orange Fanta was gone, but the rim was sticky with sugar. "I hate to bring this up," she said finally, "but you don't have any children."

"I know that. But one day, I *will* have children. The co-op would be a great opportunity for me to practice. You don't mind, do you?"

"Mind? I'd let Jack the Ripper babysit my kids, if he was willing to do it."

"You're not serious!" Lissa asked. Here was a woman who was easily shocked.

"I don't think so. But some days, I get so desperate I'd consider it. Do you really want to join the co-op?"

"If you'll let me." Lissa blinked her goldfishiest blink. "I'll bet you're each taking two days a week. Why don't I take the fifth day? Then you'll both have three days of freedom. I bet you'd like that."

"I sure would," Kate agreed. "Why don't you talk to Fangs? This is all her idea; she's in charge of it."

"I'll *do* it." Lissa stood, and Kate realized the visit was over. Lissa wanted Kate to go home so she could call Fangs immediately. Lissa was deadly serious about the babysitting co-op.

When Lissa opened the door, Jessie and Sam were gone. Finished with their soft drinks, they had obviously wandered home. Kate was embarrassed to see that some Orange Fanta had dribbled down the concrete steps. Lissa took the children's empty glasses and returned with a damp sponge to wipe the stains away. Kate stood helplessly as Lissa cleaned Sam's and Jessie's mess.

As Lissa straightened up, a car honked from the street. Kate shielded her eyes to see a grey Porsche convertible drive by. The occupant of the car was tall and lean and tanned, or maybe naturally dark-complected. His head was as bald as Boffo's bottom. In thirty-one years of watching men, Kate had never seen anyone so handsome. She wondered how Martin would look with his head shaved. No, she thought, he wouldn't have the head for it. He'd have a flabby scalp or a bony skull; *something* would ruin it. Heads like this one came along once in a lifetime.

"Who is *that?*"

"Close your mouth," Lissa said. "You're drooling. Besides — he's married. That's Gus, my husband. He just bought that car, and he's driving around the block to show it off for me. That's one handsome devil."

Kate wondered if Lissa was talking about the car or the driver. She realized that it didn't matter; both the car and Lissa's husband were equally attractive.

"Gus has Yul Brynner Syndrome — shaved his head when he starred in 'The King and I' in high school. The girls went bananas; you can see why they did. He's been shaved ever since, except for the two years he was on his mission. He's the only person I know who had to *grow* his hair to get a mission call."

"If that's your husband, I'm off," Kate said. "I'm sure you'll want to go for a ride in that car."

Lissa nodded absently.

"I'm glad to get to know you," Kate said. "Thanks for inviting me over."

"I'm glad you came," Lissa said. "I can't wait to call Fangs. I'm so excited about that co-op."

Her brow furrowed. She put her lip between her teeth as if she were going to chew on it. Then she asked, "Are your kids allergic to cats? Jessie wouldn't be allergic to Phideaux, would she?"

"Not that I know of. If she is, she'll have to develop a tolerance. A good babysitter transcends allergies."

Waving goodbye to Lissa, Kate walked up the street toward home. She didn't think that Jessie would be allergic to Phideaux. She only hoped that Phideaux wouldn't be allergic to children.

Chapter 5

On Saturday morning, Kate finally met the dog owners. It was an unhappy meeting. They were lurking Neanderthals — a matched pair of them. Evidently of the same genetic stock, they looked like the Cave Brothers. Call them Thag and Thor, or Fred and Barney. Which one's which? she wondered. Does it make a difference?

Kate, who had walked up to the fence with a pan of Pillsbury cinnamon rolls she had baked as a peace offering, turned back to the porch and hid the pan. These men hadn't evolved beyond raw meat.

"Beautiful dogs you have there," she said, returning to the chain-link fence.

"Yeah," Thag grunted. He was doing sit-ups on a mat while Thor held down his feet and counted the repetitions. Stripped to the waist, his every muscle stood out in glistening relief. Either the two men had oiled their skin, or they had majored in sweat production at Cave Man University.

"The dogs are quite — uh, active, too." Kate tried to smile.

"They like to run," Thor said, sandwiching the words between 246 and 247. Kate wouldn't have guessed Thor could count so high.

Kate surveyed the samoyeds, pretending to admire them. Their fur was tall and white and fluffy, and their tails curled in an upright circular arc. Evidently there was a zoning regulation on

Farley Street: pets could only be fluffy and white and cute. But unlike Phideaux, the samoyeds were equipped for sound. Their barks were as piercing as smoke detector alarms.

Having feigned admiration, Kate took a deep breath and got to the heart of the matter. "I don't think you realize it, but our bedrooms are all on your side of the house."

Thag grunted. "So?"

"The problem is, the dogs bark incessantly. We can't sleep at night, and they drive us crazy all day long."

Thor stopped counting at 269. His eyes narrowed, as if he were devoting all the wattage of his two-volt brain to the question of murder. Would a garrote be more painful, or should he skin Kate alive?

"They're not barkin'," Thag finally grunted between sit-ups. There was a note of finality in his voice. Both dogs cheerfully barked their agreement.

"They're barking *right now.* They haven't stopped barking since we moved in." Kate was losing her patience. The dogs' barks were so constant they sounded like a siren; when one samoyed stopped to breathe, the other dog filled in the gap.

Thor looked at her thickly. "That's not barkin'," he said. "That's just talkin'."

"THEN TELL THEM TO HOLD THEIR CONVERSATION SOMEWHERE ELSE!"

Retrieving her pan of cinnamon rolls from the porch, Kate stalked back inside. As she turned to go, she saw Thag and Thor exchange puzzled looks. The samoyeds' discussion continued unabated.

"What number am I on?" she heard Thag pant as she opened the front door to go inside.

"I dunno. Lost count."

"Damn! Now I have to start all over."

Kate smiled. Maybe Thag would choke on his own sweat — assuming he had evolved enough to develop lungs.

Just as Kate thought she would scream if she heard one more bark, the barking was no longer a problem. Thag had finished his sit-ups. He, or Thor, turned on the stereo. Discordant metal music shook the windows of Kate's kitchen, drowning out the dogs' conversation.

"Neato!" Sam called from his bedroom. "When I put my hand on the wall, I can feel the music. Come see!"

Kate put her fingers on Sam's bedroom wall. She could feel the vibrations thumping out the beat.

Her hands trembling in anger, Kate looked up the number of the Salt Lake police. Fangs was right: Thag and Thor were human hairballs. They deserved to be locked up and forced to listen to Lawrence Welk music. If she couldn't shut the Cave Brothers up, the police would have to do it.

To Kate's horror, the policeman who answered the telephone didn't even take Kate's name or address. He said rock music was legal until 10 P.M. There was nothing the police could do about the dogs. "Dog owners pay their taxes, too, you know." He hung up the phone.

Slamming down the telephone receiver, Kate watched for a moment as Sam and Jessie delightedly held their hands to one wall of the house and then another, feeling the music. She was only glad that Martin had taken Angela to the supermarket; Angela would have taken on both Thag and Thor singlehandedly. Martin would only raise his eyebrows in wonder that she let mere rock music and barking dogs bother her.

Leaving Jessie and Sam with their hands on the walls, Kate went over to Fangs's house for sympathy. She found Fangs and Lissa sitting on the sofa drinking red juice. Phideaux was no where in sight.

"I'm glad to see some real people," she said, waving away Fangs's offer of a drink. "I just had a run-in with the Cave Brothers next door."

Fangs raised an eyebrow. "Dogs, or rock music?"

"Dogs. Do you know what those idiots said to me?"

"I can guess," said Fangs. "Their dogs don't bark."

"Bingo. 'They're just talking.'"

"It sounds like they're *arguing*," Lissa said. "It's bark bark bark, all day long. Dog owners are so irrational. I don't know what people see in dogs."

"My first reaction was to call the police," Kate admitted. She left out the part that she had already called the police, waiting for Fangs's response.

Fangs only shook her head. "Don't bother." She obviously spoke from experience. "They can't do a thing."

"Or *won't* do a thing." Kate was furious at the dogs and the police department and the Cave Brothers and the world in general.

"Why do they always side with the dogs?" Lissa asked, wide-eyed.

Fangs gave her a look of disgust. "Think about it. You don't suppose your stereotypical policeman is a cat lover, do you?"

"I never thought about it," Lissa said. "Unless I see a dog, I assume people have cats."

That didn't surprise Kate. "By the way," she said, "where's Phideaux?"

"He didn't want to come today," Lissa said, taking a sip of her red juice. "He's at home, watching television."

Kate tried not to look shocked.

"He has one of those kitty videos," Fangs explained. "You know — birds and squirrels and fish in tanks. They drive cats into a frenzy."

"I'll bet they don't drive *Phideaux* into a frenzy," Kate said.

Lissa smiled. She obviously thought Kate had just complimented her cat. "Oh, no. Phideaux's much more civilized than that. But I'm sure he enjoys it."

"Doubtless," said Kate.

Fangs went to the kitchen and brought Kate a glass of cranberry juice. By now, Kate was ready to drink it. "I'm glad you came over," Fangs said. "We're talking about the co-op. Lissa wants in, and I think it's a good idea."

"Do you want us to pay you for your day?" Kate asked. "It only seems fair."

Lissa smiled benignly. "Nope. I'm doing this for the experience. I want to practice at being a mother."

"You've never spent any time around children," Fangs said. "Are you sure you know what you're getting into?"

"They're just innocent babies." Lissa blinked liquidly.

"That's what I was afraid of," Fangs said. When she shook her head so vigorously, she didn't look elegant at all. "I don't think children are necessarily born without guile. I've seen children do horrible things. You may be in for a shock."

Lissa's expression appealed to Kate for support. Kate doubted that anyone who had children could think of them as without guile, but she didn't want to discourage Lissa.

"I don't know how innocent they are," she said finally, "but they *are* children. You have white furniture. You have a white *carpet*." Only now Kate realized that Lissa had decorated her whole house to match her cat.

"I will have to keep them out of the living room," Lissa conceded. "Still, anything they dirty can be cleaned. I'm excited about this. Please let me help."

Kate shrugged. Fangs shrugged.

"Then it's settled." Lissa grinned broadly, and she looked just like a wide-mouthed bass. A *fluffy* wide-mouthed bass. "You won't be sorry about this. The kids will love me."

Outside the line of Lissa's vision, Kate thought she saw Fangs roll her eyes.

Fangs's tape of ocean waves ended. As the tape deck re-cued the cassette to play again, Kate realized that the rock music was still going, as loudly as ever. In Fangs's house, with the ocean waves pounding, Kate could forget about the music and the dogs.

"Where did you get those tapes?" she asked. "I have to get some."

"You don't want these tapes," Fangs said. "They're just waves."

Kate was puzzled by Fangs's reluctance. "I'll take waves over electric guitar," she said. "Remember — I'm one house closer to the band and the dogs than you are. Have mercy."

"You don't want *these* tapes," Fangs said. The discussion was closed.

"Would you like to be in a co-op?" Kate asked Jessie when she got home.

"SURE, MOM! WHAT'S A CO-OP?"

"Every day while Sam and Angela are in school, you can play with R.J. and Boffo. Two days a week, you'll all play here. Two days a week you'll go to Sister Stevenson's house. Do you remember who Sister Stevenson is?"

"YEP. SHE'S FANGS."

"You're right. And the other day, you'll all go visit Sister Chrousos."

"THAT'S PHIDEAUX'S MOMMY."

"Well, sort of."

"BUT WHAT ARE WE GONNA *DO*?" That was a hard question. Kate had no idea what *she* was going to do with Jessie and Boffo and the perfect R.J. Stevenson, two days a week.

"It's going to be a surprise," she said at last, unable to think of anything else. "You like surprises, don't you?"

"OKAY." And Jessie trotted off to feel the rock music in her walls.

As far as Kate knew, Jessie immediately forgot about the babysitting co-op. But later, as Kate was making carrot and raisin salad for dinner, Jessie reappeared.

Kate shaved off a sliver of thumbnail with the carrot grater. She checked to make sure she wasn't bleeding. Finding the fingernail sliver in the carrot and raisin salad, she dug it out and threw it away.

"Jessie, come here and help Mommy measure the pineapple. If you're good, I'll give you a bite."

As Jessie supervised, Kate opened a can of pineapple bits and drained the juice into a metal bowl. Pouring the juice into a cup, she gave the prize to Jessie. Jessie managed to get more than half of it down her throat. The rest landed on her front. What didn't soak into her shirt, dribbled onto the floor.

"MOM! I DON'T WANNA BE SURPRISED. WHAT DO YOU DO IN A CO-OP?"

"I don't know," Kate admitted. "I've never done a co-op before. What do you want to do?"

"I DON'T KNOW. I'VE NEVER BEEN IN A CO-OP, EITHER. CAN I DO IT NAKED? BOFFO DOES EVERYTHING NAKED."

Kate wiped pineapple juice off Jessie's chest and then knelt to mop juice off the floor. "I think Boffo's going to be awfully cold when winter comes," she said. "Wouldn't you rather wear clothes?"

Jessie furrowed her brow, considering. Finally, reluctantly, she said, "SOMETIMES. BUT SOMETIMES, CAN I GO NAKED LIKE BOFFO?"

"Only after I'm dead," said Kate. She wondered if Jessie's personality would rub off on Boffo, or if it would be the other way around. Maybe they would combine into two naked shouters.

She imagined the Hairball Brothers leaving their cave next door to complain, dragging a dead mastodon over for a peace offering. "Our dogs can't hear themselves think with those kids screaming," they would grunt.

"They're not screaming. That's just the way they talk."

As the dogs barked and the rock music throbbed over the weekend, Kate kept thinking about Fangs's ocean waves. She wanted a set of those tapes. She didn't want to make illegal copies of Fangs's tapes; she only wanted to buy a set of her own. Fangs was so reasonable otherwise; Kate couldn't imagine why Fangs was so determined to keep her ocean waves to herself.

Next time she saw Lissa, she asked her.

"You don't want Fangs's tapes," Lissa said. "They'd turn you into Fangs."

Kate snorted. "If you mean smart and competent and beautiful, I can live with that."

"I'm serious," Lissa said, blinking her wide-eyed blink. "Those tapes were made just for Fangs. You don't need them."

Kate was disgusted with both her new neighbors. Fangs had the one weapon that would protect Kate's family from the Cave Brothers, and neither she nor Lissa thought Kate was worth sharing it with. Kate determined to find her own ocean waves. One way or another, she would insulate her family from the barking dogs and the incessant rock music.

Chapter 6

Kate anticipated Labor Day and the beginning of the co-op with excitement and dread. It would mean freedom, yes, but Kate's days would be nerve-wracking. What if she couldn't control R.J. and Boffo?

The first day of the co-op followed Labor Day, and Kate had drawn the Tuesday and Thursday shift. To Kate's surprise, Fangs had easily found a doctor's office to share on Tuesdays and Thursdays, leaving her Monday and Wednesday to co-op and Friday to do Relief Society work. Lissa took the Friday co-op shift.

Because Kate would begin the co-op, the day after Labor Day, all the pressure was on her. She had to do it right, or Fangs and Lissa would know what kind of a mother she really was. Kate's reputation was on the line. She couldn't screw up.

Kate spent August bedtimes staring at the ceiling, deciding what to do on her co-op days. She arranged the weeks of the year alphabetically, beginning the first week appropriately enough at A. Aviaries. Airports. The first week would be a winner.

The Friday night before Labor Day, she put all her ideas down on paper. Propping a pillow behind her back, she filled a notebook with suggestions for every week of the year. Martin watched her from his side of the bed.

"You've been making charts and lists for hours," he said when he finally caught Kate's attention. "It's just a babysitting job. It's only two days a week."

Kate tucked her calendar inside her notebook and capped her pen. "It's not a job I'm suited for," she said. "I don't have a talent for motherhood."

"People don't have a talent for motherhood, Kate. They just do it."

"I don't just do it," Kate said wearily. "I have to work at it every moment of my life. But now, at least I'm ready for the co-op. Let me tell you my plan."

She held up her notebook and referred to its pages as she talked. "Every week I'm going to feature a different letter of the alphabet. The first week will be A week, so I'll take them to the airport on Tuesday. On Thursday, we can visit the aviary and feed the ducks."

Martin lowered the business section of the Salt Lake *Tribune* and pushed his glasses up on his nose. "You took all those notes for *that?*" he asked. "You can't feed the ducks without writing it *down?*"

"I don't want to make a fool of myself." There was annoyance in Kate's voice as she responded to Martin. The answer was so obvious.

Martin seemed unimpressed. "How many children are you tending, anyway? Are you taking on the whole neighborhood?"

"You know it's only three," Kate said. "It's Jessie and R.J. and Boffo."

"You're already taking care of three children," Martin said. "Jessie and Angela and Sam. I don't see you filling out charts and calendars for that."

"Of course not." Kate hated when Martin was so pragmatic. She sounded less patient than she wanted to sound, but Martin was so obtuse. "Those are *our* children. I don't need charts and graphs for Sam and Jessie and Angela."

Martin nodded sagely. "Then all this effort is for Fangs Stevenson's kids," he said. "Why do you love R.J. and Boffo more than you love our own children?"

Kate inched over toward her own side of the bed. She had passed annoyance and was quickly getting furious. "Why would you say anything like that?" she asked. "That was a cheap shot."

"You haven't taken your *own* children to the aviary and the airport, have you?"

"Martin, this is a *job*."

"I thought being a mother was a job."

Kate blushed to the roots of her fingernails. The aviary forgotten, she put the notebook and the calendar under the bed. Turning her back on Martin, she lay on her side and seethed until she finally fell asleep.

On Tuesday morning, after sending Martin off to work and Sam and Angela off to school, Kate found herself putting on makeup. Angrily she wiped her face clean. Then she decided that a little lipstick wouldn't hurt, and she put just a smidgen of lipstick back on her lips. She did look better.

She watched the procession from next door, as Fangs dropped off R.J. and Boffo on the way to work. They arrived at exactly 8:30 A.M. Fangs seemed delighted to have a day of freedom, and she waved farewell to her sons with a cheery goodbye wave. Kate wished she had as much faith in herself as Fangs apparently had in her.

When Fangs's back was turned, Kate said hello to R.J. and Boffo. Boffo was fully clothed, and Kate took that as a good omen. R.J. carried a thick book under his left arm.

"You won't need that book today," Kate said in her children voice as she ushered Boffo and R.J. inside. "Do you know what today is?"

"It's Tuesday, Sister Carbine," R.J. said helpfully. He smiled broadly and looked Kate straight in the eye.

"That's right; it's Tuesday. And call me Kate."

"All right, Sister Carbine. I'll call you Kate."

Kate smiled. She liked R.J. already. He was so normal compared to Boffo, who was already sitting on the floor, studiously removing his shoes. Fangs had double-tied the laces of Boffo's sneakers, and the little boy's pudgy fingers picked hopelessly at the knots. Jessie knelt on the floor next to Boffo. Tugging the ends of the shoelaces to loose them, she only pulled the knots tighter.

Ignoring Boffo and Jessie, Kate returned to her conversation with R.J. "Yes, it *is* Tuesday," she agreed, raising her voice to capture the interest of all three children. "It's Tuesday of the first week of the co-op."

When the children looked at her blankly, she continued, "Does anyone know the first letter of the alphabet?"

Boffo and Jessie looked at Kate as if she had lost her mind. "Do you have a knife?" Boffo asked, ignoring Kate's question.

Knives were not on Kate's agenda. "I *said*," she repeated, speaking just a little more firmly than she had before, "does anyone know the first letter of the alphabet?"

Again, Boffo and Jessie ignored her. To her relief, she saw R.J. patiently raise his hand, waiting to be acknowledged.

"Yes, R.J.?"

"It's *A*, Sister Carbine. The first letter of the alphabet is *A*."

Kate could have kissed R.J. right on the forehead. "You're right," she said, including all three children in her comments, "*A* is the first letter of the alphabet. Since this is the first week of the co-op, this will be *A* week. Everything you do when you're with me on Tuesday and Thursday will begin with an *A*. Won't that be fun?"

"Help me get my shoes off," Boffo demanded. He hadn't yet grasped the *A* concept, being more preoccupied with his shoelaces.

Kate shook her head. "No, sir. If your mom tied your shoes that tightly, she must have wanted them to stay on. Can any of you think of words beginning with *A*?"

Jessie watched, transfixed, as Boffo tried to pry off one shoe with the toes of his other shoe. Again, Kate turned to R.J.'s raised hand.

"Alligator," R.J. said. "Albatross. Avalanche."

Kate smiled, impressed with the words R.J. chose. R.J. was Fangs's child: He was smart. Kate would have to stay on her toes to keep him entertained.

"Afghanistan," R.J. continued helpfully. "Army ant."

"That's good, R.J. That's excellent. Jessie, can you think of a word that starts with *A*?"

"VOLKSWAGEN!" Jessie boomed triumphantly. "MOM, CAN WE GET A VOLKSWAGEN?"

Kate knelt in front of Jessie. This was a teaching moment. She barely saw Boffo leave the room as she put her arms around Jessie's shoulders.

"Jessie, Volkswagen begins with a V. That's kind of like an upside-down A. Can you think of any words that begin with A?"

"MOM, I WANT A VOLKSWAGEN. SAM SAYS THEY LOOK LIKE LITTLE BUGS."

"That's true," Kate said. "They look like *little* bugs. They're so little, our whole family wouldn't fit inside."

"OH," yelled Jessie, considering. "THEN CAN WE GET A VOLKSWAGEN WHEN DADDY DIES?"

"Jessie!" Kate was shocked. This wasn't going at all the way she had expected it. "Daddy is going to live for a long, long time."

"THAT'S OKAY," Jessie yelled agreeably. "WE'LL PUT HIM IN THE TRUNK."

Kate saw that R.J. had raised his hand for attention. "You don't have to raise your hand here," she said. "What do you want to say?"

"Anchor. Aardvark. Alabama."

"Very good, R.J.," Kate said. Then, realizing she had lost one of the troops, she raised her voice: "Boffo! Where are you?"

"Boogers!" Boffo sounded royally disgusted. "Double boogers!"

Kate stood and followed Boffo's voice to the kitchen. Boffo was sitting on the kitchen floor. His left shoe was off, the laces hacked through with one of Kate's steak knives. The knife, which had obviously slipped from Boffo's grasp, was lodged in the linoleum of the kitchen floor. Boffo was sucking blood from a fingertip.

It was 8:39 A.M. Boffo had been in Kate's custody for eight minutes and fifty-three seconds.

She ran to Boffo and squatted next to him on the floor. She inspected his index finger and was relieved to find a cut that was so tiny she wondered why it had bled at all. Things could have been much worse. Pulling the knife from the floor, she sighed and sawed the frayed shoelace of Boffo's right shoe until it, too, broke. Boffo shed his right shoe and sock. He wiggled his toes as if they had been freed of a tourniquet.

From the corner of her eye, Kate saw R.J.'s upraised hand. "Yes?" she asked.

"Aspirin," R.J. said.

Kate shook her head. "No, this is just a little cut. Boffo doesn't need an aspirin. He doesn't even need a Band-Aid."

R.J. smiled patiently. "No, Sister Carbine," he said. "Aspirin is an *A* word. So is Aerostar. That's a Ford."

"I WANT A VOLKSWAGEN," Jessie said. "CAN WE GET A VOLKSWAGEN TODAY?"

Kate sighed. None of the children had read the script. If she didn't regain control of the situation, the day would be lost.

"This is *A* week," she said doggedly. "Volkswagen begins with a *V*. On *A* week, guess what we do?"

"Eat alphabet soup?" R.J. asked. Mentally, Kate kicked herself. She should have thought of that.

"Good idea, R.J.," she said. "Maybe we'll do that on Thursday. But *A* also stands for airplane. We're going to make paper airplanes and have an airplane contest. Then we're going to make airplane cookies."

"Can I watch television?" Boffo asked. His shirt was lying in a crumpled heap on the floor. "Cartoons come on HBO."

Kate forced herself to smile maternally. "Not today. This is *A* week. Cartoons begin with C."

"Astroturf," said R.J. "Accident. Axe."

"I think we get the idea, R.J.," Kate said. R.J. was almost too cooperative. "Thanks for your help."

Kate got out a stack of erasable bond paper and a handful of marking pens. By the time she returned to the kitchen, Boffo had doffed the rest of his clothes.

"Boffo? Don't you want to put those clothes back on?" she asked.

"Nope."

Kate saw Jessie grin, apparently delighted that Boffo defied her mother. Somehow, she had to take control. She knelt next to Boffo and said, "I thought that was a pretty t-shirt you wore. It had mountains on it, and a great big fish. Will you wear the t-shirt for me?"

"Nope."

Jessie's grin widened.

Kate saw R.J.'s hand climb skyward. Maybe he could help. "Yes?" she asked. Her voice was almost desperate.

"Boffo doesn't *like* to wear clothes," R.J. said, stating the obvious.

"I'm sure that's true," Kate agreed. "All of us do things we don't like to do."

R.J. shook his head. "Not Boffo. Mom doesn't make him wear clothes."

R.J. was right. Fangs didn't mind Boffo's nakedness. Jessie didn't seem to notice it, either. But if Kate pressed the issue, maybe Jessie *would* start to think about it. Kate had lost this battle.

"Who knows how to make airplanes?" she asked, changing the subject in defeat.

Boffo extended both arms and zoomed around the kitchen, a bare-bottomed 747. Jessie followed, making more noise than the Concorde. R.J. patiently raised his hand. Kate *liked* R.J.

"Jessie! Boffo!" Kate raised her voice a little louder than she had intended, and two airplanes stopped in their flight paths. "R.J. knows how to make paper airplanes. Let's all make paper airplanes together. Then we can go outside and fly them."

Reluctantly, Jessie and Boffo sat at the kitchen table. Neither of them folded paper into airplanes the way R.J. and Kate tried to teach them. Jessie drew a pink airplane on her first sheet of paper, sticking her tongue between her teeth in concentration. She drew a big smile on the snout of the plane, resurrecting a dim memory in Kate of an airline that once did the same thing with its whole fleet. Boffo drew dinosaurs — green ones and purple ones.

"That's an allosaurus," R.J. said solemnly, ever aware that it was A week. "Allosauruses look like Tyrannosaurus rexes, except for the hands."

Kate nodded in agreement. Privately, she thought Boffo's rendering looked more like a tree.

Lunchtime came, only eighty-seven hours after R.J. and Boffo had arrived. While Boffo and Jessie battered each other with dinosaur airplanes and R.J. read in the corner, Kate made tuna salad with celery. She split English muffins and spread the tuna on top of each half. Then she criss-crossed pieces of cheddar over the tuna and melted the cheese under the broiler. She poured apple juice to drink and sliced apples for dessert, keeping with the theme of A week.

Jessie prayed over the food. "DEAR GOD," she yelled. Jessie always began her prayers as if she were dictating a letter. Usually she looked skyward, too, in the off chance that God was hard of hearing and needed to read her lips. "THANK YOU FOR THE CO-OP. BLESS THE TUNAFISH AMEN."

Jessie attacked her sandwich, licking the cheese and tuna off the English muffin as if she were divesting an Oreo of its shortening cream. R.J., ever the gentleman, ate his sandwich in the traditional manner. He wiped his lips with his paper napkin after every bite.

Boffo picked up his sandwich and set it down again. "I can't eat this muffim," he said indignantly. "It has sand on it."

Kate peered underneath Boffo's open-faced sandwich and saw grains of cornmeal imbedded in the bottom of the muffin. As far as Kate knew, every English muffin on earth had cornmeal on the bottom of it.

"That's just cornmeal," she explained. "The people who make English muffins put cornmeal on the bottom so the muffins won't stick to the bottom of the pan. Isn't that a good idea?"

"Nope," said Boffo. "Looks like sand to me."

Kate persisted, "That's the stuff they use to make taco chips. You eat taco chips all the time, I'll bet."

"Yep," said Boffo, "but I won't eat this muffim. It's got sand on the bottom. Got any Wonder Bread?"

Cleaning up after lunch, Kate chewed thoughtfully on Boffo's untouched English muffin. Four hours had marked Kate as a failure. Boffo had barely escaped serious injury, the new kitchen floor was marred, and Jessie was planning to bury Martin in a Volkswagen. After all Kate's preparations, nothing had gone the way she had planned.

It was all Boffo's fault, she knew. Boffo wouldn't keep his clothes on, so Kate had lost face with Jessie before the day even began. Boffo wouldn't make paper airplanes, and the paper airplane contest had been canceled when Jessie followed Boffo's lead. Boffo didn't even like sand in his food. Without Boffo in the group, Kate may have had a chance of success. But Boffo spelled disaster. It was going to be a long, long year.

As soon as the kitchen was clean, Kate gathered cookie ingredients. She had found three airplane cookie cutters at ZCMI — one for each child to make airplane-shaped cookies as a climax for the day's activities. She had also purchased pink-capped bottles of silver candies and sugar sprinkles and candy confetti, along with tubes of frosting in several colors. Maybe she couldn't keep Boffo clothed. Maybe the children were too young to make paper airplanes. But as sure as Kate was a mother, all three children would enjoy making cookies.

When the ingredients were assembled, Kate called the children. No one came. Sighing, she put down the measuring cup and searched for Boffo and Jessie and R.J.

She found them in the living room. R.J. was sitting on the floor in the corner, absorbed in his book. Kate had seen it earlier: *Ivanhoe*. She suspected it was not a child's version of the book.

Boffo and Jessie stood in front of the television. Boffo held the remote control switch at arm's length, frantically changing channels. He was a crafty child, doing his dirty work with the mute button on.

"Your TV's broke." Boffo said it accusingly, as if Kate had broken the set on purpose. As he flipped from channel to channel, the picture shone with perfect clarity.

"Your TV's broke," Boffo repeated. He stopped on channel 32, and the screen filled with snow. "This is the station for HBO, and I can't get HBO."

"Maybe the cable's out," R.J. said, without looking up from his book.

"The cable's not out," said Kate, reaching for the remote control. "We don't have cable."

"Wow," said Boffo.

"Wow!" said R.J. reverently. This time, he did look up from his book.

Jessie yelled, "MOM, WHAT'S CABLE? CAN WE GET SOME?"

"No," said Kate. She pressed the power switch, and the television screen went blank. "We're going to make cookies."

"Do we have to?" said Boffo.

"DO WE HAVE TO?" yelled Jessie.

"Do you *have* to?" Kate thundered. "No! You *want* to. Into the kitchen. March!"

Politely, as if he were submitting to oral surgery, R.J. put down his book and went to the kitchen. Less politely, Jessie followed. Boffo brought up the rear.

Jessie looked at the candied confetti and the sugar sprinkles. She opened the silver candies and sniffed them; then she closed them again.

"WHAT'S ALL THIS?" she yelled. "I THOUGHT WE WAS GONNA MAKE COOKIES."

"This *is* for cookies," Kate said, glad she had finally piqued Jessie's interest. "We're all going to make airplane-shaped cookies and decorate them with frosting. Won't that be fun?"

Jessie's face fell. "DO WE HAVE TO MAKE AIRPLANES? I WANT TO MAKE CHOCOLATE CHIPS."

"Me, too!" said R.J. and Boffo at the same time.

Sighing, Kate put the cookie cutter and the colored frosting tubes away and rooted through the cupboard for chocolate chips. When she opened the package, Jessie took a handful of chips and arranged them neatly about a half inch from the edge of the kitchen table. Jessie always arranged her food: Peas were organized by rank and file; mashed potatoes were squared off and eaten with geometric precision.

Boffo, on the other hand, favored chaos. Holding his left hand like a snowplow, he shoveled Jessie's neatly arranged chocolate chips into his mouth, chewed twice, and swallowed. Jessie punched Boffo in the stomach. Boffo, unperturbed, only burped.

Fangs arrived at 4:43 P.M. Kate knew the exact time, because she had one eye on the clock and the other on Fangs's driveway, waiting. She tracked down Boffo's clothes, folding them neatly before Fangs knocked at the front door.

When the door opened, Kate held out Boffo's shoes for inspection. The severed laces proclaimed Kate's ineptitude: Boffo could have killed himself under Kate's supervision. She expected a reaction from Fangs, but the response she got was surprising.

"I guess I should have warned you about that," said Fangs. "I'll be glad when he graduates to loafers. Any trouble with R.J.?"

Kate snorted. "R.J.? I'd like to have a houseful of R.J.s. What a vocabulary! He's a perfect child."

"So he seems," Fangs said cryptically. "I'm just glad you survived. It's my day tomorrow. Spending a day with adults relaxed me so much that I'm ready to take on the little beasts. I'll see Jessie at 8:30."

She pursed her lips and whistled once, a piercing shriek that sent the dogs next door into a frenzy. Boffo and R.J. appeared, still alive and apparently none the worse for wear.

"There was sand in our lunch," Boffo said.

"Cornmeal. There was cornmeal on your English muffin." Kate tried not to sound defensive, but she was more than a little embarrassed. She had hoped the open-faced sandwiches would be such a big hit that the boys would brag to Fangs. Instead, *sand.* No more English muffins for Boffo.

Changing the subject, she continued, "I'm glad you enjoyed your day, Fangs. Of course, it may be a little more hectic when you get some patients." Kate envisioned Fangs's sitting in an empty doctor's office while she drummed up a practice. That didn't sound great to her.

"I had tons of patients," Fangs replied. "I'm subbing for an O.B. friend of mine who's recovering from knee surgery. He'll be out another six weeks. By then, I'll have patients of my own to pick up the slack."

"Tomorrow is *my* day of freedom," Kate said. "At last, I'll remember what it's like to spend a day without children."

"I heartily recommend it," Fangs agreed cheerfully.

Kate waved as Fangs marched home with her two sons. Only when the Stevensons were out of sight did Kate sink to the sofa with a sigh. She was dead tired, and she was even more discouraged than she was exhausted.

This was only A week. The alphabet stretched before Kate with relentless certainty.

Chapter 7

After Kate's unmitigated disaster with the babysitting co-op, she was anxious to see how *Fangs* would handle a day with Jessie and Boffo together. As much as she wanted the co-op to succeed, she almost hoped Fangs's day would be as miserable as hers had been. Instead of looking for a physical therapy job, Kate spent the day at home. She didn't even call medical centers in the vicinity to see if part-time work was available. Secretly, she was keeping the telephone lines free, just in case Fangs needed her help. The telephone never rang.

Martin came home from work early with a migraine. Kate pretended that Martin needed her, pouring him a Coke and giving him some Tyrox to ease the pain. She put his feet up on a pillow and looked after him until the headache had receded. Taking care of Martin filled the afternoon.

When Martin's migraine had subsided into a dull ache, Kate felt useless and bored. She went to the kitchen to empty the dishwasher. Martin followed her there, obviously as bored as she was. Sam and Angela returned from school, but both of them immediately disappeared. Kate heard Sam playing with trains in his room.

Jessie bounded home at 4:25, five minutes before Kate would have gone to pick her up. Kate watched her scamper across the lawn, smiling the way Jessie always smiled. Then she slammed the front door hard enough to rattle Kate's teeth, just as she did whenever she entered the house.

"MOM!" she screamed. "MOM!"

Martin clutched his temples and winced.

"I'm in the kitchen, Jessie. I'm just checking on dinner."

Jessie ran pell-mell to the kitchen. She had peanut butter on her cheek and in her hair, and she was breathless with excitement. Filling her lungs with air, she screamed, "IT WAS FUN, MOM. WE PLAYED IN A BOX!"

"You played in a box?" Kate rubbed the peanut butter off Jessie's cheek with her thumb.

"YEP. HI, DAD!" she yelled, noticing that Martin was home. "FANGS BOUGHT A NEW FRIGERATOR. SHE LET US PLAY SPACESHIP IN THE BOX."

Kate was dumbfounded. "That was *all*? You played spaceship in a *carton*?"

"WE PLAYED GROCERY STORE IN THE BOX, TOO. IT WAS FUN. I BOUGHT A ROLL OF POTTY PAPER, BUT FANGS WOULDN'T LET ME KEEP IT. WE EATED PEANUT BUTTER AND JELLY SANDITCHES FOR LUNCH, TOO. I PUT MY POTATO CHIPS ALL IN A LINE."

Kate lifted the lid from the crockpot and turned her head away to avoid the steam. Finally she asked, "Did Fangs play in the box with you?"

Jessie grimaced. "MO-OM! FANGS IS A MOMMY. MOMMIES DON'T GET IN A BOX."

"Oh," Kate said. It had been a stupid question. Then, "If Fangs didn't play in the carton with you, what did she do all day?"

Jessie shrugged. "I DUNNO. SHE CLEANED THE HOUSE AND TALKED ON THE TELEPHONE. CAN I GO BACK TOMORROW?"

"I don't think so," Kate said. "Tomorrow, R.J. and Boffo will come here. We're going to feed the ducks."

"OH." Jessie sounded disappointed. "CAN WE GO BACK THE NEXT DAY?"

"Not the next day, either. That's the day you're going to play with Phideaux — remember? You'll go back to Fangs's house next Monday."

"OKAY." Jessie's shoulders slumped in resignation. "MONDAY'S A LONG TIME. I WISH IT WAS MONDAY NOW."

Martin giggled. Kate gave him a withering look.

"Don't worry, Pumpkin," he said. "Maybe Mommy will talk to Fangs for you. Maybe Fangs will keep the box until you go there next week."

Jessie jumped up and down. Pulling Kate toward the telephone, she yelled, "CALL FANGS, MOM! CALL HER *RIGHT THIS MINUTE*."

"I'll do better than that," Kate said. "I'll go over to Fangs's house and tell her in person."

Turning to Martin, she added, "I want to check on a few things with Fangs."

"You mean, you want to know if Fangs survived. Go right ahead. I'll play Monopoly with Jessie and Sam."

Martin grinned. Kate knew he was gloating. For a cruel moment, Kate wished the migraine would return.

"Have fun," she said. "I won't be a minute." Privately she thought she might visit with Fangs until Saturday, weather permitting. It would serve Martin right.

Fangs's house was so spotless that a stranger would guess she was childless. In fact, the house was cleaner than that; Kate had met plenty of childless people whose homes were more cluttered than this one. There was no evidence that three children had spent a day on the premises, playing in a box. Fangs's make-up was fresh, and she looked as chipper as if she'd had a long afternoon nap.

"I've just come to check on you," Kate said, surveying the cleanliness. "I can see you've survived."

"I'm still in one piece," Fangs said. "Want some raspberry juice? I was hoping you'd come over."

Kate smiled inwardly as she realized why Fangs wanted the visit. Jessie and Boffo had driven Fangs crazy. Kate hoped the problem was surmountable; after all, she *did* want the co-op. Still, the idea that Fangs had suffered was a big consolation. Fangs's house may be clean, but Kate wasn't the only one who had been beaten by the Boffo-Jessie combination.

While Fangs was in the kitchen pouring juice, Kate envisioned Fang's day. Had Jessie broken anything? Had Jessie's yelling driven Fangs completely crazy? Kate only hoped that Jessie had kept her clothes on. That was the last habit that Kate wanted Jessie to learn from Boffo.

But when Fangs did speak, she caught Kate completely off balance. She handed Kate a glass of raspberry juice and put a bowl of potato chips on the coffee table. "I have a ward job for you, if you want it," she said, settling on one end of the couch with her own glass of juice.

"You what?"

"A ward job. Do you want a ward job?"

"I guess so," Kate said. She took a sip of raspberry juice and licked her upper lip. "You just surprised me. I thought you were going to talk about the co-op."

"Heavens, no," Fangs said breezily. "The co-op's a piece of cake. Why? Don't you think so?"

"Absolutely," Kate lied. "Piece of cake. Now, what's this about a ward job?"

"It's nothing major, really," Fangs said. This time, Kate suspected that Fangs was the one who was lying. In Kate's experience, 'nothing major' usually meant just the opposite.

Please, she thought. Not the nursery. I'll do anything but the nursery.

"It's not the nursery," Fangs said. Only then did Kate realize she had said at least the last part of her prayer aloud. "It might be worse, though. Do you like jobs with a lot of status?"

Kate shook her head vigorously. "Not I. Normally the status jobs go hand in hand with work."

Fangs sighed. "Then you may not want the job. This job has no status, but there's a lot of work in it anyway. I've been looking for someone to fill it for months. You're the first person I've thought could do it."

Kate's interest revived despite herself. Fangs knew exactly which buttons to push.

"The reason it's secret," Fangs continued, "is that we'd call you for one job and you'd do another. I have the authority to call women to ad hoc positions in Relief Society, and that's how you'll be sustained. Officially, you'll be called to send out Relief Society birthday cards. Not counting you, there are now 199 Relief Society members in the ward — two moved in at about the same time you did."

"That's a lot of birthday cards," Kate said.

"It is. That's about a card every other day. Of course, we supply the cards and the stamps. All you have to do is address 'em and sign 'em and put them in the mailbox."

"That's my whole job?"

"Officially," Fangs said. "As I said, the important part of the job is off the record."

Kate couldn't wait to hear her assignment. She loved secrets. "What's the rest of it?" she asked. "I'll do anything short of burglary. I don't know where to fence jewelry in Salt Lake City."

"It's not *that* bad. But the pay's not as good, either." Fangs took a sip of raspberry juice. Kate thought she was stalling for time. Finally she said, "I want you to visit people whose visiting teachers miss them."

Kate's eyes rolled involuntarily. After all that buildup, it was only a visiting teaching job. Kate thought visiting teaching was almost as pleasant as nose hair.

"I get it," she said. "You want me to beef up your visiting teaching statistics. I'm supposed to visit everyone who was missed, and you can count the Relief Society as being a hundred percent visited."

Now it was Fangs's turn to look disgusted. "I don't give a rat's eyelash for the statistics," she said. "In fact, your visits won't even go on the visiting teaching records. There are people falling through the cracks because their visiting teachers don't see the vision of visiting teaching. I want you to save them."

Kate ate another potato chip. "You've picked the wrong cookie," she said after she swallowed. "*I* don't see the vision of visiting teaching."

"You will. The people I'm sending you to are desperate. They'll reach out to you like...." Fangs's voice trailed off.

"Like what?"

"I don't know what," Fangs said. "The only analogy I could think of was leeches. But they *will* reach out to you. You can change their lives."

Kate picked another potato chip from the bowl. It was dark and greasy and covered with salt. It tasted delicious. "This is a great concept," she said, licking salt from the corner of her mouth. "But if I'm not their official visiting teacher, why will I visit them? What excuse will I use?"

Fangs shrugged, a gesture that said, that's not important. "I'll help you. Maybe you'll interview them for the Relief Society newsletter. Maybe you'll go to ask favors of them. The best way to help some people is to let them help you."

"I can use lots of help," Kate said.

"We all can. Then you'll take it?"

Kate shook her head. "I don't know." She didn't want the job, but she also didn't want to disappoint Fangs. She looked forlornly at the potato chip bowl, as if the bowl of chips could solve the problem for her.

If Kate thought Fangs would drop the subject, she was wrong. Fangs obviously knew she had her foot in the door. She reached down and took a potato chip from the bowl, but instead of eating it, she held it between her thumb and her finger, waving it for emphasis as she talked.

"This is a great job, if you think about it," she said. "You can keep your own hours. You can still take bubble baths and eat bonbons for two days a week if you want to. Then, on the third day, you can do your church work. Sundays you'll be home free."

Kate opened her mouth to protest. "I was kind of hoping to go back to work," she said apologetically. "You seemed to enjoy it so much yesterday that I've been feeling a little envious."

"No problem. Do like I do — work two days a week and spend the third day on your church job. You'll still have Sundays off, which is more than most Mormons can say."

"You can't promise me I won't have anything to do on Sundays," Kate said. "You can't guarantee that this will be my only job in the ward."

"I can in a ward this size," Fangs said, still waving the potato chip. "Almost nobody here has more than one job. Besides, I'll tell the bishop you're off-limits. Take this job, and you won't have any others."

Kate smiled. She had been afraid that in this new ward, she would be called to work with children. This bishop didn't know Kate; he wouldn't know that children didn't like her. This way, she would be safe.

"Who are the people, and what cracks have they fallen through?" The questions were academic. Kate knew she would take the assignment.

Fangs finally ate the potato chip. She even looked elegant chewing junk food. Kate suppressed pangs of envy. "They won't be the same people all the time," said Fangs. "Right now I'm worried about Lizbet Appleton and Joanna Fries. Myra Frost is another problem. Myra's a walking crisis center. She's imagined enough illnesses to fill a wing of LDS Hospital. She's cried wolf so many times that when the wolf really comes to the door, everyone hopes it will eat her. You're new blood. Maybe you can reach her."

Kate didn't want to reach Myra Frost. She didn't care about Joanna Fries or Lizbet Appleton, either. But there sat Fangs, the only person Kate had ever met who could eat potato chips without getting her lips greasy. If Fangs could be a perfect mother and a perfect housekeeper and a doctor and a Relief Society president, all at the same time, Kate couldn't refuse such a simple request.

"I'll do it," she said.

Fangs shook her head. "Think about it for a few days. This is a big job. Don't make a decision all at once."

"I have to decide all at once," said Kate. "If I think about it, I'll say no. This is the only way you'll get a yes out of me."

"Then it's settled." Fangs smiled. Then the smile widened into a grin. "Spend the rest of the week with your bonbons" she said. "You'll be sustained on Sunday. Right after that, I'll be putting you to work."

Chapter 8

Thursday's co-op was as bad as Tuesday's had been. Only thoughts of Friday kept Kate sane until the day was over. On Friday morning, she was awake at six and ready to drop Jessie off at Lissa's. Today was the day she would look for a job.

Before taking Jessie over to Lissa's, she cut a cartoon from the Salt Lake *Tribune*. It featured Garfield in a comatose pose that reminded Kate of Phideaux. Kate hoped she would make points with Lissa by giving her a present for Phideaux's art gallery.

No sooner did Lissa open her front door than Jessie disappeared inside the house. She sank in front of the television and watched Phideaux's video tape for cats as intently as if she were viewing it for college credit.

Lissa, who was carrying a paintbrush and wearing a smudged artist's smock, smiled maternally as Jessie joined Phideaux on the living room floor. "Come on in for a minute," she said to Kate. "I want your opinion on something."

She led Kate to the breakfast nook, which was laid out with artist's supplies.

"I'm a graphic artist," she said proudly. "At least, I *would* be if I weren't waiting to get pregnant. Now I'm working on a Relief Society project — we're going to stencil 'SuperMom' on t-shirts."

"Are you going to make one for yourself?" Kate asked.

"Sure I am. Naturally, I'll have to alter mine. I think 'Future SuperMom' will do nicely. You're going to make one, aren't you?"

Kate only laughed. The more she thought about it, the harder she chuckled. Some people could get away with a SuperMom t-shirt. Fangs, for example — if Fangs wore it, the words wouldn't be a lie. But Kate?

"I don't think so," she said finally. "I'm all thumbs. But you're doing a great job."

"Do you think so?" Lissa smiled demurely. "What do you think of the artwork?"

The calligraphy was so full of curlicues and flourishes that Kate felt her blood sugar skyrocket, but the artwork was professionally done. "You do know what you're doing," she said, accentuating the professionalism rather than the design.

"Are you sure I can't sign you up to make one?" Lissa looked hopeful. Maybe she was getting a royalty for each t-shirt the Relief Society produced.

Kate only laughed. "I'm not *super* anything," she said. "Except, after this week, I do feel like a super failure."

"Oh?" Lissa's eyes widened, and her lips pooched out in a little O. "Whatever happened? Are you sick?"

"Only tired. You'll be tired too, after a few hours with Boffo. He's a handful. He's *more* than a handful."

Lissa looked solemn. "Did you have trouble?" she asked.

"It depends on what you mean by trouble," Kate said. "I didn't check my agenda with Boffo. He sabotaged everything I wanted to do all week."

"What did he do?"

"Just what you'd expect. Yesterday he jumped into the duck pond at Liberty Park. He said R.J. pushed him in. If Boffo had pushed *R.J.* in, I could understand it. By the way, have you ever taken a three-year-old boy out in public with no clothes on?"

Lissa wrinkled her nose. "No. Whenever I take three-year-old boys out, I'm fully clothed."

"Very funny. But count on it. If you leave the house, you'll leave the house with Boffo naked."

Lissa smiled, but her face retained a vacant expression that made Kate wonder if Lissa was paying attention. "We aren't going anywhere today," she said. "I want the children to get to know me and get familiar with the house. Other than Boffo, how was your week?"

"The usual. Jessie fell in a pile of duck poop."

"Duck poop?"

"Jessie said it was duck poop. *I* think an elephant's roaming loose in Liberty Park. And Boffo led a food rebellion: He doesn't like English muffins."

"I was planning to send out for pizza," Lissa said. "Will they like that?"

"Almost as much as they liked playing in the refrigerator carton over at Fangs's. You and Fangs have an instinctive talent for co-ops. I'm just a natural failure."

Lissa nodded sympathetically. "You'll learn," she said. "Give yourself time."

Friendly advice from a Future SuperMom was not what Kate wanted to hear. Backing out of the breakfast nook, she said, "I have to leave. By the way, I brought you a present." She held out the Garfield comic, but Lissa didn't extend her hand to take it.

"Phideaux doesn't like Garfield," she said.

"Did Phideaux say why?"

The sarcasm rocketed over Lissa's head. It left the atmosphere and headed for Venus. "Garfield's far too snide," Lissa explained earnestly. "He doesn't act like a *real* person."

Free at last, Kate went home to start her job search. She laid out a plan. First she would check the want ads. If that didn't pan out, she would call all the physical therapists' offices in the Yellow Pages. Only after that failed would she go through an employment agency.

She made herself a big cup of cocoa and resolutely drank it even though the temperature in the house was pushing eighty. Cocoa had always made Kate feel secure. After a week spent with Boffo, Kate needed a little security. Curling her feet under her legs, she sat with the cocoa in one hand and the want ads in the other. Balancing the newspaper on the crook of her arm, she looked for a part-time job.

And didn't find one. Either there were no openings available or physical therapists didn't advertise in the newspaper. Kate washed the newsprint off her hands and put the cocoa cup in the sink. She got out the Yellow Pages and opened them to the appropriate heading. There were lots of possibilities. Sanity was at hand.

Then the telephone rang.

"Mrs. Carbine? This is the school nurse at Uintah. Your daughter is here. She needs you to pick her up."

For a brief, frantic moment, Kate wondered how Jessie had escaped Lissa and walked all the way to the elementary school. Then she remembered Angela. "Is it anything serious?" she asked.

"Angela threw up in her classroom." The nurse's voice was accusing, as if Kate should have predicted Angela's illness and kept her home. Then Kate wondered if Angela *had* been sick this morning. Maybe Kate had been so preoccupied with getting a job that she missed the signs.

"I'm sorry," she said. "I'll be right there." She found her car keys after only a few minutes' searching, and off she went to Uintah School.

A sick Angela was even less communicative than a well one. She leaned against the door of the car as if Kate were the one who was contagious. After Kate tucked her into bed, she spent the day making demands.

"I want some 7-Up." "I need some sherbet." "I want some comic books." "Come talk to me."

On one of her frequent trips to Angela's room, Kate put the telephone book away. First, Martin's migraine had kept her from finding a job. Now it was Angela. For the second time in a week, Kate's career was on hold.

With nothing to do but wait on Angela, Kate missed Jessie and Sam. Sam thought everything Kate did for him was neato; Angela only seemed to expect it. And Jessie made sickness an adventure. She was so full of happiness that even illness was something to savor.

At last Sam came home. Then it was time for Kate to get Jessie. Leaving Sam to wait on Angela, she marched up the street to Lissa's house. She was almost disappointed to see that the house was still standing. Everyone could handle Jessie and Boffo except for Kate.

"HI, HON!" Jessie barely looked up as Kate entered the room, but the salutation was for her.

Hon? Kate wondered. Where did Jessie get *Hon?* "Hi, Hon, yourself," she said.

She looked up to exchange shrugs with Lissa, but stopped in mid-shrug. Lissa was white-faced.

"Well, here I am," Kate said. It was an obvious statement, but Lissa looked as if she needed reassuring. Kate thought there was a good possibility that Lissa might faint. "How was your day?"

Lissa's reply was almost inaudible.

"Come again?" Kate asked. "I thought you said something about Phideaux and the refrigerator."

"*That's. What. I. Said,*" said Lissa, emphasizing every word. "*Boffo. Put. Phideaux. In. The. Refrigerator.*"

Kate almost laughed, thinking of kitty footprints in the Jell-o and kitty hairs in the butter. But Lissa wasn't even smiling.

"Are you all right?" Kate asked.

Lissa shook her head. "I don't know. I've never been so upset in my life. *Look* at Phideaux. He's been traumatized."

Kate looked at Phideaux, who was coping with the tragedy in the only way he knew: He was sound asleep.

"I think he'll recover," she said. "Did Boffo say why he did it?"

"Boffo said he *didn't* do it. That little monster put Phideaux in the refrigerator, and then he lied about it."

"Are you sure it was Boffo?" Kate didn't know why she asked. Putting a cat in the refrigerator sounded just like something that Boffo would do. Hunched in front of the television set next to Jessie, Boffo looked just like the kind of child who would torture cats.

"Absolutely." Lissa was insistent. "R.J. said he saw Boffo going in the kitchen with Phideaux."

"I'd say that was pretty good proof." Kate hesitated, then she continued. "Are you sure Jessie didn't have anything to do with it?"

Lissa raised both eyebrows and blinked her goldfish eyes. "Jessie? Jessie's an angel. Jessie loves Phideaux. She would never hurt him."

Kate sighed with relief. She didn't have nearly as much faith in her daughter as Lissa did. Even though Jessie was innocent this time, Kate would have to make sure Jessie knew that Phideaux was off-limits.

After a discreet pause, she said, "How was the *rest* of the day?"

"That *was* the rest of the day," Lissa said. "Phideaux was so *cold* when I pulled him out. He was so still that I thought he'd frozen to death. I took him to the vet, just to make sure he was all right. Jessie threw up in the car."

"That must have been *after* the pizza. Jessie gets carsick after lunch. I have a carpet shampooer at home. I'll clean the upholstery for you."

Lissa shook her head. "No need. I took the car right to the car wash and had it detailed. Even the smell is gone. But I'm worried sick about Phideaux. I don't know what to tell Fangs." She cleared her throat. "Maybe you'll tell Fangs for me."

"I think that's between you and Fangs," Kate said. "But I will tell Jessie to watch out for Phideaux. With both of you keeping your eye on him, I think he'll be safe from Boffo."

Despite Lissa's reassurances, Kate had a nagging suspicion that Boffo hadn't acted alone. At bedtime, Kate sat on Jessie's bed to see what she could learn.

"I HAD FUN TODAY, MOM," she yelled. "I FREW UP IN PHIDEAUX'S CAR AND WE GOT TO GO TO A CARWASH. THE MAN VACUUMED OUT THE FROW-UP WITH A BIG MACHINE."

"That sounds fun, Jessie," Kate said. "Why were you *in* the car?"

"WE WENT TO THE CAT DOCTOR. THERE WAS LOTS OF CATS AND A POODLE AND A BIG DOG THAT DROOLED. CAN WE GO TO THE CAT DOCTOR NEXT WEEK?"

"I doubt it, Jessie. We don't have a cat."

"OH." Jessie bit her lip. Then she brightened. "THAT'S OKAY. I REALLY WANT TO PLAY IN A BOX. CAN WE GET A NEW FRIGERATOR?"

Kate smiled briefly. Heaven knows, she wanted a new refrigerator. Despite truckloads of Arm and Hammer, her refrigerator still smelled like dead frog. Then she shook her head. "We'll have our own things to do next week. I know we'll have fun.

"Tell me something, Jessie," she continued. "What else did you do at Lissa's house today?"

"WE PLAYED PLEECE STATION. I WAS THE CRIMBINAL AND BOFFO WAS THE PLEECEMAN. R.J.'S NO FUN. HE READED."

"If you were that busy, when did Boffo put Phideaux in the refrigerator?"

"HE DIDN'T, MOM," Jessie protested. "HE PLAYED WIF ME ALL DAY."

"Then how did Phideaux *get* in the refrigerator?"

"I DUNNO. HE JUST WENT THERE. MAYBE HE GOED THERE BY HIMSELF."

Kate kissed Jessie on the forehead and tucked the sheets up to her chin. If Jessie were marooned on the Sahara, she would insist on sleeping with a full contingent of bedclothes. She turned out Jessie's light and left the door open so that refrigerated air from the swamp cooler would reach Jessie as she slept. She tiptoed outside Jessie's room, only to be stopped by a piercing shriek from Jessie's bed.

"GOODNIGHT, HON!"

Kate stopped at the doorway. "Why do you call me that?" she asked.

"I DUNNO." Kate could visualize Jessie shrugging under the covers. "THAT'S WHAT SISTER CHROUSOS CALLS ME. WHAT'S HON?"

"That's short for honey, Jessie. Lissa thinks you're real sweet. Goodnight, hon." As she went to the kitchen to put the dinner dishes away, Kate heard Jessie giggling in the dark.

The first week of the co-op had ended. Lissa almost lost Phideaux; Kate almost lost her sanity. Only Fangs emerged unscathed. Fangs, like a cat, would always land on her feet.

Pondering the experience, Kate realized that the highlight of Jessie's week was the time she spent playing in Fangs's stupid box. Even the trip to the carwash paled by comparison.

Kate sighed, feeling sorry for herself. Despite all her plans, Kate's *A* week had backfired. The airplane cookie cutters sat unused, and the prizes for the paper airplane contest were still tucked away in a cupboard. Not even Boffo's dive in the duck pond was as exciting to Jessie as the time she spent with Boffo, buying toilet paper in their corrugated cardboard supermarket.

Kate would just have to try harder on *B* week.

Chapter 9

As Angela's nausea evolved into a full-fledged case of the flu, Kate decided that she was the most selfish mother on earth. The school nurse was right: Kate *should* have seen that Angela was sick before even sending her to school on Friday. If Kate hadn't been so anxious to find a job, she would have noticed that Angela was ill. It would serve Kate right if everyone else in the family got the flu.

But no one did. By Sunday, Angela was even well enough to see Kate sustained as an ad hoc worker in the Relief Society.

"What does ad hoc mean?" Angela asked after meetings were over.

"It means I'll be sending out birthday cards and writing interviews for the Relief Society newsletter. Nothing exciting, I'm afraid."

But Kate *was* excited, if only a little bit. If she did her job well, she could prove to herself that, all evidence to the contrary, she wasn't the most selfish person on earth.

When she took Jessie over to Fangs's house for co-op on Monday, she asked Fangs for her first assignment.

"I'm impressed," said Fangs. "I didn't think you'd dive in this fast. What happened to the bubble baths and bonbons? What happened to the *job*?"

Kate blushed. "My fingers got wrinkled, and I'm too lazy to look for a job. Seriously, Fangs, I want to do this right. You mentioned three women that I should visit. Which one needs a visit the most?"

"Myra Frost *thinks* she needs visiting the most. That makes her a good candidate. She's a late sleeper for an old lady — she's suffering from terminal hypochondria, and she spends a lot of time in bed. She gets up at about nine, and she'll be ready for you by 9:30 or so."

Kate felt a tremor of apprehension. "*Ready* for me? She doesn't even know me."

"Trust me. She keeps one ear on the doorbell, waiting for visitors. She assumes that people are standing on the curb, waiting their turn to take care of her."

"Why aren't they?" Kate asked.

Fangs only laughed. "You haven't met Myra. She consumes people like potato chips. She's burned out every visiting teacher in the ward. *You'll* see."

"I can't wait." Kate tried to keep the sarcasm from her voice, but she was unsuccessful.

Fangs laughed harder.

"Are you sure I'm the right person for this?" Kate persisted.

Sobering, Fangs shook her head. "I'm not sure about anything," she admitted, "but I've got a good feeling about this. I think you can help people. This may be a good job for you."

Privately, Kate disagreed. She was too selfish to help Myra Frost or anyone else. Still, she didn't want to disappoint Fangs. Ignoring her doubts and her fears, she got Myra's address from Fangs and promised to report after the visit.

Kate hoped she could learn something from the outside of Myra's house, but Myra Frost lived in a bungalow. Except for the distinctive house number, it looked about the same as the houses on either side — and about the same as Kate's own house, or Fangs's. Bungalows were like most people: If there was any beauty in them, it would be found within. Kate knocked.

When the door opened, Kate was greeted by a female version of Howdy Doody's clown. Her face was so pallid that it looked as if it had been powdered white. Her lips were a cherry red gash in her face, and her arched eyebrows had been painted stark black. Her hair was an orange color that no natural process had created, and it was cut like a poodle's fur; tufts of it stood out on the top of her head and above each ear. To set it all off, she wore a baggy polka dot dress. From the moment Kate got her first glimpse of Myra, Myra Frost became Clarabell forever.

"Come *in*." Clarabell extended the invitation without knowing who in the world Kate was. Kate felt sorry that anyone could be so desperate for company that she would invite a total stranger inside to visit, but she obediently stepped inside.

Having been met at the door by a bona fide clown, Kate expected to find a house that was decorated in Early Barnum & Bailey. A three-ring living room, perhaps, with dancing bears and caged lions. But indoors, Clarabell's home was as bleak as the outside. The furniture was clean and sturdy. Some pieces looked relatively expensive, as if they had come from Ethan Allen rather than from Sears, but none of the pieces quite matched any of the others. Some were Early American; some were Scandinavian; some were Oriental. Whatever Clarabell liked, she bought, with no concept of an overall theme.

The television was tuned to Home Shopping Club. A chipmunk-cheeked show host sang the praises of a battery-operated insect that hopped around the screen. Its yellow wings were covered with red hearts, and four of its six fuzzy legs held a heart-shaped fabric cushion that said, "I love you." The lavender-colored insect was so hideous that even the show host, who was trained to treat every item on the screen as if it were a cure for cancer, had trouble keeping a smirk off his face.

"You'll have to excuse me for a minute," Clarabell said. "I just have to order that love bug. I've been waiting for it for months. It's only six dollars — imagine!"

Turning her back on Kate, Clarabell picked up the telephone. While she placed her order, Kate was free to examine the focal point of the room. In the place of honor, right above the television, was a huge pen and ink rendering of a singer, framed in black. The portrait was so badly done that Kate wasn't sure who the singer was, but the trousers were so tight over the jutting pelvis that she assumed the subject was Elvis Presley.

"That's — interesting," Kate said politely when Clarabell hung up the telephone.

Clarabell beamed. "Did it myself. I never had a lesson, either. Just copied it from a picture in a movie magazine."

"How creative of you!" Maybe creative wasn't the right word. *Brave* was the word Kate had in mind. It took courage to hang up a picture of a celebrity, particularly a homemade drawing that was so spectacularly bad. Kate would never have had that much confidence.

"I've got others," Clarabell confided. "You should *see* my bedroom."

"I can imagine. My name's Kate Carbine."

"You're from the ward, aren't you? I was expecting somebody. Got milk and cookies for you in the kitchen." Clarabell stalked toward the kitchen, motioning Kate to follow her. She put on an apron that told Kate, *I'd rather be rocking!* and opened the refrigerator to pour two glasses of milk.

Dutifully, Kate sat at the kitchen table to eat her snickerdoodles. Instead of sitting at the table with her, Clarabell leaned against a counter, mommylike. Kate had played out the same scene in her own kitchen countless times — but then, *she* was the one leaning against the counter while Angela and Jessie and Sam ate their cookies out of the sack. Looking up at Clarabell, Kate could remember how it felt to be eight years old.

"You're the first person who's visited me *all day*." Clarabell's voice was accusing, and Kate shrank in her chair. Then she straightened herself up. At 9:34 A.M., it was only four minutes after Fangs had said Clarabell would be open for business. Besides, it wasn't *Kate's* fault that no one else had visited Clarabell. Clarabell should be happy that Kate was even there.

"I'm new in the ward, and I wanted to meet the people I go to church with," Kate explained. For Clarabell's sake, she added, "You were the first on my list."

Clarabell's smile said, *Of course I'm the first one you'd visit.* Fangs had been right: Clarabell had been expecting company.

Like Catherine the Great on her throne, Clarabell waited for people to come to her.

"I don't get to church much," Clarabell confessed.

"I didn't think I'd seen you." If Kate had seen Clarabell before today, she would have remembered it.

"I'm sick, you know."

"No, I didn't know. I'm sorry to hear it. What can I do to help?"

Kate's offer pushed a magic button. Clarabell took a deep breath and exhaled in a satisfied sigh. "Lots of things," she said. "I've got a grocery list this long. The leaves need raking. Haven't cleaned my toilet for a week."

Kate laughed weakly. "I haven't cleaned my toilet for *two* weeks. I haven't raked my leaves, either, but I'll be glad to go to the grocery for you. Give me a list and write me a check."

"Check'll bounce." Clarabell didn't sound a bit embarrassed at that admission. "Go to the bank first, and deposit my Social Security check. I bank at Zion's on Second South."

"Can't I go to any Zion's?" Kate asked. There were lots of branches closer than the ones downtown.

"Second South is my bank. They know me down there. Wouldn't want 'em to think I took my business to another bank. Here's the grocery list. Here's the checkbook. The Social Security check is tucked right inside it. You'll have to find your own pen."

"I think I can manage."

Before Clarabell could issue any other orders, Kate escaped out the front door. Only after she had driven to the corner and was stopped at the stop sign did she inspect Clarabell's grocery list. It was a short list, with a note underneath it. Everything was written in a schoolgirl's penmanship. Age had not robbed Clarabell of her manual dexterity.

3 lbs. ground beef, Xtra lean
1 doz. Lean Cuisine dinners, assorted — NO lasanna
SPAM, 3 large
lettuce, not Iceburg
wish-bone dressing

2 loaves Wonder bread
oleo
7 tomatos
potato chips & onion dip (plastick container)
chocolate cake (with cherries, NOT Germen chocolate!)
french cruelers, 1 doz.
Maxwell House coffee (FOR GUESTS I DONT DRINK COFFEE)
National Enquirerer
Star magazine
Globe magazine — if UFO ship is not on cover (I have that one)
Kotex, extra large box

The grocery list raised as many questions as it answered. Kate dredged into her past and remembered that her grandmother used to call margarine *oleo*, so that wasn't a problem. But Clarabell looked like a woman who was centuries beyond her Kotex years. Did the potato chips and dip and cake and crullers and coffee mean that Clarabell was having a party? If so, who in the world would come? Maybe the Elvis Presley fan club met in Clarabell's home. That would explain the Spam.

Then Kate read the note underneath.

Go to the bank on 2nd south. Depposit all the Social Security check except for $75 — the depposit slip is attached to the check. Then go to the ZCMI for a Playtexx Cross Your Heart Bra — size 34 B. Then stop at Bill and Nada's Cafe (North of Trolley Square) for the chocolate cake. Get the rest of the groceries at Smith's on Eighth South. BRING ME ALL THE CHANGE!!!

Kate almost turned the car around. She had offered to do an errand; she hadn't volunteered to go on a scavenger hunt. Then she thought of Fangs. Fangs had a feeling that Kate would succeed at this job. If Fangs had faith in Kate, Kate couldn't let her down. Sighing, she aimed her car toward 2nd South.

"Did you see anything unusual?" Clarabell asked the question even while Kate stood on the doorstep with her arms full of groceries. Her eyes narrowed into a squint as she quizzed Kate.

"Not particularly," Kate said, dropping the box of Kotex so she could get a better grip on the chocolate cake. "Was I looking for something?"

Clarabell shrugged. "I saw Elvis at Bill and Nada's once. I like to keep an eye out for him there."

Kate squeezed past Clarabell and took the groceries to the kitchen. She set the chocolate cake on the first available counter. She unpacked the groceries on Clarabell's kitchen table. She stacked up the tabloid newspapers and put them on the counter. After returning from the front step with the box of Kotex, she pulled out a kitchen chair and placed the box on the seat. Finally she said, "I wasn't exactly looking for Elvis. Elvis has been dead for years."

"He has not!" Tears sprang to Clarabell's eyes. "People see him all the time. It's in my papers."

Clarabell slapped the supermarket tabloids so forcefully that Kate thought she had broken her hand. She rubbed both hands together as if to soothe her stinging palm. Then, calmer, she added, "If I see him, I'll get millions. I keep a lookout for him. If I don't turn him in, maybe he'll buy me a Cadillac."

"That would be nice."

Clarabell arranged the groceries on her kitchen table with nervous fingers. She lined up the tomatoes in a row, and she inspected the Lean Cuisine dinners. No lasagna. Then she opened the bag of french crullers and counted them. She opened the box of Kotex and ran her hands inside the box as if she were counting those, too.

Finally she said, "If I found him, he might come to stay with me."

Kate only nodded, unable to think of a suitable answer.

"No one *else* comes to visit me, that's for sure."

"I'm here," Kate said.

"You're here today, but will you come back?"

Again, Kate didn't know how to answer.

Then, in a little voice, Clarabell asked, "Why don't people like me?"

Kate hedged. "How do you know they don't?"

"They've stopped visiting me. They've stopped doing things for me."

"When was the last time you did something for someone else?" Kate asked. She was still bitter about the list of errands. She didn't think Clarabell would return the favor.

"Why should I help other people?" Clarabell demanded. "*I'm* the one who's sick."

"Oh." Kate couldn't argue with that. "What exactly do you have?"

"Well, I got tested for a heart attack last month, and I thought I had breast cancer last Thursday."

"But you didn't."

"Not *this* time," Clarabell said pointedly. Then Kate understood that even Clarabell knew nothing was wrong with her.

"Then what *is* wrong with you, Myra?" she asked, playing the game.

"I don't know," said Clarabell. "Maybe they'll find something next week."

"And maybe they won't. Don't go looking for trouble. Think positively."

"But I'm *sick*." Clarabell wore sickness like a badge of honor.

"What are your symptoms?" Kate asked. Clarabell looked stronger than Martin. If *she* was sick, Martin was at death's door.

Clarabell thought long and hard. Finally she said, "I don't know."

"Are you tired?"

Clarabell shook her head.

"Do you hurt anywhere?"

Another shake of the head.

"Do you just *ache*?"

"Well, no."

"Is anything bleeding or swollen or not working right?"

Clarabell's eyes narrowed suspiciously. "You don't believe me," she said.

"That's not it. I'm just trying to understand how you know you're sick."

"I just know. My mother died last year. Now I'm getting old. When people get old, they get sick. And nobody even cares."

"I care," said Kate, lying because she knew the lie was expected. She didn't really *care* about Clarabell, even though she felt sorry for her. Clarabell was so afraid of loneliness that she manufactured illness just to keep people beside her.

"No, you don't." Clarabell didn't believe her for a minute. She must have also known that Kate wanted to escape, but she wouldn't give Kate an out. Instead she added, "If you *really* cared, you'd stay with me."

"You don't see me standing up to leave, do you?" Kate asked. She put out her hand and took Clarabell's fingers in her own. Clarabell clutched her like an eagle catching a mouse in its talons.

"That's better," Clarabell said, as Kate tried not to grimace. Then, "Tell me about your life. What are the names of your children?"

Kate told her. She talked about Angela's flu last weekend and how she would have diagnosed the illness herself if she hadn't been so preoccupied with other things.

Clarabell sniffed. "Children get sick," she said, still gripping Kate's hand with her talons. "It never means anything. They're always well tomorrow. When they grow up, they'll forget all about you anyway."

"Do you have children?" Kate asked.

"A daughter. Haven't seen her since Christmas. She flew in to get her presents. Then she flew home again. She's forgotten me. Everyone's forgotten me."

Clarabell relaxed her grip on Kate's hand. Relieved, Kate stretched her fingers. As fast as a Venus flytrap snapping shut on a fly, Clarabell's hand closed down on Kate's. Kate patted Clarabell's claws with her own free hand. Clarabell smiled.

"Maybe I'm not sick." Clarabell looked intently into Kate's eyes, as if awaiting her reaction.

Kate brightened. She thought Clarabell would want to see a big, cheerful smile. "*That's* good news," she said.

Clarabell only shook her head. "If I tell 'em I'm well, they don't come to visit me anymore."

"I'll come to visit you," Kate said. "Now I have to go home."

"I knew it," Clarabell said with a sigh. "Nobody ever stays."

"If I stayed here all the time, it wouldn't be special anymore. This way, I can come again."

"*I'd* like it if you stayed," Clarabell said. Nevertheless, she released Kate's hand. Kate stood and gave Clarabell a hug. With one last look at the pen and ink drawing of Elvis Presley, she shut Clarabell's door behind her.

"What about my toilet?" Clarabell called when Kate was halfway down the sidewalk. "Aren't you going to rake my leaves?"

Kate knew that if she did everything Clarabell wanted, she would never escape. Clarabell would manufacture one chore after another, bleeding her dry of energy for anything else. "Sorry." she said. "I have to run. It was wonderful meeting you. I'll come back another time." Kate rooted through her purse to find her keys.

"If Elvis were here, *he* wouldn't ignore me," Clarabell said as Kate opened the door of the car. "One day I'll find him. Even for a zillion dollars, I wouldn't turn him in."

When Kate went to pick up Jessie, Fangs met her at the door.

"Well? What did you learn about Myra — other than that she's one tile short of a tight roof?"

"I do know she needs more help than one person can give her," Kate said. "I felt so inadequate."

"Nobody's adequate to handle Myra," Fangs agreed. "How do you deal with someone who named her daughter after Elvis Presley?"

Kate's eyebrows arched.

"She didn't *tell* you?" Fangs asked. "She named her daughter Elvia."

"That doesn't surprise me," Kate said. "What does surprise me is that she's young enough to have a daughter who was born that recently. When she sent me to the store for Kotex, I thought she was crazy."

"She *is* crazy. She tapes the Kotex to her feet and dances around on them to buff the floors."

Kate didn't think that sounded like a half-bad idea. Extending the concept, Kate thought she could also tape sponges to her feet and dance around to *mop* the floors. That could be a real time-saver. Obviously Fangs didn't agree, so instead of pursuing the idea, Kate turned her thoughts to Clarabell. She said, "Myra did tell me that her daughter never comes to visit."

"Do you blame her? Myra's a human black hole. The more you do for her, the more she wants."

"She's unwell," Kate protested.

"Only in her mind."

Kate shrugged. "I suspect that hypochondriacs feel just as bad as people who really are sick."

Now it was Fangs's turn to raise her eyebrows. "I do believe you *like* Myra," she said.

"I think she's sad," Kate said.

"Sure she's sad, but it's her own fault. People make their own unhappiness." Fangs shrugged. "Maybe you *are* right for this job. Heck — maybe you should be the Relief Society president."

"Hardly," Kate said, but she smiled with pleasure. This morning, Kate had thought she was the most selfish person in the world. Now she knew that Clarabell could give her lessons.

Kate was still a rotten mother, and she was far more selfish than most people. But if she felt empathy for Clarabell, there was hope. That hope buoyed her spirits for the rest of the day.

Chapter 10

As the year progressed, Kate continued to visit Clarabell. She never did all that Clarabell wanted; she never stayed long enough to satisfy Clarabell. Nevertheless, she visited the old lady once or twice a week, running errands and doing chores and holding Clarabell's hand.

She also tried to call the other two women on her list, but nothing worked out. Lizbet Appleton was perpetually busy or out of town, and Joanna Fries was even worse. Joanna always seemed delighted to hear from Kate and was more than eager to set up an appointment to see her, but whenever Kate knocked on her door, nobody answered. Kate felt like a failure in her church assignment, but Kate always failed. She couldn't remember the last time she had done anything right.

She couldn't even find a job. She called every physical therapy office in town, looking for work. Several times she was even offered a job, but there was always a catch. Either she had to work odd hours or she had to commute. Each time, something stood in her way.

The one constant in Kate's life was the co-op. The weeks of Kate's co-op alphabet passed with clockwork regularity. *B* stood for barbecue; C stood for canyon. During *D* week, Kate helped her charges build a dam in a stream not far from home, causing only minimal damage to the nearby flora and fauna. *E* was harder, but Kate solved the problem by giving eye exams from a rudimentary eye chart in her kitchen. Mercifully, *F* stood for fire station, an experience that would have been a total success if Boffo hadn't burned his private parts by sliding down the fireman's pole naked.

Then came G week. G stood for gas stations and grocery stores. It also stood for grown-up. Kate decided to spend Thursday of G week having a grown-up day with the children. She would learn what the children wanted to be when they grew up and take it from there.

Again, none of the children followed Kate's script.

"I WANT TO BE A BUNNY."

Kate raised her eyebrows. She and Jessie and R.J. and Boffo were gathered around a toy metal gas station that had been resurrected from Martin's childhood. Jessie had just wrecked her toy Ferrari on the retaining wall of the second story of the building. Kate thought that was a good opportunity to ask the children what they wanted to be when they grew up.

"Why in the world would you want to dress up in a bunny suit?" she asked.

"NOT A PERSON IN A BUNNY SUIT. I WANT TO BE A BUNNY."

Kate ruffled Jessie's hair. For a moment, her bangs stood straight up, as electric as Jessie's personality. Finally she said, "You can't be a bunny. You're a little girl."

"OH. THEN I WANT TO BE THE TOOTH FAIRY."

"You can't be that, either," said Kate. "There's only one tooth fairy, and the job is already taken."

Jessie exhaled loudly, obviously disgusted. "IF I HAVE TO BE A PERSON," she yelled, "I WANT TO BE A CHECK-OUT LADY."

"That's good enough," Kate said, mollified. There were a lot of things that Kate could do with that. The children could play supermarket, and Jessie could be the checker. Suddenly, things started looking up.

Jessie picked up the wreckage of her Ferrari and pushed it over the edge of the gas station's retaining wall. It fell to the carpet with a thump.

"BUT I REALLY WANT TO BE A BUNNY."

"We'll see, Jessie. We'll see. R.J., what do *you* want to be?"

R.J. smiled and straightened up from his slouch over the gas station. He looked Kate straight in the eye and said, "I want to be president of the church."

"Oh," Kate said. "That's nice." For once, the ever-helpful R.J. hadn't helped her at all. Kate didn't know how in the world she could play a game about being church president. Maybe R.J. could give a sermon, but Kate didn't think for a minute that Boffo and Jessie would sit still for it.

Besides, the whole thought of a child aspiring to a position like that made Kate more than a little nervous. It even seemed just a little sacrilegious to make a game out of being the prophet. Kate would have to think about this one.

Kate pushed her toy Mustang down the ramp from the parking level and pulled up at one of the gas pumps. Pulling the rubber hose from its cradle, she filled the car with imaginary fuel. Boffo wiped off the windows of Kate's Mustang. Kate didn't know where Boffo's parents bought their gasoline; Kate hadn't had her own windows washed by a gas station attendant since before Boffo was born.

"Thanks for the window wash, Mr. Boffo," Kate said. "You're a great gas station attendant. Is that what you want to be when you grow up?"

"Nope." Boffo polished Kate's front window again, just as thoroughly as he had done it seconds before.

"Then what *do* you want to be when you grow up?"

"Nothing."

Kate laughed, an indulgent mother's laugh. "You *have* to be something, Boffo," she said. "All daddies go to work. You can work in a bank or be a doctor or ride on a fire truck. You liked that, didn't you?"

"Yep."

"Well, maybe you want to be a fireman."

"Nope," Boffo said. "I'm not gonna be anything."

As far as Kate was concerned, there was only one criterion for a successful grown-up day: Everyone had to have *some* sort of career in mind. Kate didn't care if Boffo wanted to be a nudist or an axe murderer or an Indian. All she cared was that Boffo decide on *something*. Without everyone's cooperation, grown-up day would crash and burn before it ever got off the ground.

"You'd get awfully bored if you didn't do anything at all," Kate said.

"I'm gonna do things."

"*Now* we're cooking," Kate said. "So what do you want to be when you grow up?"

Boffo's eyes filled with tears. "I'm not gonna grow up," he said. "I don't *have* to, and I'm not *gonna*."

Boffo picked up Kate's Mustang and threw it across the room. Then, as if Kate had banished him there, he picked himself up and sat in the corner of the room.

Kate stood up to go to Boffo. She didn't know what had touched him off, so she didn't know what to say to him. She was still making up her mind when she felt Jessie pulling on the corner of her blue jeans.

"I DON'T WANT TO BE A BUNNY ANYMORE," she announced.

"That's nice," Kate said, her mind still on Boffo.

"I WANT TO BE A GARBAGE TRUCK."

Pleased with herself, Jessie ran all the cars in the parking lot over the retaining wall and onto the carpet.

Once Boffo was in the corner, Kate didn't know how to get him out of it. He sat as if the corner were his second home — a daily penance he had to pay for being a little boy who didn't want to grow up. Finally Kate appealed to the little boy in him, a childhood characteristic that most men carried with them all their lives.

"This is G week," she said. "G stands for gas station and grown-up, but it also stands for grocery store. How would you like to go to the grocery store and get some ice cream?"

Boffo quivered as though Kate had tickled his backbone with a feather. "Chocolate?" he asked, in a tremulous voice.

"If that's what you want."

"Strawberry?" Boffo's voice sounded even more hopeful.

"Sure," Kate said. Kate hated strawberry.

"Pralines and cream?" Now Boffo sounded like Boffo. He craned his head around to give Kate a tentative smile.

"I think that can be arranged. Why don't we all get in the car and see what kind of ice cream we can find. Then we'll come back and have a party."

"Me, too," said R.J.

"ME, TOO!" Jessie's eighty-decibel voice guaranteed that no one could possibly forget her.

"Me, too," Kate said, and the led the procession to the station wagon.

But of course, even a trip to the grocery store was fraught with calamity if Boffo was there. While Kate and R.J. and Jessie were absorbed in the assortment of ice cream flavors, Kate was startled by a muffled yelp from a freezer case nearby. She turned around to see Boffo sitting in the freezer case, as naked as a penguin on an ice floe. His tongue was firmly affixed to a can of frozen lemonade.

Kate picked Boffo up in one arm, holding the lemonade can to Boffo's tongue with her free hand. As she lifted Boffo to the grocery cart, cans of juice that had been stuck to Boffo's skin fell to the floor and rolled in every direction. Ignoring the fallen cans, she put Boffo in the cart and guided the cart around the periphery of the store with her stomach and one arm until she found a water fountain. Just as she leaned over to turn on the water, Boffo's saliva melted the ice of the lemonade can, and his tongue was free.

"I'm cold!" Boffo's first words were predictable. After all, he had just been sitting in a freezer case in the altogether.

A blue-haired lady pushing a cart past Kate sniffed. "I'm not surprised! Taking a naked child out in the dead of winter!"

It was only mid-October, but the lady had a point. Kate shot her a malevolent glance, and the blue-haired shopper scurried away with her grocery cart.

Trying not to look embarrassed, Kate rolled Boffo back to the freezer aisle. At least Jessie and R.J. were still there. They had gathered up the lemonade cans that had fallen to the floor and set them neatly on a shelf opposite the freezer case. Jessie's handiwork was evident: The cans were neatly lined up on the shelf. Only one of the cans leaked lemonade concentrate. Kate considered this a minor miracle.

After all the humiliation that Boffo had just put her through, Kate expected the rest of the grocery store visit to be easy. After all, things couldn't get any worse. She didn't figure on the children, each of whom had a different ice cream selection in mind. R.J. wanted a drumstick, and drumsticks were only available in packages of six. Boffo had his heart set on pralines and cream, but Jessie saw cherries jubilee and decided she couldn't live without that.

Kate, seeing no compromise, finally put all three ice cream containers in the cart.

"THANKS, MOM!" Jessie yelled.

"Thank you, Sister Carbine." R.J. was always so polite.

But there was no agreeable *yep* from Boffo. Boffo was missing.

"Boffo!" Kate's half-whispered call met with no response.

"Boffo!" Louder this time, but again Boffo didn't answer. Kate picked up Jessie and R.J. and put them both in the grocery cart with the ice cream and the leaking can of lemonade. Even though R.J. was far too old for grocery carts, imprisoning both remaining children on wheels would at least keep *them* from getting lost.

Kate circumnavigated the supermarket once, then twice. No Boffo. She was about to check the parking lot when an announcement broke into the Muzak version of "Wake Up, Little Susie."

"Will Bosco's mother please meet your little boy at the bakery department?"

Kate stopped in her tracks, trying to remember where the bakery department was located. She had only shopped in this store every week since July.

Then, "Will the mother of the little naked boy who answers to the name of Bosco, *please* retrieve your child at the bakery department."

The second announcement jarred Kate's memory. She rolled the cart with Jessie and R.J. and three varieties of melting ice cream pell-mell through the store, knocking shoppers aside like bowling pins in her quest to find Boffo. Her progress was marked by dripping lemonade, which left a trail on the shiny floor of the supermarket.

She found Boffo in the bakery department, as advertised. He had managed to open a self-serve bakery case and extract two chocolate-covered doughnuts. One of the doughnuts had been nearly devoured; chocolate frosting was caked in Boffo's hair and smeared all over his face and up and down his front. The second doughnut was relatively unscathed.

The bakery department manager descended on Kate. "Is this your little boy, ma'am?"

From the manager's tone, Kate was proud to say that Boffo didn't belong to her. "No, this is a neighbor's child," she said.

The manager didn't believe her, Kate could tell. Nor did the half-dozen shoppers who had gathered in the bakery section to see the little naked boy named Bosco. Kate could hear the snickers. She knew that every person who was laughing in Salt Lake City at that moment was laughing at her.

"We'll pay for the doughnuts," she said. Picking up Boffo and setting him in the grocery cart, she pretended to be oblivious to the chocolate he transferred to her clothes and her face.

Leaving the snickering shoppers behind, Kate fled to the express check-out line, threw a wad of money at the cashier, and abandoned the store.

All the ice cream flavors were ice cream soup by the time Kate arrived home with the grocery sack. None of the children would eat it.

That night in bed, Kate recapped the day's events for Martin in all their exasperating details. When he laughed at the grocery store caper, Kate knew that confiding in Martin was hopeless.

"You're putting entirely too much effort into this co-op thing," Martin said when Kate told him of Boffo's rebellion. "So what if grown-up day fell through? I think Jessie and Boffo and R.J. will be just as happy if you let them play on Thursday instead of making yourself jump through all those hoops."

"I won't," Kate said. "I made a commitment to do this co-op, and I'm going to do it the best way I know how. Maybe I *don't* have a talent for it. Maybe the kids *don't* care if we do something on G week that begins with a G or an X or a Q. But *I* care. I'm not going to let myself down."

"You're not going to have grown-up day, that's for sure," Martin said. "At least, not on your own terms. Find another G. Take 'em to the zoo to see the giraffes."

"Then what would I do on Z week? Grown-up day is all I can think of, and Boffo has ruined it."

"Great Salt Lake begins with a G," Martin said.

Kate smiled. "So it does. You've saved my life."

But Martin didn't smile back. "I've saved your life *this* time," he said. "The root of the problem remains. This co-op is driving you crazy. What happened to the job you were going to get?"

"I don't have time for that right now. Maybe after Christmas. I don't know. I keep waiting for life to settle down."

"Life won't settle down until you're dead."

"*I* know that," Kate said irritably. Then, repenting her sharpness, she added, "There's never any *time* to look for a job. Either I'm teaching the co-op or planning the co-op or doing my Relief Society visiting. There's never any time left."

"It's your own fault," Martin said. "Fangs asked you to visit Myra Frost. Once. Or twice. She didn't intend for you to be her best friend."

"I know that, too," Kate said. This time, her voice was quieter. "It's just that when I look at Clarabell, I see myself in thirty years. It scares me. I think that if I'm nice to her, maybe someone will be nice to me when my time comes."

"You're too hard on yourself," Martin said. "From what you've told me about Myra, you're not like her at all. The way you've worked on this co-op shows me that. You haven't thought of yourself ever since you started this thing."

"You're wrong," Kate said. "Myself is all I ever think about. It's so *hard* to be a mother. I sit through those Relief Society classes on motherhood, and they make it sound so easy. What they don't tell you is that some of us just might not have the aptitude for motherhood. If I were only good at it, maybe I'd be happy."

Martin put down his newspaper and put his arm around Kate. "You *are* happy," he said. "You've been happy all along. You just don't know it yet."

"Sure. And when you come home from work and tell me how tired you are, you're not really tired at all. You're chock *full* of energy. You just don't know it."

Martin squeezed Kate's shoulder, but Kate wriggled away. Martin had no right belittling her frustration. That was part of just being a mother. Nobody ever took Kate seriously. Not even her husband — the one person who *should* know exactly how inept and how miserable Kate felt.

On Thursday, Kate took the co-op for a picnic at the Great Salt Lake. She was sorry that it was too cold outside for the children to float-like-a-cork on the water, but she guessed it was just as well. Fangs had assured Kate that the lake wasn't as salty as it used to be. She didn't want to be responsible if Boffo stubbornly refused to float at all. It would be just like Boffo to sink under the waves and drown, just to ruin Kate's day.

"Who wants to offer the prayer on the food?" she asked, when lunch was served. She was glad there were four of them — one to anchor each corner of the blanket. It was a windy day, and chilly. They wouldn't be at the lake for much longer than it took to eat lunch and taste the water.

She was gratified to see Boffo wave both hands in the air. "Okay, Boffo. You'll be our prayer-sayer for us."

Boffo folded his arms in a militant stance. He squeezed his eyes shut, and Jessie and R.J. followed suit. "Help us not to have tunafish sanwiches for lunch," he prayed. "We hate tunafish. Amen."

Kate looked miserably down at the sandwiches. They were still tuna. Prayer hadn't turned them into peanut butter and jelly.

Boffo examined the sandwiches in dismay. "Damn!" he said. "Double damn!"

"We don't use those words in our family," Kate said, trying not to sound annoyed. "If you promise not to use those words again, I'll make peanut butter and jelly next week. Today you can eat your celery sticks, and I have alphabet soup in this thermos. R.J. and Jessie will eat your sandwich."

"YUCKO!" yelled Jessie. "I HATE TUNAFISH."

"No, you don't." Kate knew Jessie liked tuna sandwiches. This was Boffo's fault. *Everything* was Boffo's fault.

Inspired by Boffo, none of the children ate their sandwiches. Kate ate all three sandwich halves in disgust, demonstrating how delicious tuna sandwiches were. One bite of tuna salad stuck in her throat, and she coughed until tears streamed down both cheeks. All three children nodded knowingly.

Chapter 11

Taco Bell and the Invisible Men

Autumn in Utah was a miracle. The air was electric with energy. Leaves turned crimson and gold. They withered and fell to the ground, where they crunched underfoot until soaked by October rain.

"MOM! THE LEAVES ARE LIKE RICE KRISPIES. LISTEN!" It was Jessie's first autumn away from California; thus, it was Jessie's first autumn. Jessie liked Rice Krispies.

"KRAP! SNACKLE! POP!" she yelled, jumping on the leaf-covered sidewalk.

Kate stopped raking leaves for a moment. Leaning on the rake handle, she watched as Jessie crushed maple leaves into oblivion. Jessie stomped. Then she knelt to inspect the fragmented leaves before she stomped again. Jessie was an automatic mulching machine. If there were a dozen Jessies, they could crumble a whole yardful of leaves to their atomic components. Then Kate wouldn't have to rake.

After a particularly enthusiastic crushing of leaves, Jessie squatted over them for several seconds. Kate watched as Jessie pulled up a glob of Utah dirt. She ran to Kate with her treasure.

"LOOK, MOM! IT BLINKS! I'VE NEVER SEED ONE THAT BLINKED BEFORE."

Kate peered at the dirt and saw a tiny piece of quartz, glistening in the sunlight.

"WASH IT, MOM!" Jessie said. "IT'S ALL DIRTY."

Kate went to the side of the house and turned on the spigot. Martin hadn't winterized the house yet, and the outside water was still turned on. Kate dribbled some water on the clump of dirt, instantly transforming it to a handful of mud. The bit of quartz disappeared. Jessie beamed.

"IT'S STOPPED BLINKING NOW," she yelled. "THANKS."

She ran back to the pile of maple leaves, leaving Kate to wash the mud off her hands.

Jessie's shouts caught her attention. "MOM! THESE BUGS IS DANCING TOGETHER!"

Kate loped over to Jessie, who was squatting at the edge of the sidewalk. She looked over Jessie's shoulder to see two centipedes mating, their two hundred legs interlocked like jigsaw puzzle pieces. Kate, who personally thought that centipedes were the only creatures on earth that were more loathsome than spiders, squashed both centipedes with her tennis shoe before they could make more centipedes. At least the centipedes died happy.

Kate worried briefly that the carnage might be too much for Jessie. Her fears were unfounded.

"YOU MADE BUG SOUP," Jessie yelled happily. Inspecting the former centipedes with satisfaction, she grinned and turned her attention to other garden creatures.

In a moment she was tugging on Kate's shirttail. "MOM! IS THERE SUCH THINGS AS WITCHES?"

"I've never met one," Kate said. "Why do you want to know?"

"SAM DREW ONE IN FIRST GRADE. HE SAYS WE GET FREE CANDY ON HALLOWEEN. WHAT'S HALLOW-EEN?"

Kate hadn't even thought about Halloween, and she smiled because Jessie had forgotten. That was one thing about children: They forgot the first few years of their lives. It was a gift that God gave parents, just like repentance; the mistakes that parents made when the children were young were forgotten as the children got older.

Or were they? Maybe the reason Angela was so bitter was that she *did* remember all the mistakes that Kate had made. Kate stored the idea in her mind, ready to resurrect the next time she brooded about Angela.

"MOM!" Jessie tugged hard on Kate's sleeve. "I *SAID*, WHAT'S HALLOWEEN?"

"Halloween is a holiday at the end of October," she explained, raking leaves into a pile. "All the children dress up in costumes and go to people's houses asking for candy. It's called trick-or-treating. You went trick-or-treating last year, Jessie — you just don't remember. You were a ghost. Do you want to be a ghost again this year?"

The last was spoken hopefully. Ghosts were easy. They required a white sheet and a pair of scissors. Even Kate could make a ghost costume. She wondered which box in the basement held all the white sheets.

But Jessie had her own ideas. "NO GHOSTS," she yelled. "I WANNA BE TACO BELL."

"Wonderful," Kate said. "Do you want Sam to be Burger King?"

"SILLY," said Jessie. "I WANNA BE *TACO* BELL."

McDonald's, yes. Kate always took the kids to McDonald's. But as far as she knew, Jessie hadn't seen a Taco Bell since they moved to Utah. "Where did you see Taco Bell?" she asked.

"ON TV. CAN I BE TACO BELL, MOM?"

"If that's what you want."

Satisfied, Jessie returned to the autumn leaves. Kate shook her head and bent over the rake, trying to decide which would be easier — to dress Jessie like the restaurant itself, or to deck her out like a giant taco.

Dressing Jessie up as a whole restaurant was just too much, Kate thought, but the taco idea was workable. She only hoped that Sam and Angela weren't quite as demanding as Jessie was.

On Friday, while Jessie was at Lissa's and the other two children were in school, Kate designed the taco costume. She felt like the Wright Brothers, concocting a contraption that might or might not fly. But if Jessie wanted to go trick-or-treating as Taco Bell, Jessie would *be* Taco Bell. Jessie would be the best darned Taco Bell in Salt Lake City, Utah. Sam and Angela might go as ghosts, or Kate could buy their costumes at Sears. But one Carbine child would have the costume of a lifetime, and that costume would tell the world that Kate wasn't a failure. Only a good mother would go to that much trouble for Halloween.

She went to a fabric shop and bought fabrics. Then she went from store to store, searching for chicken wire to hold up the taco shell. She carried all her treasures when she walked over to Lissa's to pick up Jessie at the end of the day. Lissa was an artist — at least, she would be if she weren't trying to get pregnant. Her professional opinion carried a lot of weight.

As usual on her co-op days, Lissa was grim-faced.

"What happened this time?" Kate asked. She was always afraid that the culprit was Jessie, and always relieved that Boffo had caused the day's calamity.

"It's Boffo again," she said. "Do you know how many weeks we've had this co-op?"

"Sure," Kate said. "It's *H* week. That's *A-B-C-D-E-F-G-eight!*"

Lissa looked at her blankly. "I don't know why you're counting that way, but it *is* eight weeks. These have been the worst eight weeks of my life. I don't know what I'm going to do with Boffo. Phideaux doesn't like Boffo at all."

"What happened?"

"What happened *today*, you mean. Every week, it's something different. Today Boffo dressed Phideaux in doll clothes. Last week, he put Phideaux in the dryer. I found him asleep on top of our underwear. What if Phideaux had *suffocated*? What if I had turned the dryer *on*?"

"Have you talked to Fangs?" Kate asked.

Lissa shook her head. "I thought of doing that, but I decided not to. I'm practicing to be a mother. If I can't handle children, what am I doing being a *woman*? I'm going to solve this problem on my own."

"You don't *have* to solve the problem," Kate said. "No one says you have to be in the co-op."

"*I* say it. Boffo isn't going to get me down. I'm going to break that kid. I can't have children till I do. How can I have children if I can't control Boffo?"

Kate said, "Your own children would be different." Then she thought of Angela and looked away. The moment was saved by the taco costume Kate was carrying. Motioning for Lissa to follow her, she upended the sack on a table. Brown and red and lime green and gold fabrics tumbled out.

"Let me show you how much fun your own children can be," she said. "This is what I'm doing for Jessie for Halloween. Voila! a giant taco. I'm tearing the green stuff to make shredded lettuce, and I'm wrapping the red around styrofoam to make tomato bits. I'll stuff pads of brown for the ground beef. The taco shell is the worst part. I've got the fabric and some chicken wire, but I'm open for suggestions."

Lissa smiled weakly. "That's an — interesting idea," she said. "I've never seen a person dressed as a taco."

"Me, either. But Jessie wants to go as Taco Bell. Her heart's set on it. You know how children are."

"Tinker Bell," said Lissa.

"Pardon?

"Tinker Bell. Every Friday, Jessie and Boffo watch a *Peter Pan* video after lunch. Jessie calls the fairy Taco Bell. I've never corrected her."

Kate blushed. She grabbed the lime green material and stuffed it into the sack. Then she wadded up the brown and the red and the gold and stuffed *it* in the sack. The paper sack split at the seams, and two spools of thread rolled off the table onto the floor.

"Tinker Bell it is, then," Kate said, smiling bravely as she chased the thread across the floor. "Maybe Sam wants to be a taco."

"Maybe so," said Lissa. "A taco costume is a *great* idea."

Lissa was a terrible liar.

*

To Kate's relief, Sam thought being a taco for Halloween was neato. All of Angela's friends had costumes from Sears, so Angela was just as happy to pick her costume off the rack. And Jessie became Tinker Bell — not an elaborate Tinker Bell, but an acceptable Tinker Bell. Halloween was underway.

Kate made three batches of Halloween cookies on Halloween afternoon — one for each of the ladies on her Relief Society secret visit roster. She decided to have the children give cookies to the three ladies, in addition to taking candy on the regular trick-or-treating route. It would be a good lesson in giving as well as receiving. It would also provide an excuse for Kate to meet Lizbet Appleton and Joanna Fries.

She put orange frosting on the pumpkin-shaped cookies, adding candy corn for facial features. Then, licking frosting from her fingertips, she set the cookies aside and got the children ready for Halloween.

As Kate was dressing Sam in his taco suit, the telephone rang.

"Kate? It's me — Fangs. Just my luck. I've got a baby to deliver, and it won't wait. Rob's in surgery, so *he* can't take the kids trick-or-treating, and Boffo *insists* on going. You know how kids are. Could you take him and R.J. when you go?"

"I guess so," Kate said. "Actually, I was looking forward to going with you so you could tell me which houses are the good ones."

"Good ones? I don't know. I take R.J. and Boffo everywhere — except maybe to the Hairball House. Those jerks passed out dog biscuits last Halloween. Boffo ate 'em anyway. Look — I've got to run. R.J. and Boffo will be over in a minute. If you could watch them until one of us gets home, you'd be a lifesaver."

"Sure," said Kate, but the smile in her voice wasn't reflected on her face. Halloween was a family thing. Kate could watch Fangs's kids, but she couldn't remember Halloween for Fangs. It was sad that Fangs would miss the excitement of Halloween.

She returned to Sam, who was waiting patiently to be transformed into a taco. She dressed him in gold tights and a buff-colored t-shirt. Then she steadied him while he stepped into the golden tortilla shell.

As she arranged the taco filling around Sam's torso, she said, "Guess what? Boffo and R.J. are going trick-or treating with us!"

Sam brushed shredded lettuce away from his neck. "How come?" he asked. "Why can't they go with Fangs?"

"Fangs has a baby to deliver," Kate explained.

"But this is Hallo*ween*. Why can't she wait till tomorrow?"

Kate laughed. "Babies don't wait for anything. I barely got to the hospital before you were born."

"I still think it's rotten," Sam said. "I'm glad you're not a baby doctor."

The front door opened, and two gauze-wrapped boys marched inside.

"I'm The Invisible Man," R.J. said proudly.

"*I'm* The Invisible Man," said Boffo, with just as much pride as R.J. Kate was relieved to see that Boffo's version of The Invisible Man included gauze.

"I thought of it first." R.J. was wrapped in enough gauze to raise the stock prices of Johnson & Johnson.

"Yep," agreed Boffo, fully comfortable with R.J.'s claim.

Although R.J. was tightly swaddled in bandages, Boffo's costume had already begun to unravel. Kate could see that before the evening was over, there would be no duplication of costumes. R.J. would still be The Invisible Man, but Boffo would look like a bedraggled version of The Mummy.

Then R.J. laughed. "You look just like a taco," he said, pointing at Sam.

"That's what I am," Sam said. "Mom made it. I bet I'm the only taco in town."

"Wow!" said Boffo.

"Wow!" said R.J.

Kate's taco costume had passed inspection. Sticking the edges of the taco shell to Sam's shoulders with Velcro, she called,

"Angela! Jessie! Are you ready to go?"

Angela appeared in her plastic mask. "Mo-om! The holes are too small. I can't *see*!"

"You don't have to wear the mask," Kate said. "You look just like a rabbit without the mask."

"But I don't look like *Bugs Bunny*." Angela's whine filled the living room. "Make me another costume."

"I can make you a ghost," Kate offered.

"I want to be a taco, like Sam."

"It's too late for that. You can be Bugs Bunny with the mask, or *a* bunny, without the mask, or you can be a ghost. It's your choice."

Angela's lower lip quivered. Kate couldn't actually see it, because Angela's plastic mask was frozen in the likeness of Bugs Bunny. But Kate knew Angela. She was experiencing the pause that came just before tears.

Miraculously, Martin appeared. "I'll cut Bugs's eyes bigger," he said. "How about that?"

Angela ripped off the plastic mask. "Thank you, Daddy," she said gratefully. "*You* always know how to make things better."

Despite the autumn chill, Boffo was naked underneath his surgical wrappings. Kate saw a flash of his fanny as he stepped outside the house.

"Don't you want to wear a jacket?" Kate asked hopefully.

"Nope. It'd ruin my costume."

Kate persisted, "Won't you get cold?"

"It ain't winter yet."

Resolutely, Boffo headed directly to the one place that Kate was determined not to go — the Hairball Brothers' cave. "Mom says they give dog biscuits," he explained, as Kate tried to call him back.

"Neato!" said Sam. "I never got dog biscuits before."

Jessie ran ahead and reached the front door first. She made an angelic Tinker Bell. Kate knew that even the Hairball Brothers couldn't trick such a little girl by giving her a dog biscuit on Halloween.

Standing on the sidewalk below the front step of the cave, Kate watched as Thag dropped a bone-shaped goodie in Jessie's bag. Without comment, he reached around Jessie and gave each of the other children an identical treat.

"Gross!" Bugs Bunny said. "They *do* give dog biscuits."

"That's what my mom said," Boffo agreed delightedly. "If you don't want yours, I'll trade you."

"Thank you. I'm sure," Kate called disgustedly after each child had thanked Thag for the treat.

Thag grunted.

Kate stalked off, holding Tinker Bell firmly by the hand. Two Invisible Men, Bugs Bunny, and a giant taco had to hurry to keep in step with her.

Fortunately, the rest of the neighborhood had caught the Halloween spirit. Each of the children had their bags filled with delightful, tooth-rotting treats.

When they had collected enough candy to keep them climbing the walls for a month, Kate herded them home. "The *first* half of Halloween is over," she said. "Now we're going to give something away."

"Not *my* candy," Boffo said.

"Not MY candy," Angela protested.

"You're right," Kate said. "You can keep every miserable piece of candy you collected all night. We're going to give cookies away to the ladies I visit in the ward. Won't that be fun?"

"I wanna eat cookies," Sam said.

"I like cookies better than candy. Why can't *I* have cookies?" Angela always wanted whatever she didn't have.

Kate said, "I'll give each of you one cookie, if you'll help me. The rest are for the ladies I visit. Hop in the car. I'll get the cookies, and we'll be on our way."

Kate retrieved the cookies from the kitchen. She balanced all three plates of cookies on her arms and got in the car. Five pairs of hands reached for the treasures. Smiling, she passed out cookies to each of the children. For once she had done something right.

But she hadn't counted on Angela. Although everyone else ate their cookies with gusto, Angela held her cookie at arm's length. Her nose wrinkled.

"These cookies are *orange*," she whined.

Kate tried to smile. "The last time I checked, that was the color of jack-o-lanterns."

"But I don't *like* orange. I won't *eat* orange."

"Fine. Eat candy instead. Somebody else can have your cookie."

"I will," said Boffo and Sam.

"I WILL," yelled Jessie.

"If nobody else wants it, I'll take it," R.J. said helpfully.

"*I* want it," Angela said, unable to give away even something she didn't want. "I just wish they weren't orange."

"Well, they *are* orange," Kate said. "Just quit complaining, or next year I won't take you trick-or-treating at all."

Angela sank into her seat. She pushed the Bugs Bunny mask up on her forehead and nibbled on her cookie as if it were laced with battery acid. Kate had tasted the cookies; she knew they were as delicious as anything she could make. Angela was just being Angela.

They stopped at Clarabell's house first. R.J. beat on the door with a closed fist. Clarabell came to the door and opened it wide.

"I don't participate in Halloween," she announced loudly. Then, squinting myopically at Kate, she brightened. "Oh. It's *you*. Come on in!"

Jessie held out a plate of cookies to Clarabell, and Clarabell took the gift with a broad smile. "Now *this* is the way Halloween should be," she said. "It's nice to see people who don't have their hands out. Come on in. I've already invited you, and you're still standing on the front steps."

All five children obediently marched indoors. Kate hoped that after Clarabell's speech, none of them would shout, "Trick or Treat!" None of them did, and Kate counted her blessings.

But as soon as the door was shut, Boffo spoke up. "You got any food for us, or don't you?"

Clarabell only smiled. "Got some food right in the kitchen," she said. "I had chicken wings for dinner."

Boffo led the way as if he had been in Clarabell's house a hundred times before. Then Kate realized that Clarabell's house was built on exactly the same floor plan as Fangs's. She had never noticed that.

Boffo climbed on a kitchen chair and fell right off again, tripping on a loose tail of gauze. He picked himself up and, carefully this time, climbed back up on the chair. Dropping his trick-or-treat sack on the table, he took a chicken wing in each hand.

"Happy Halloween!" he said.

Clarabell smiled. "Happy Halloween yourself."

"Happy Halloween," Sam said.

"HAPPY HALLOWEEN," yelled Jessie.

"Happy Halloween, Sister Frost," said R.J. politely.

Angela mumbled something from the corner.

Each of the children ate chicken wings except for Angela, who stood by the door as if planning her escape. Clarabell smiled as each child gnawed on the chicken. She seemed delighted to share her chicken wings, but Kate thought she wanted the group to leave so she could eat the cookies by herself.

Sure enough, Clarabell herded everyone out the door as soon as the chicken wings had been distributed. "It's my bedtime," she said. "Old ladies have to get their rest. It's time for you to be on your way."

All five children scampered to the car, letting Kate follow at an adult's pace.

"Thanks for the cookies," Clarabell called. "It was a darned *nice* thing for you to do."

Kate smiled, genuinely pleased. This was the first time that Clarabell had shown real gratitude for anything Kate had done. Maybe she and Clarabell were developing a friendship. Perhaps this was a good omen, and the other two people on Kate's list would also be home tonight.

But Kate's hopes were dashed quickly. Lizbet Appleton's house was almost dark. Unable to leave without at least knocking, Kate herded the children to the front door and knocked anyway. Again, R.J. supplemented the knock by beating on the door with his closed fist. Lizbet Appleton's house didn't quite fall down.

Just as Kate was about to give up, the door opened just a crack.

"TRICK OR TREAT!" everybody yelled.

Kate heard an audible sigh. Then, "Is it Halloween already? I'm sorry. I just got in from Paris. I was sound asleep. I don't even know what day it is."

"It's Halloween! *That's* what day it is! Trick or Treat!" Boffo held out his bag for candy.

Kate stepped in front of Boffo. "We didn't mean to wake you," she said. "I'm new in the ward. My name's Kate Carbine, and some of these children are mine. I made some cookies for you. We'll give you the cookies, and then you can go back to sleep."

Sam held the cookies out, but Lizbet didn't take them.

"I'm sorry," she apologized again. "I don't eat cookies. I have to keep a trim figure. Why don't you children keep the cookies and pretend I gave them to you for Halloween. Is that all right?"

"Neato!" said Sam.

"YAY!" yelled Jessie.

"You don't have any *candy* for us?" Angela asked.

"Not this year," Lizbet said. "I'll have something for you next year. Happy Halloween. It was nice to meet you."

Without waiting for Kate to respond, Lizbet Appleton shut the door.

Fully disheartened, Kate herded the children into the car and drove to Joanna Fries's house for the last stop of the night. The house seemed ready for trick-or-treaters, so Kate and the five children marched up to the front door with the last plate of cookies.

When they got to the door, they found a chair on the porch, next to the door. There was a big bowl on the chair, filled with small plastic packets. A note was stuck to the chair above the bowl.

HAVE A CLEAN HALLOWEEN,
COMPLIMENTS OF CLEANWAY SOAP.
ONLY TAKE ONE.

CALL US FOR ALL YOUR CLEANING NEEDS.
CONRAD AND JOANNA FRIES.

Kate picked up a plastic packet and held it up to the light. It was a tiny sample of shampoo. Glued to the back was a business card for Conrad and Joanna Fries. Kate wondered if Joanna was any better at keeping her business appointments than she was at staying home for church visitors.

R.J. rang the doorbell. When no one answered, he beat on the storm door with his closed fist. Again no one answered, even though Kate saw a shadow moving inside the house.

"I guess no one's home," she said brightly.

"Good," said Boffo. "Do we get to keep the cookies?"

"I guess so. I don't have a pen and paper to write a note."

"Hot dog!" said Sam. This was his lucky day.

"I still wish they weren't orange," Angela said.

R.J. smiled at her beatifically. "It's okay," he said. "I'll eat your cookies for you if you don't want them."

Chapter 12

The Thanksgiving Rebellion

As Thanksgiving approached, Kate realized that she had never in her life cooked a turkey dinner. At home in California, they ate holiday meals at her parents' house — or at Martin's parents' condominium. Usually, to keep the peace, they ate a Thanksgiving dinner with one set of parents and a Christmas dinner with the other. Kate never cooked; everyone knew that Kate *couldn't* cook. Her contribution was to help set the table or wash dishes at the end of the meal.

But this year, Mom and Dad weren't a fifteen-minute ride away. Thanksgiving dinner was Kate's responsibility. And Kate learned a sobering truth about herself: She was afraid of turkeys. She was only glad the co-op was suspended for the week, because schools were out for the holiday. That gave her a whole week to plan Thanksgiving dinner.

As it turned out, Kate didn't have time to plan. Fangs's patients kept reproducing, as relentlessly as hamsters. On Monday morning, Fangs was summoned by her beeper. She left R.J. and Boffo in the hands of Kate, leaving Kate to watch five children instead of the usual three.

Fangs arrived to retrieve her children long after the normal co-op would have ended. As Boffo and R.J. shuffled home through the remaining autumn leaves, Fangs took a fifty-dollar bill from her wallet and handed it to Kate.

"What's this?" Kate asked.

"It appears to be money. If you watch my children, you get paid for it."

Kate tried to shove the bill back in Fangs's hand, but Fangs's fingers closed into a fist. She put the fist in her pocket. "I'm serious," she said. "I won't let you watch my children for free."

"Great," Kate said. "So when I have an emergency and ask you to watch *my* children, I'd better have a fifty-dollar bill on hand. What happened to the idea of doing favors for friends?"

"This is more than a one-time favor," Fangs said. "I'm getting more patients than I know what to do with. I suspect every last one of them got pregnant on Valentine's Day. I delivered three babies today, Kate, and I'm expecting more of them this week. If you *don't* take money, I won't be able to bring my kids over here next time. Then I'll be in trouble."

Kate stared at the fifty-dollar bill, wanting to keep it and needing to give it back. Fangs settled the dilemma by adding, "Do you know how much money I'll make for delivering *one* baby today? You're being grossly underpaid. Take the money, buy a dress, and hush up about it. Then I can call you again."

"I'll take the money," Kate said. "At this time of the year, I can use it. But I need something besides money. Turkey cooking eludes me. Tell me how to do it. Thanksgiving has me scared to death."

"What's to be scared about?" Fangs asked. "You take the guts out; you spray the carcass with Pam; you cook it at 325° until the red button pops out. Of course, there are all sorts of extra things you can do that might be tricky. I can teach you how to debone a turkey before you carve it, and still leave the bird intact. *That* isn't easy, but it impresses your guests like crazy."

"Not interested," Kate said. "You're talking to someone who probably won't even be able to get the red button to work. I'm not kidding about this — I'm developing a real phobia about turkeys."

Kate wanted to see a turkey that had been deboned before carving. She hoped that Fangs would invite her to Thanksgiving dinner, and spare her the agony of cooking the holiday meal. That would be worth more to Kate than a fifty-dollar bill. But Fangs didn't take the hint.

"Everything will be fine," she said. "Don't you worry a bit. Speaking of turkeys, you reminded me that we're flat out of hickory chips for the smoker. You don't have any, do you?"

"Just used the last one yesterday." Kate couldn't tell a hickory chip from a buffalo chip, but she would never admit that to Fangs.

Fangs returned from the store with a large box of fist-sized hickory chips for Kate, and Kate regretted her sarcasm. She had no idea what to do with hickory chips, and she certainly couldn't ask Fangs for advice. She wondered if she could put a hickory chip in the oven. She resolved to try it the next time she cooked a chicken.

On the Tuesday before Thanksgiving, Fangs again spent the day delivering babies. Again, Kate watched five children instead of just three. Again Fangs pulled out a fifty-dollar bill at the end of the day and insisted that Kate take the money. Kate contemplated using the week's babysitting money and taking Martin and the kids to a fancy hotel buffet for Thanksgiving dinner, but Martin would never stand for it. Martin enjoyed his leftovers.

After Fangs had disappeared with her own children home and Martin had arrived home from work, Kate resolutely went to the supermarket to buy ingredients for Thanksgiving dinner. She got all the way to the store before she remembered that Clarabell would doubtless want some shopping done for her. Without even parking the car, she backtracked to Clarabell's house for the additional grocery list.

Clarabell already had the list written down.

3 lrg. SPAMS (not lo soddium it tastes bad)
2 doz. or so Lean Cuisine dinners — NO lasanna or Italian Food
1 Swanson's Hungry Man TV Dinner — TURKEY!!!!
bear claws or apple fritters, 10 or so

ice cream, vanilla (Allways good to have around the
House!)
all my magazines, globe, star, ect.
Kotex, extra large box

Kate shook her head at the Kotex. Come to think of it, Clarabell's floors were always spotless. But the item that caught her attention was the Hungry Man TV dinner from Swanson. Maybe Clarabell was expecting a guest who didn't enjoy Lean Cuisine.

"That's my Thanksgiving," Clarabell said, when Kate asked about the dinner. "Swanson's does a good job of it. There's lots of food — I can get two meals out of it, if I'm careful. I'll eat the white meat the first time around, and the dark meat on the rebound. I never was able to save the best for last."

The thing that broke Kate's heart was that Clarabell said all this without an ounce of self-pity. Clarabell was skilled at the art of angling for sympathy; Kate had spent enough time with her to be well aware of that. But on this occasion, Clarabell sang the praises of Hungry Man dinners as though Kate might be considering TV dinners for her own family's Thanksgiving meal. That was just Clarabell's way of celebrating Thanksgiving: She got a big enough TV dinner that even she could have leftovers the next day.

Kate studied Clarabell's grocery list as if looking for inspiration. She mentally calculated the amount of food she was preparing for Thanksgiving dinner. A turkey could always stretch to feed one more, but she had only planned to make one pie. She could make two.

"I suppose you're going to be busy on Thanksgiving Day," she said. "You wouldn't want to eat Thanksgiving dinner with us, would you?"

"Could I?" Clarabell's eyes lit up like neon slot machines. For a brief moment, her eyes were even brighter than her lipstick.

Kate, seeing the hopeful expression on Clarabell's face, was immediately sorry she had broached the subject. She hadn't checked with Martin; she hadn't asked the kids. Thanksgiving was a family holiday, and Clarabell certainly wasn't family.

But Kate saw tears glistening in the corners of Clarabell's eyes, and immediately she repented her hesitation. Clearing her throat to give her courage, she continued, "We'd love to have you eat Thanksgiving dinner with us."

Clarabell smiled so broadly that her jowls jiggled with the sudden motion. Extending her talons to take Kate's hand in hers, she said, "It would be delightful to spend Thanksgiving with you."

Wincing in the pain of Clarabell's grasp, Kate remembered the turkey. She couldn't cook turkey for her own family. What in the world had made her think she could fix dinner for somebody else — especially someone as demanding as Clarabell? But she had gone too far to back down. Quickly, she added, "I'm a horrible cook. You'd probably be disappointed. Maybe it was a bad idea."

"It was a *great* idea," Clarabell said agreeably. "Don't worry about me. My taste buds are shot anyway. You get to be my age, you sorta lose your taste for food. You could feed me shredded newspapers and tell me it was turkey — I probably couldn't tell the difference."

Once again, Kate scrutinized Clarabell's grocery list. Again, the words offered no advice. Finally she said, "I guess you won't be needing the Hungry Man dinner."

"Maybe you'd better get it after all, dearie," Clarabell said. "If you're as bad a cook as you say you are, I can heat it up when I get home."

At 12:30 P.M. on Thanksgiving Day, Kate took off her apron and stood back to inspect her dinner. The pies were lopsided. They were burned on one side, and just a little undercooked on the other. Kate had no memory of removing the wax paper lining from the pre-made pie crusts, and she suspected there would be a layer of wax paper between the crusts and the filling.

The dinner rolls would be fine. They were heat and serve; even Kate could pop them in the oven without ruining them. The mashed potatoes, corn and stuffing looked okay, although Kate was a little nervous because she couldn't find her favorite stuffing mix in the local grocery store. She hated to rely on a substitute for such an important occasion.

In a burst of energy, Kate had made cranberry sauce from scratch. The cranberries burst open in the pan, spraying red freckles on the wall above the range. Nevertheless, the cranberry sauce was passable. Kate was proud of that.

There was also a green salad. Nobody ever ate green salad on Thanksgiving, but it looked good on the table. It was part of a balanced meal.

As predicted, the red button on the turkey never did pop out, but Kate suspected the turkey was sadly overcooked.

Relieved that the cooking — for better or worse — was behind her, Kate went down to the basement to dress for dinner. She nudged Martin away from the closet and chose a dress for the occasion. Pulling it over her neck, she tugged at the seams nervously. Then she rooted through her jewelry box and pulled out a necklace that Martin had given her about a million years ago. She smiled as she placed it around her neck. In the mirror's reflection, she saw that Martin also looked pleased.

"MOM!"

Kate jumped. She hadn't seen Jessie enter the room.

"CAN I HAVE THAT NECKLACE WHEN YOU'RE DEAD?"

Kate, staring at herself in the mirror, watched her eyes go round. After taking a moment to compose herself, she said, "It's '*May* I have that necklace when you're dead?'"

"WELL, CAN I?" Jessie demanded. She was oblivious to the nuances of grammar.

Kate hedged. "We'll see. What if Angela wants it?"

"I ASKED FIRST."

"So you did," Martin said. "We'll take the matter under advisement."

Jessie giggled and scampered upstairs.

"Why does she say these things?" Kate asked. She no longer felt pretty. Now, she only felt fragile and old.

"What things?" Martin asked.

"She wants my necklace when I'm dead. She wants a Volkswagen when *you're* dead. That doesn't bother you?"

Martin shrugged. "Why should it? She gets it from you. You're always saying, 'Not while I'm alive,' or, 'Not while I'm your mother,' or, 'Not in this life.' It's only natural for Jessie to talk the same way you do. Besides, I'm glad she knows that this life isn't permanent."

"I think it's frightening," Kate said.

"*I* think it's healthy. She's okay, Kate. Jessie probably has a better outlook than either one of us."

Martin opened his mouth to add something else, but he was interrupted by Angela. She appeared in the doorway like an avenging angel. "When are we eating dinner? I'm *hungry*."

Kate straightened the necklace around her neck. After a last look in the mirror, she said, "We'll eat as soon as Sister Frost gets here."

"Who's Sister Frost?"

"She's a widow in the ward," Kate said. "You remember — the one who gave us the chicken wings on Halloween. She didn't have anywhere else to go today, so I invited her to eat here."

"I don't want to eat Thanksgiving with an old lady," Angela complained. "Why can't it just be us?"

Martin glared. "Your mother has already invited her — that's why."

"She didn't ask me." Angela sounded just like a table saw when she whined.

"She doesn't have to ask your opinion. You don't want Sister Frost to spend Thanksgiving by herself, do you?"

Angela folded her arms stubbornly across her chest. "I don't care *what* she does," she said, "but she'd better not do it here. I won't eat with her, and if she eats here, I won't eat with any of you."

"That's fine," Martin said. "You can eat Thanksgiving dinner in your room."

Angela ran up the stairs to her bedroom and slammed the door behind her, but Martin didn't follow. Kate felt a surge of love for Martin. She knew how hard it was for him to take sides, and she was pleased he had stood behind her.

A few minutes later, as Kate was scooping a dollop of butter onto the mound of mashed potatoes, she heard the creak of Angela's bedroom door. She watched Angela go to the living room and kneel on the sofa to peer outside the living room window. Angela looked as if she were standing sentinel against an interloper. Kate hoped that Angela wouldn't say anything rude in front of Clarabell.

When Clarabell's ancient Buick pulled to a stop in front of the house, Angela wailed in anguish. Instead of throwing open the front door to greet the guest, she reported to the kitchen.

"She looks like a clown," Angela said. "I'm *not* eating Thanksgiving dinner with a clown."

Angela was nothing if not perceptive. Kate looked out the front window to see that Clarabell was wearing the same baggy polka dot dress that Kate had seen so many times before. She was wearing an extra gallon of day-glo lipstick, and she must have applied a fresh coat of Elvis Black Eyebrow Paint to celebrate the occasion.

Seeing Clarabell's lips, Kate scurried to the dining room to remove the cloth napkins from the dinner table. She tucked the napkins away in the china closet and hurried to the front door, opening the door just as Clarabell raised her hand to the doorbell. Behind her, she heard Angela slam the door to her bedroom.

Clarabell kissed Kate right on the mouth. "Happy Thanksgiving!" she cried. "It's a *wonderful* day."

As discreetly as she could manage it, Kate licked lipstick from her teeth.

"Sit down," she said heartily. "Jessie and Sam are watching the Macy's parade. I'm putting dinner on the table right now. You can just sit here and relax till we're ready to eat."

"Don't mind if I do," said Clarabell. "Nothing beats a good parade, except maybe Home Shopping Club. You know, they're having a great sale today...."

Sam and Jessie looked at Kate in horror.

"I'm *so* sorry," Kate said. "We don't have cable. I'm afraid you'll have to make do with the parade. We'll be eating in a minute anyway. Just let me fill the water glasses."

Leaving to watch the parade with Clarabell, Jessie, and Sam, Kate filled the water glasses and popped a batch of dinner rolls in the oven. Making one trip after another, she filled the table with Thanksgiving food as Martin carved the turkey in the kitchen.

Then she heard the front door slam. Looking out the kitchen window, Kate saw Angela march resolutely to Fangs's house. She felt a surge of anger and hopelessness, but she took a few deep breaths to calm herself. This was Thanksgiving; she had to be happy. Worrying about Angela wouldn't help things a bit.

When the front door opened just a few minutes later, Kate sighed with relief. Fangs had talked some sense into Angela, bless her. And the timing was perfect — everyone was sitting around the table, waiting for Martin to say the prayer. Maybe Thanksgiving *wouldn't* be a disaster.

But the newcomer wasn't Angela; it was Boffo, wearing his Thanksgiving Day birthday suit. "It's Fursday," he said. "I'm sposed to be here on Fursday." He pulled out Angela's chair and sat at the place that had been set for Angela. Taking the big paper napkin from underneath his fork, he spread it demurely across his lap. The white paper covered his private parts, and he looked like a little old man with white boxer shorts. He was a fitting date for Clarabell, being considerably more alive than Elvis Presley.

Clarabell inspected the children sitting around the table. "This is two boys and a girl," she said. "I thought you had two girls and a boy."

"We do," Kate explained. "Our oldest has apparently gone next door for dinner. Boffo Stevenson is here to take her place."

"I'm Boffo," Boffo said proudly. "I always come over here on Fursdays."

"So I've heard," said Clarabell. "What happened to your clothes, young man?"

Jessie tugged insistently on Clarabell's sleeve. "BOFFO DOESN'T GOT ANY CLOTHES. HIS BROTHER SENT 'EM TO OUTER SPACE."

"That happens," Clarabell agreed solemnly. Kate smiled at the way Clarabell handled children. Kate would have scolded

Jessie for making up stories, but Clarabell played along like a professional. Kate could learn a lesson or two from Clarabell.

Then Kate realized that Clarabell might not be playing along at all. Anyone who read the tabloids and spent her afternoons looking for a dead man could believe anything. She looked at Clarabell with new misgivings.

Martin cleared his throat and said the blessing. He prayed for peace in the home as well as in the rest of the world. Kate appreciated that. She only wished that Angela were there to hear it.

Then the food was passed. Boffo hadn't grasped the concept of counter-clockwise. Letting his napkin fall to the floor, he ran around the table with his plate, a two-legged garbage truck making pick-ups on his route. He reached over Sam's arm and grabbed a turkey wing off the platter. He scooped the pool of butter from the top of the mashed potatoes, leaving the potatoes virtually intact underneath the butter. He mounded his plate with corn and bypassed the stuffing and the cranberry sauce altogether. He took four of the dozen dinner rolls, prompting Kate to run to the kitchen and stick another package of heat-and-serve rolls into the oven.

To Kate's surprise, Clarabell's table manners mirrored Boffo's. Kate was appalled to see that Clarabell couldn't or wouldn't eat anything on the table.

"Cranberry sauce is too tart for my taste," Clarabell said cheerfully. "Puckers my mouth all up." She turned down the turkey, saying that the dark meat was too greasy and the light meat was too dry. Lettuce gave her gas.

Clarabell put a mound of mashed potatoes on her plate, but she declined gravy. Kate blushed; she knew the gravy was lumpy, but she didn't think it was *that* lumpy. The only other thing Clarabell took from the serving dishes was a pair of dinner rolls, without butter.

Kate was humiliated. Clarabell's plate was nearly bare. She couldn't understand Clarabell's sudden food fetishes. After all, Clarabell had been planning to eat a TV dinner for Thanksgiving. This was a woman who consumed *Spam*.

"At least have some candied yams," Kate said, glad she had opened a can of S&W and melted some marshmallows on top.

Clarabell waited until her mouth was full of dinner roll before she answered. "Not today, dearie. Sweet potatoes get caught in my dentures. It causes an unholy mess."

"You have fake teeth?" Sam asked. "Neato!"

"Take 'em out!" Boffo cried. "I wanna see your mouf naked."

Before Kate could say, "Not at the dinner table," Clarabell lowered her face into her napkin. Kate heard a loud sucking sound, and Clarabell raised her toothless head.

"Neato!" said Sam.

"THAT'S A NEAT TRICK!" Jessie agreed.

Boffo wrinkled his nose. "Your mouf looks like a raisin," he said. "I wish I could do that."

Clarabell smiled proudly. "You have to be *real* old to do that trick," she said.

Jessie clapped her hands in delight. "*YOU* DO IT, DAD!" she yelled.

"I'm not old enough. Ask your mother."

"OKAY, MOM! TAKE YOUR TEETH OUT FOR ME!"

Martin giggled. Clarabell giggled, and the noise reverberated hollowly inside her toothless mouth. Then Boffo and Sam and Jessie giggled. Kate scowled at each of them in turn.

Somehow, they got through dinner. Jessie spilled cranberry sauce on the carpet, and Sam dropped mashed potatoes in his lap. Boffo polished off nine of the twenty-four dinner rolls singlehandedly. Everyone only picked at the stuffing, which was much more tasteless than the brand that Kate usually made, and the turkey was so dry that everyone put a lot of gravy on it. But food disappeared, and nobody complained. Kate felt herself starting to relax.

Clarabell left immediately after Thanksgiving dinner, even refusing to eat a small piece of pie.

"This is the best Thanksgiving I've ever had," she said fervently as Kate opened the front door. Her eyes shone with happiness, and she smiled so broadly that Kate could see every one of her false teeth.

"How can you say that?" Kate protested. "You didn't eat anything."

"Food isn't what's important. I could have gotten food at home."

Clarabell chewed on the inside of her lip with her dentures. Then, she put her hand on Kate's arm. She kept her hand there as if she didn't touch people very often, and she didn't know how long to touch them or when to take her hand away. "Don't worry about your little girl," she said. "She'll come home."

"I know that; she's only eight years old. She *has* to come back, if only because Fangs won't keep her. I only wish Angela liked me. Nothing I ever do for her is right."

Clarabell shook her head sadly. "You can't force your children to like you," she said. "You can't even force them to respect you. I tried to do it for years. The harder I tried, the harder my daughter pulled away. Don't do that with *your* daughter."

She kissed Kate again, leaving only a pound or two of lipstick on her face because the rest had been sopped up by the dinner rolls. She pulled out her false teeth and made a hideous face for the children. Jessie clapped her hands in delight.

"Thank you for coming," Martin said as Clarabell lowered her face to return her dentures to her mouth. He walked Clarabell to the car and opened the door for her. Kate, watching from the front porch, was sure that Martin's courtliness charmed the socks off Clarabell. She waved as Clarabell drove off.

Returning to the living room, Martin leaned down and shook Boffo's hand. "And thank *you* for coming. But now it's time for you to go home."

"Do I have to?" Boffo asked.

"You sure do," Martin said. "We're going to trade you for Angela. She's our little girl. You belong with your own mom and dad. Send Angela over here when you get home."

Boffo swore: "Damn! Double damn!" Seeing Kate's glare, he amended, "Boogers! Double boogers!" Still, he left the house without further protest.

Angela arrived home a few minutes later, as happy as Kate had ever seen her.

"You should have seen it," she said. "We had smoked turkey and chestnut stuffing. There was a whole plate of crab legs and shrimp. Fangs made *seven* pies, too — for four people! Isn't that crazy? It was the best Thanksgiving of my whole life."

"I liked *our* dinner," Sam said loyally. But instead of complimenting the meal, he added, "Sister Frost plays games with her false teeth. She's neato."

"That's gross," Angela said. "Fangs makes mashed potatoes out of real potatoes, not just flakes. She mashes up a cooked carrot with them. It looks really weird, but it tastes great. She's the best cook in the world. I wish I lived with Fangs all the time."

"Angela!" Kate had never been so furious with Angela.

Angela noticed the anger. Her lip quivered. Then, defiantly, she said, "It's true. I can't lie about it. I wish I lived with Fangs."

Kate clenched her fists. She was the worst mother in the world, but she had never struck one of her children. Now she was afraid she would hit Angela if she didn't control herself. She wanted to knock Angela across the room.

Trying to keep her voice level, she asked, "Other than the cooking, do you have any *other* complaints?"

"Sure," Angela said. "Fangs is pretty. Fangs wears nice clothes. Fangs doesn't drive a beat-up old station wagon. She's a doctor, and you're only a mother. There's nothing interesting about you."

"Is that *all* that's wrong with me?"

Angela didn't notice the sarcasm. "You act like you're my boss," she continued. "Fangs doesn't act like my boss. She acts like my friend."

"That's enough," Martin said. His voice was so quiet that Angela's mouth slammed shut like a mousetrap. "Angela, go to your room. I don't want to see you again until you apologize to your mother. Do you hear me? You are not to leave your room. Not to eat. Not to go to the bathroom. I don't care if you stay there till Christmas. You will stay in that room until you apologize."

"That's not fair!" Angela cried. "I was only telling the truth." Nevertheless, she obeyed Martin. She slammed her bedroom door, and the house echoed with her sobs.

Although Kate had planned to wash the dishes, she went downstairs to escape the sound of Angela's crying. Martin followed her.

"It doesn't mean anything," he said. "You know how cruel children can be."

Kate shook her head. "The reason we think they're being cruel is that adults have learned to hide the truth. Angela was telling the truth as she perceives it."

"That's the key," Martin said. "'As she perceives it.' But she's perceiving it from a child's perspective. As she gets older, her perspective will change."

"*You* heard Myra," said Kate. "Her own daughter has never changed. She only visits Myra once a year."

"You aren't Myra Frost," Martin said. "One day, you and Angela will like each other. I have a feeling about that, and I've learned to trust my feelings."

Tears stung Kate's eyes. "I don't care if Angela likes me," she said. "I only know I don't like her. Sam and Jessie will be just like her in a few years — wait and see. But you don't care. You have a *feeling*. Isn't that wonderful?"

"Do you know what I think about your feelings?" she continued. "I don't think you *have* any feelings. *Your* daughter didn't say those things to *you*. My daughter *did*. You don't know *what* I feel. Don't try to tell me you do."

The 10 o'clock news was just starting when Kate heard Angela's door open. Angela padded up the hall to the living room and stood next to the television.

"I'm sorry I said those things, Mom," she said. "I know your Thanksgiving dinner was good, too."

Angela's voice sounded wooden, and she refused to look at Kate as she apologized. Angela squirmed just a little as she offered her apology, too. This was no apology. Angela didn't mean a word she said.

Kate felt her anger surge anew, but she controlled herself. Even if Angela and she were enemies, they had to live in the same house. A truce was better than nothing.

"I know you didn't mean to hurt my feelings," Kate said. "Now go put on your pajamas. It's time to brush your teeth and go to bed."

As if she had been furloughed from prison, Angela immediately disappeared. The subsequent flushing noise confirmed Kate's suspicion that Angela's apology was centered more in her bladder than her heart. For the four hundredth time that day, Kate felt a surge of anger and self-pity and hurt.

She supervised the children's bedtime, making sure that each of them was tucked in for the night and all the lights were off. Then she lumbered through the kitchen and downstairs to the basement to go to sleep.

As she turned to douse the kitchen light, Kate saw the mound of unwashed dishes in the sink. A good mother would load the dishwasher before going to bed, she thought. Then, after only a moment's hesitation, she proceeded down the stairs to her room. Martin would hold her tonight. The dishes would be stuck with leftover food tomorrow.

Chapter 13

Martin's Christmas present to Kate was a family trip home to California. He told her the good news shortly after Thanksgiving, wrapping the itinerary in an oversized Christmas card. Kate was delighted with the opportunity to go home, and she couldn't wait to tell the children.

Wanting to break the news right, she planned an elaborate family home evening early in December. She bought a California-shaped ice cream cake from Baskin-Robbins for dessert. When she carried the cake out to the family, she was greeted by three blank stares.

"What's that?" Sam asked.

"IT'S ICE CREAM!" yelled Jessie.

"Yeah, but what's it *shaped* like?"

Angela grimaced. "That's California. Why do we have a California cake?"

"It's your Christmas surprise," Kate said. "Your dad and I are going to take you home for Christmas. Won't that be fun?"

Kate waited for cries of excitement from Angela and Jessie and Sam. Their reactions surprised and dismayed her.

"We won't miss any school, will we?" Sam asked. "The last day before Christmas, we're going to have a Christmas party in the room. I'm supposed to take cookies shaped like Santa Claus and two Christmas ornaments and a present for the present exchange; I forgot to tell you."

"WHERE'S CALIFORNIA?" Jessie asked.

"It's home," Kate said. "*You* remember home."

"WE'RE ALREADY HOME. IS THIS CALIFORNIA?"

Angela rolled her eyes. Blowing her bangs off her forehead in exasperation, she said, "California is where we used to live. It's okay if we go, but I have to be back for the ward Christmas party. There's going to be a manger scene, and I'm a sheep."

"I'm really sorry about that," said Martin. "You're going to miss the last day of school, and I'm afraid we're going to miss the ward Christmas party, too. We have to go when my boss lets me off work. We'll all have to adjust."

Sam scowled. Angela wailed. Jessie yelled, "DO WE HAVE TWO HOUSES? I WANNA SEE THE OTHER ONE."

Sam said, "If we go to California, our Christmas tree will get lonely."

Martin laughed. He was trying to help the situation. "We won't even *have* a Christmas tree this year," he said. "You'll have presents under Grandma Carbine's tree, and Grandma Hollister's tree, too."

"NO CHRISTMAS TREE?" Jessie yelled.

"No *Christmas* tree?" Angela dissolved into sobs. Running to her room, she slammed the door behind her.

The family home evening that began as a surprise ended in disaster. Angela was so busy crying herself to sleep that she didn't even taste the ice cream cake, and Kate felt like a ruthless tyrant. All Kate wanted was a vacation. She couldn't even go home without ruining her children's lives.

As the days passed, the California trip loomed ahead like a prison sentence. Jessie pressed her nose against the car window every time she passed a Christmas tree lot. Sam refused to sit on Santa's lap at the ZCMI mall, claiming that Santa wouldn't know where in the world to find him. As usual, Angela was the worst of all. In July, Martin and Kate had torn Angela away from San Francisco by her fingernails. Now being a sheep in the ward Christmas pageant was more important to Angela than seeing San Francisco again. Unfairest of all was that Angela's anger was completely directed against Kate. It wasn't Martin's fault she would miss her debut as a sheep in the ward manger scene; it was Kate's. As far as Angela was concerned, every evil in the world was Kate's fault.

The vacation that Kate so sorely needed was only a burden on everyone else. She felt guilty every time she anticipated the holiday. She dreaded the departure and the tears that would accompany it.

She drove guilt from her mind with a frenzy of activity. She filled her days with the purchasing and wrapping of Christmas presents, mailing her gifts to California so the children wouldn't see them before Christmas. She also made elaborate, edible Christmas trains for Clarabell and Lizbet Appleton and Joanna Fries, carefully assembling them from miniature candy bars, LifeSavers and Hershey's kisses. The day before the Carbines left for California, Kate loaded the three Christmas trains in the station wagon and made her Christmas delivery, hoping to put a little joy in the lives of the three women who were her responsibility.

Even the Christmas trains were jinxed. When she delivered the first train, Lizbet Appleton refused to take it.

"I don't eat candy," she said, frowning at Kate as if it were Kate's fault she didn't eat sweets.

"That's all right," Kate explained. "This train isn't to eat, unless you want to. It's a Christmas decoration."

"Oh." Lizbet's lips turned downward, and tiny wrinkles etched themselves into her mouth. "If it's a decoration, I'm afraid it's a dust-catcher, and I'm extremely allergic to dust. You're a wonderful visiting teacher, and I'm sorry I don't seem more grateful, but I really can't take your gift. Why don't you give it to somebody with children?"

"I'm not your visiting teacher. I'm just a person who's here to help you," Kate said, but she didn't say it out loud. She said "Merry Christmas" instead, and she almost managed a smile. Balancing the train in front of her, she retreated, stepping carefully on the ice-covered sidewalk.

Just as she leaned over to open the door of the station wagon, she slid on a patch of ice. The Christmas train flew into the air, and pieces of candy scattered all over Lizbet Appleton's frozen parking strip. Kate skinned her knee, and she hoped that Lizbet would run to her side to help. But Lizbet was gone, the door firmly shut behind her. Kate kicked the scattered candy into the gutter, bitterly hoping that Lizbet would find the candy and feel guilty about refusing Kate's gift. Then she limped to the driver's seat of the car, where she mopped blood off her knee with a crumpled tissue.

The second train went to Joanna Fries. At least, it would have gone to Joanna Fries if Joanna had been home. Her mailbox was full, and rolled-up copies of the *Deseret News* littered the front porch.

"Fries aren't home," an old lady said, calling over from the next porch. "They're in Palm Springs at a Cleanway convention. Can't imagine giving a convention at Christmastime, but Cleanway does it every year. I'm supposed to pick up the papers for 'em, but I'm eighty-three years old. Can't just hobble over there every afternoon. If you're a friend of theirs, maybe you can do it."

Setting the Christmas train aside, Kate stacked up the rolled-up newspapers and took the mail from the mailbox. She carted the whole mess over to the house next door. The old lady obligingly held the front door open for Kate, but she bristled when Kate set the mail and the papers on her dining room table.

"At least you could put it in the bedroom," she said. "I don't want that junk littering my house all through the holidays."

Kate stuffed her arms with mail and papers and limped to the bedroom, where she piled the assortment on a chair by the window. It wasn't fair. She didn't even know the Fries, and the Fries would never know what she'd done for them. This wasn't any way to fellowship a neighbor.

Kate retrieved the Fries's Christmas train and put it back in the station wagon. Favoring her injured knee, she eased herself back in the car. She had one stop left to make. She could only hope that at least Clarabell appreciated her efforts.

At last she was rewarded. When Clarabell saw the gift, she burst into tears.

"Somebody gave me a Christmas present," she said. "And it's candy! Can I eat it?"

"If you want to."

Clarabell speared a chocolate-covered raspberry log from the log car of the train, using a clawlike forefinger and thumb to separate the log from its fellows. She lifted the raspberry log to her lips and then held it there as if debating what to do with it. Sighing, she returned the log to its place on the train.

"What's wrong?" Kate asked.

Clarabell stuck out her lower lip. "If I eat it, it won't be here anymore. Now I don't know *what* to do."

"I have a solution. There's an extra train in the car. You can keep one train and eat the other."

She waited for Clarabell to protest, but Clarabell beamed. "Now that's *real* nice. I can eat candy all day, and still have a train to show off under the Christmas tree. I'll hold this one. You can go get the other one."

As Clarabell watched from the doorway, Kate limped down the front steps and picked her way down Clarabell's icy walk. She returned with the remaining Christmas train, just a little annoyed that Clarabell was so willing to take two trains instead of one. Then she looked up and saw the tears streaming unchecked down Clarabell's cheeks.

"You're a *good* friend," Clarabell said. "You always do nice things for people. You're walking funny — do you know that? Do you hurt? No matter. You sit right down in this chair and rest. I've got a little present for you."

Clarabell disappeared. Everything was quiet for a few moments. Then, in the other room, Clarabell whispered, "Goodbye, little fellow. I'll miss you." After that, there were banging sounds as Clarabell slid drawers open and slammed them shut again. She muttered a running commentary as she worked. "*There's* the scissors, right where I put 'em." "I'll use this wrapping paper; it's almost gone anyway." "Dammit! Where the *hell* did I put the tape?"

Finally she reappeared, carrying a hastily-wrapped box before her. It was covered in crumpled green paper that was secured to the box with masking tape. Atop the box was a polka-dot stick-on bow that had seen better days. It clashed miserably with the pattern of the wrapping paper. There was no gift tag.

Clarabell thrust the box into Kate's hands. "Merry Christmas."

"Thank you, Myra. This is real sweet of you."

"How do you know? You haven't opened it yet. Well? You *are* going to open it, aren't you?"

Kate obediently removed the wrapping paper to reveal a white box that was covered with red hearts. Blazoned across the sides of the box were the words, "Battery Operated LOVE BUG". Kate opened the lid and pulled out the lavender-colored love bug that Clarabell had ordered from Home Shopping Club the first day that Kate had met her. It was even uglier in person than it had been on television, with bright yellow legs and antennae and wings, and garish orange feet. It carried a red satin heart that proclaimed "I Love You" in feminine script. The love bug's creators had missed an opportunity by coloring the creature's eyes black and white. If only they had used blue and green, the love bug would have boasted every color of the spectrum.

Rubbing the top of the love bug's head with an index finger, she said, "It certainly is soft and fuzzy."

"Turn it on!" Clarabell demanded. "That's the good part."

Kate turned the creature over and found an "on" switch. When she pushed the switch, the love bug's orange feet churned.

"Put it on the floor! It's not going to do anything if you just *hold* it like that."

Kate put the love bug on the floor, where it took a few frantic steps and then stopped to wave the satin "I Love You" pillow up and down for a few moments before it lurched across the floor again. All the while, it chirped hoarsely. The love bug was the most pathetic thing Kate had ever seen.

"Isn't it sweet?" Clarabell asked. "No matter how sad I am, that love bug always makes me smile."

Kate felt tears sting her eyes. Clarabell had sacrificed something that was dear to her, just to give Kate a present for Christmas. "It's a wonderful gift," she whispered. She picked up the love bug and watched its orange feet churn in the air for a moment before she turned off the switch. "Are you sure you want to part with it?"

Clarabell sighed. "I'll miss him, that's for sure, and I hope you put him away real fast before I change my mind. But I want you to have him — yes, I do. That's what Christmas is all about."

By the time Martin drove the family across the Bay Bridge, everyone's enthusiasm for Christmas had surfaced. Even Angela forgot the ward Christmas pageant in Utah and was excited to see San Francisco again. But when Kate went to church in her home ward, she realized it wasn't *her* ward anymore. There were a lot of new people, and none of them knew that Kate was the same Kate Carbine whose roadshows always used to win the stake competitions. Nor did they know that Martin was the best Scoutmaster that San Francisco had ever seen. Now somebody else was the Scoutmaster, and Kate's roadshow trophies gathered dust in the trophy case. As far as the new people were concerned, she and Martin were just visitors, displacing them from their accustomed seats in the chapel and garnering far too much attention.

Even her friends, as happy as they were to see her, didn't quite know what to do with her on a temporary basis. They had learned how to live without Kate, and her return threw some of them just a little off-balance.

Their visits to her parents and in-laws, while enjoyable, were not what she had expected, either. Everyone treated her like company, and that made Kate nervous. She didn't fit in anywhere the way she had done before.

More than once during the holiday season, Kate found herself thinking of R.J. and Boffo. She spent so much time with the two little boys that she felt the family was somehow incomplete without them. She wondered if R.J. had received the new set of encyclopedias that he wanted from his parents. She worried whether Boffo's firm belief in Santa Claus had been shaken by R.J.'s lack of faith.

When Kate turned on the Weather Channel to see that a blizzard had dumped a foot of snow on Salt Lake the day after

Christmas, Kate worried about Boffo's nakedness. She had seen no evidence that Boffo was smart enough to wear clothes if the house got cold. Neither had she seen any indication that Fangs would stay home from work to keep Boffo dressed and well.

Kate noticed that she was almost as excited driving back to Utah as she had been on the way out to California. She caught herself leaning forward in the seat of the station wagon — a childhood habit of hers when she was in a hurry to get somewhere. She forced herself to relax, only to find herself leaning forward again a few minutes later.

At last the station wagon pulled in the driveway. Martin and Kate unloaded the car, unpacking Christmas presents and souvenirs as well as suitcases and kids. Kate sent Martin and the children off to pick up a pizza while she inspected the house. She was relieved to see that the windows hadn't leaked and the pipes hadn't frozen, even though Martin never had managed to prepare the house for winter.

She went next door to Fangs's house to get the mail, carrying a loaf of cranberry nut bread as a thank-you present. Fangs met her on the front step.

"I thought you'd never get back." Just as Kate was smiling at the thought of being missed so much, she added, "I've really come to depend on that co-op."

"I didn't miss the co-op at all," Kate said. "Well, I *did* miss R.J. and Boffo. How was their Christmas? I've been wondering."

Fangs checked Kate's forehead for fever. "You're amazing," she said. "When my kids are out of my sight, they're out of my thoughts. I can't believe you'd miss children who aren't even yours. Next time the ward needs a new Primary president, I'm suggesting your name."

"I don't *like* children," Kate persisted. "I was only curious about R.J. and Boffo because I see them so much. Besides, I like the church calling I already have. Going to California made me realize I don't belong there anymore. I don't belong here yet, either. If I do my church job better, maybe this ward will feel like home."

"The only way you'll do a better job is to have Myra Frost move in with you. I still can't get over that *insect* she gave you for Christmas. What in the *world* was she thinking of?"

"That's not an insect," Kate said. "It's a love bug she bought from Home Shopping Club. As ugly as it is, it was one of her prized possessions, and I treasure it for that reason alone. Besides, I'm not worried about Myra. You've given me two more women to visit, and I still haven't talked to them."

"It's not *your* fault. You've been to their houses half a dozen times. Lizbet won't let you in, and Joanna isn't ever home."

"I don't know what to do about her," Kate said. "I've set up appointment after appointment, and whenever I get to her house, there she isn't. It's so frustrating. I can't help these people if I can't talk to them."

"I don't have any advice," said Fangs. "If anyone else had gotten through to them, I wouldn't have given them to you. You're my last resort. You get all the people nobody else can help."

That was the last thing Kate needed to hear. If she failed, Fangs would abandon both Lizbet and Joanna. She resolved to visit at least one of them before the month was out, even if she had to pitch a tent on a doorstep until Joanna or Lizbet let her inside.

On Friday, Kate dropped Jessie off at Lissa's and then hurried home to call Joanna Fries. When she asked for an appointment to see her, Joanna turned her down flat.

"I'm just too busy this month," she said. "I'm training three couples to sell Cleanway. I have to stock their inventories and teach them all about pricing. You wouldn't *believe* what some people don't know about multi-level marketing. Why don't you try me next month?"

"Okay," said Kate, and she sighed. That left the elusive Lizbet Appleton. If Lizbet didn't cooperate, Kate's new resolve would end in failure.

She called Lizbet and hung up without speaking when Lizbet answered the phone. It was a despicable thing to do, but it told her what she needed to know. Lizbet was in town and on the premises.

Before Lizbet could leave the house, Kate drove to her bungalow and knocked. She saw Lizbet inside, and she felt Lizbet's eyes on her through the curtained window. When Lizbet didn't answer the door, she stood at the doorstep and knocked again. Finally the door opened.

"You're the most persistent visiting teacher I've ever seen," Lizbet said.

"I'm not your visiting teacher."

"Then who *are* you?"

"I'm Kate Carbine." Kate smiled her warmest smile. "I'm new in the neighborhood. My job is to interview women for the Relief Society newsletter. Alphabetically, you're first in the ward. I'm glad you were home."

Lizbet sighed. She smiled, but it wasn't a smile with warmth. "Come inside," she said. "I can give you a few minutes." She didn't need to add, "Then maybe you'll leave me alone."

When Kate stepped indoors, she was almost overcome by jealousy. Lizbet's house wasn't a bungalow on the inside. It was straight out of "House Beautiful." Every item Kate could see was color-coordinated. Kate's red pantsuit was woefully out of place in the forest of teals and grays. First Fangs, then Lissa — now Lizbet. Kate wondered if people in this neighborhood actually lived in their homes.

Lizbet's person was as beautiful as her house. Like Fangs, Lizbet was tall and slender and beautiful. But where Fangs was exotic, Lizbet was tailored right down to her underwear. Even her panties were probably monogrammed.

Lizbet sat on the edge of her seat, as if she were waiting for Kate to ask her questions and then leave. Kate pulled a notebook and pen from her purse and held them ready for use.

"Why do you want to interview me?" Lizbet asked. "I don't make it to church very often."

"That explains why I've never seen you," Kate said. "Do you travel a lot?"

"Tons. I'm a buyer for ZCMI. I spend a lot of time in New York and Dallas and Chicago. I get to Paris a couple of times a year. I've even been to Italy once or twice."

Envy welled up in Kate. Lizbet was free to come and go as she pleased. Her house was spotless, and none of her furniture was stained with grape juice or chocolate. She made her own money and lived her own life. She wasn't at all like Kate, whose own child wanted somebody else for a mother.

As Kate wrote down the things that Lizbet had said, she felt Lizbet's eyes on her. When Kate stopped writing, Lizbet asked, "What do *you* do?" She was only being polite. Lizbet didn't care what in the world Kate did with her time.

"I'm just a mom," said Kate.

"That's it? You're a rare duck. Most mothers I know have jobs, too."

Kate blushed. Lizbet was judging her. Compared to Lizbet, Kate was only a household drudge. "Motherhood *is* a job," she said defensively. "If you were a mother, you'd know what I mean."

"Excuse me." Lizbet's voice was cold. "I forgot. I'm not a member of your club. You change diapers and make cute little trains out of candy bars. People who aren't married aren't even real to you."

Kate's anger welled up and overflowed. She was only trying to help Lizbet. She didn't even want to be here. "You're real, all right," she said. "I've been to your house six times at least, and you're too important to be polite. Either you're just going somewhere, or you're just getting in, or you're lurking inside and won't answer the door. My cookies are too fattening, and my candy bar train is a dust-catcher. I only wanted to be friends with you. I'm sorry I'm not good enough."

Before Lizbet could say another word, Kate stuffed her notebook in her purse and stalked to the door. Her exit was ruined because she couldn't open the door at first; she pulled at it and then realized that Lizbet had locked the door behind her. Unlocking the door, she marched out to the station wagon. Lizbet didn't try to stop her.

Kate drove to Fangs's house, looking for sympathy. Fangs wasn't there, so Kate took her anger home with her. She vacuumed the house with a vengeance. Later she cut the stew vegetables in such tiny pieces that she had to make soup instead. At dinnertime, she burned the garlic bread because she forgot it was in the broiler. She smiled at Martin and the children whenever they needed smiles, but she felt as though her face were made of rubber.

After she put the children to bed and went downstairs for the night, Martin lowered his newspaper.

"I've been waiting to hear what happened to you today," he said. "Maybe you'd better tell me about it."

"Is it that obvious?"

"Let's just say you've had better days. Even Angela noticed. She asked if you were having PMS."

"I didn't know she'd ever *heard* of PMS."

"She's in second grade, and she watches television constantly. There isn't much she doesn't know, but that's beside the point. What *happened* today, anyway?"

Kate told Martin about her visit with Lizbet. The telling made her angry all over again. When she finished talking, she rubbed her temples to ward off a headache.

"Well?" she asked, dropping her hands to cross her arms over her chest. "What do you think?"

"You don't want to know," Martin said.

"What do you *mean*, 'You don't want to know'? You can't possibly be on her side."

"It's not a matter of taking sides. I love you, and I don't even know her. But you messed up. You have to know that."

"I do not know that. Didn't you hear me? She was rude to me from the moment we met."

Martin shook his head. "Lizbet only responded to you. You were angry with her before she opened the door. You misinterpreted everything she said, just wanting to take offense. You owe her an apology."

"Doesn't she owe *me* an apology?"

"I don't know about that. Maybe she does. But you were the one who disturbed her. She didn't ask you to visit; she didn't ask you to take her presents; she didn't even ask you to help her. You were a stranger, just like a door-to-door salesman. She didn't have any obligation to treat you like a friend."

Kate turned over in bed. Her back to Martin, she stared at the wall.

"Now you're upset with me," Martin said.

Kate sighed. "Not necessarily with you. I'm just generally upset. I want to think about this. I need to know if I acted the way you say I did."

Martin put the newspaper aside and turned off the bedroom light. He extended his arm. Kate turned over and rested her head on his shoulder. Soon Martin's gentle snores were the only sounds in the room.

Kate was awake for hours, brooding. Sometime before dawn, she admitted to herself that Martin was right.

Kate went to the Relief Society homemaking meeting at the end of January and made a stained glass heart with miniature pink roses pressed between the pieces of beveled glass. It was a foolproof project; even Kate's heart looked professionally done. As much as she wanted to keep the treasure for herself, she wrapped it in a box with a large purple bow.

She drove to Lizbet's bungalow and stood on the front step, hoping that the package would draw her out.

The bait worked. On Kate's third knock, Lizbet opened the front door just a crack. With her eyes fixed firmly on the purple bow, she said, "I'm not lurking inside; I've answered my door. Let me guess. You liked me so much that you couldn't wait to visit me again."

"Not exactly. I acted like a jerk last time. I thought you were making fun of me because I'm just a housewife, and I guess I overreacted. I brought you this present as a peace offering."

She held forth the wrapped package and smiled. Lizbet reached out to seize the gift. Then, as if realizing that accepting the present would mean she had to invite Kate inside, she drew her hands back.

Curiosity won out. The door opened wide, and Lizbet motioned Kate inside.

"You don't have to ask me in," Kate said. "After all, you didn't invite me here."

"I know that. Why don't you come inside anyway. We'll pretend we've never met each other before. Maybe neither one of us will be rude."

Keeping a firm grasp on the stained glass heart until she got completely inside the house, Kate crossed the threshold. Taking a seat on the sofa, she relinquished the present and sat back while Lizbet opened the box. She knew full well that the heart she liked so much didn't belong in Lizbet's house. Unless a decade of strong sun faded the rose petals to dull gray, they couldn't possibly match anything Lizbet Appleton owned. Lizbet would sneer at the stained glass heart the same way that Fangs scorned Clarabell's love bug.

When Lizbet pulled the heart from the box, though, she smiled. "It's beautiful," she said. "I'd like a whole office full of these. Where in the world did you get it?"

"I made it in Relief Society."

Lizbet laughed. "Really? I thought the only thing people made in Relief Society were those tacky wreaths."

This wasn't the moment to admit that Kate had tried to sign up for the Valentine wreath class, but the class was already full. Feeling like a hypocrite, she smiled. "At least, when they *do* make wreaths, they offer an acceptable alternative."

"Well, this is stunning. Tell me, do you take presents to everyone you interview?"

"Only the people I insult the first time around. I saw how pretty your house is, and how pretty you are, and what a wonderful life you have, and jealousy just took over."

"You're jealous of *me*? You're not teasing me, are you?"

"Of course not. You've got a glamorous job, and you travel everywhere. Why wouldn't I be jealous?"

Lizbet lowered the heart into the box and carefully put the lid over it. Quietly she said, "People who have everything get their heads turned awfully easily."

"I don't have everything," Kate said.

"Don't you? You have a husband at home. Does he love you? Do you love him?"

"Yes, I guess we love each other."

"And children?"

"I have three of them, but it's not all it's cracked up to be. One of them is a real trial."

"That leaves two who aren't."

"That's true," said Kate. "I guess I've never thought about it that way. Even so, I feel so oppressed by motherhood. Everyone demands so much. We're supposed to bake bread and play the piano and take our kids to soccer games. I can't bake any bread that isn't pre-frozen from the supermarket, and I can't read music. I don't know the first thing about soccer, and I'm not even interested in learning about it. I wasn't meant to be a mother."

"What were you meant to do?"

"That's the crazy part — I don't even know. I'm old enough that I should understand what I'm supposed to do in life. I know one thing: I'm *not* supposed to be sitting at home, taking care of children who don't even like me."

"I'd trade places with you," Lizbet said.

"That's ironic. I wish I could trade places with *you*."

"For what? In the eternal scheme of things, who *cares* about fashions? And when I come home, there isn't a husband here, and there aren't two out of three children who like me."

Kate sighed.

"Do you remember being single?" Lizbet asked.

"Not very well. I got married fairly young. I think that's the problem. I hadn't lived first. I didn't have time to get to know myself."

"I've had plenty of time, and I'd rather have company. Being single means you spend Christmas by yourself. It means you try to forget Valentine's Day, and it means you don't go to church on Mother's Day. It means that everywhere you go, people keep 'reminding' you that it's time to get married — as if you'd simply forgotten to do it. Even when they don't use words, the suggestions are there. *You* try to do your grocery shopping in a store where all the food is packaged 'family size,' and you'll see what I mean. I don't want to be single, but I don't have any choice."

Kate bit her lip. She had never spent Christmas by herself.

"I've never even had a boyfriend," Lizbet said. "Married men try to pick me up, but single men are afraid to talk to me. Women say I look too intimidating, but I don't know how to look any other way."

She sighed. "I'd like somebody to kiss me. Preferably, I'd like somebody I *care* about to kiss me, but at this point I'm not too picky. You know something else? Excuse my frankness, but I want to know what sex is like. I have all the disgusting inconveniences of female plumbing, and it infuriates me to think I may never be able to use it."

Kate coughed as the dry winter air tickled her throat. Lizbet sprang up and went to the kitchen. She was gone for several minutes, but she finally returned with two glasses of mineral water.

"I may never have a boyfriend, but I *am* going to learn about sex," she said.

"How?" asked Kate. "What are you going to do?"

Lizbet looked away, staring away from Kate as she talked. "I have a plan," she said. "My thirty-fifth birthday is just around the corner. I have a few possibilities on the horizon — men I know from work; guys in the singles ward. If none of them pan out, I'm going to have an affair."

Kate took a sip of mineral water, stalling for time. The bubbles tickled her throat. She tried not to cough, because Lizbet might think she was condemning her. Her eyes watered, but she suppressed the cough long enough that when it came, it came naturally. Then she could talk.

"You're telling me you want to have a love affair?" Kate asked when she finally caught her breath.

"That's the only kind of affair I know about. Why not? What's to lose?"

"Self-respect. Your standing in the church. I can think of several things, but you already know what they are. Who's the lucky guy?"

"The first decent person who asks me after my thirty-fifth birthday — *that's* who. I don't care who he is, as long as he's reasonably healthy. I just want to see what love is like."

"That's not love," Kate protested.

"Sex, then. It's such a big part of everyone else's life that I want to experience it. What do you think?"

Kate took another sip of water.

"Well?" Lizbet asked, almost belligerently. "You must have *some* opinion."

Kate paused for a moment, trying to think of something profound to say. When she realized she wasn't going to be inspired, she said, "I think it's like fighting fire with kerosene. You don't solve one problem by creating another one."

"But I feel so *alone*. Our whole society is built around being married."

"Maybe that's why so many people are divorced," Kate said. "Marriage isn't something you do because everyone else does it. We aren't lemmings."

Lizbet sighed. "I want to be a lemming. I want to be married, just like you are."

"I've already told you — my life is nothing to brag about. I'm a rotten mother and a worse wife. Sometimes I think I should have stayed single. I would have saved Martin a lot of agony."

"But you *didn't* stay single."

"No, I didn't. Still, I don't know if Martin would marry me again." Tears came to Kate's eyes. Until that moment, she had never wondered if Martin regretted his marriage to her. Now, the question burned her like solvent.

"I like talking to you," Lizbet said. "I can say anything without shocking you."

"I hate to disappoint you, but you've shocked me plenty."

"You haven't judged me, though."

"No, I haven't. That isn't my job. I only write articles for the Relief Society newsletter."

Lizbet chuckled. "I'll bet you can't wait to write an article about me. If you write everything I told you, it may be the last issue of the newsletter."

"I'll censor our conversation. The Lizbet in my article will be as antiseptic as Listerine."

"And just as distasteful. Why don't you wait awhile? A few months from now, I'll give you something that will really raise their eyebrows."

"I hope you don't," Kate said. "I sincerely hope you don't."

Kate didn't know how to help Lizbet Appleton. Kate was such a failure at being married, and here was someone who felt just as much a failure for *not* being married. Kate wondered how she would feel if the situations were reversed, but she knew she couldn't possibly put herself in Lizbet's place. Their lives were too different. In this respect, neither could understand the other.

She *could* understand loneliness, though. She was a lone failure in a ward where every closet held a SuperMom t-shirt. Kate had three children, one more even than Fangs did, but Fangs's family was a tightly woven tapestry; Kate's family was just a tangled knot of yarn.

"It was so bizarre," she said to Martin when the two of them were in bed. "She thinks she isn't worth anything because she doesn't have a husband."

"And you think *you* aren't worth anything because you don't have a career. People are never contented, are they?"

Kate shrugged. She was quiet for a long time, summoning the courage to ask the question that was really on her mind. Then, abruptly, she asked, "Martin, if you had to do it over, would you marry me again?"

Martin didn't answer for a minute. Finally he lowered his newspaper. "Of course I would," he said. "The question is, would you marry me? You're the one who's dissatisfied."

Kate's cheeks reddened. "Is it that obvious?" she asked.

Martin nodded.

"If it makes you feel any better, I'm not dissatisfied with you. I'm dissatisfied with myself. I don't know what I expected out of marriage, but it never occurred to me that I wouldn't know how to do it."

"You're doing it fine," Martin said. "In fact, you're doing *more* than fine. I think you're a hero." He lowered his voice. "I don't even know who I'd be without you," he continued. "You're all I ever wanted in a wife."

Kate smiled briefly. She was glad to hear that. But then she sobered. "The children aren't so easily pleased," she said. "You know that. I don't do motherhood right. And because I *can't* do it right, I'll always be dissatisfied with myself."

"There isn't a right way, Kate."

"Sure there is. Look at Fangs."

"*Now* we get to the heart of the matter. Sometimes I'm sorry we ever moved here. You felt inferior before, but since the day you met Fangs, you've been comparing yourself to her."

"That isn't true," Kate said, but of course it was true.

Martin didn't even bother to argue. Instead he said, "You *aren't* Fangs. You don't look like her; you don't talk like her; you don't act like her. But I think if you could chip away every quality that makes you different from Fangs, you'd do it. And you know what? You still wouldn't be Fangs."

"Maybe I *wouldn't* be Fangs," Kate admitted, "but at least I wouldn't be a failure."

Martin raised his newspaper to his face. Kate knew it was a sign of disgust.

"Don't be that way," she pleaded. "If you've got any suggestions, I'll be glad to listen."

Martin's paper lowered a few inches. "I thought the whole purpose of this co-op was to let you go back to work," he said. "You've talked about going back to work ever since Angela was born, even though we don't need the money. You told me you'd be happier if you just spent some time with adults. Now that you have the chance, you seem determined not to do it."

"It's not that simple," Kate said. "Things keep getting in the way."

The newspaper edged higher over Martin's face. "I can see that. You're afraid to leave the house in case Fangs has a baby during co-op time or Myra Frost wants you to get her some Kotex. If everyone let worries like that paralyze them, the whole world would grind to a halt."

Martin was being grossly unfair. Kate opened her mouth to protest, but he interrupted her from behind his newspaper.

"Don't you see how *little* these obstacles are?" he asked. "You don't want to take a job; you want to be a mother. When you understand that, you'll start being happy."

As Kate glared at the sports section of the Salt Lake *Tribune*, which completely obscured Martin from her view, she thought she would trade everything she had with Lizbet Appleton, or with Fangs, or with almost anybody else — no questions asked. She didn't know what happiness was, but for her, motherhood wasn't it.

Chapter 14

The first Valentine of the season arrived before the end of January. Kate knew it was a Valentine: She could see the red heart through the square white envelope. She only knew the card wasn't from Martin. Martin never wasted a stamp when he could deliver his sentiments in person.

She turned the card over, looking for a return address. Instead of a name, she found a crimson cat's paw. The pad of the paw was heart-shaped, as were the individual toes and the tiny kitty toenails. Somebody had spent a lot of time painting that cat's paw, and the only one crazy enough to waste her time that way was Lissa.

When Kate opened the card, the Valentine wasn't a Valentine at all. It was an invitation to a birthday party for Phideaux — a party that was scheduled for the evening of February 14th.

A hand-calligraphied note from Lissa explained the reason for the date:

Phideaux was born on February 12th,
but we like to celebrate
on the fourteenth.
It's appropriate to remember him
on Valentine's Day
— don't you think? —
because, after all,

he's our own
little sweetheart.

The note went on to invite all three children to the birthday party, as well as Martin and herself. Then came the kicker, a postscript in the corner that said:

(Semi-Formal Attire)

Kate wanted nothing more than to discuss the invitation with Fangs. It was Fangs's co-op day, but when Kate called the Stevenson house, Lissa answered the phone.

"It's *me*," she said, proud as ever to be Lissa. "Fangs got an emergency call to deliver a baby. We sub for Fangs sometimes, Phideaux and I. Is there anything we can do for you?"

"No, thanks. I was calling on ... Relief Society business. Have her call me, will you?"

"Will do." And Lissa hung up the phone.

With Fangs unavailable, Kate couldn't wait until Martin got home from work. His reaction didn't disappoint her.

"There's no way I'm spending Valentine's Day with anyone but you," Martin said. "Tell Lissa you have a prior commitment. Tell her I'm allergic to birthday cake. Tell her your marriage will end if you don't have your Valentine's date."

"Will it?"

"Of course not — but Valentine's will be a lot less fun. I can think of better things to do on Valentine's Day than go to a birthday party for a cat."

Kate could think of better things to do on Valentine's Day, too. Martin always made a big deal out of Valentine's Day. He bought roses for Kate — usually pink ones — and took her someplace extravagant for dinner. Knowing Martin, he had already narrowed the site down to two or three places he wanted to try — places that were not Lissa Chrousos's white house.

When Fangs returned her telephone call, Kate asked her how to escape the party. Fangs only laughed, loud enough and long enough that Kate had to hold the receiver away from her ear until the merriment died.

"This is one party I *wouldn't* miss," she said. "Lissa has been known to drop people who refused invitations to Phideaux's party. If you slight Lissa, insults roll off her back. If you slight Gus, Lissa will eventually forgive you. But to slight Phideaux is the unpardonable sin. Do you want to keep Lissa in the co-op? Then go to the party. Celebrate Valentine's Day another night."

"But —"

"In this case, there *are* no buts. If you break your neck on Thursday morning, you'd better be at that party on Thursday night. Besides, I'd like to have someone there who can appreciate the humor of the situation. We can roll our eyes at each other. It might even be fun."

Kate was unconvinced.

"There's one other thing," Fangs added. "Lissa has the party catered. I don't care *where* Martin was going to take you for Valentine's dinner; you'll eat better at Phideaux's party. Then Martin can take you out for your own Valentine's dinner another night. You'll keep a friend, you'll make me happy, and you'll have two gourmet meals instead of one — all for the price of postponing Valentine's one lousy day."

"You have a point," Kate said.

"I'm *always* right." Kate knew that Fangs was only kidding, but Kate still accepted her words as truth. "Explain it to Martin this way: You won't have to stay at the party late because it's a school night. And the next night, sitters will be able to stay out later because it's a Friday. Valentine's Day is always better on a weekend."

"He'll go for that," Kate agreed.

"Of course. And there's one more item. Buy Phideaux a birthday present. I know it's stupid, but it's a small enough thing to make Lissa happy — especially after all the free babysitting she's done for us. And *please*, Kate, don't misspell Phideaux's name on his birthday card."

*

For the first time in living memory, Kate's alphabet week in the co-op coincided with an event that took place in the outside world. Valentine's Day fell during V week, giving Kate the perfect opportunity to spend two fun-filled days doing Valentine activities.

On Thursday, after an appropriate luncheon of Vienna sausages and V-8 juice, Kate had Jessie and R.J. and Boffo make Valentine cards that would be presented to Phideaux on his pseudo-natal day. She brought out a whole packet of construction paper and an assortment of paper doilies. She also gathered up a stack of women's magazines, which R.J. and Jessie scoured to find pictures of cats.

Boffo found it hard to participate at first. He was as naked as ever, but he wore a blanket around his body to ward off the cold. He had trouble making Valentines, because both hands were occupied in holding up the blanket. Kate finally tied the corners around Boffo's neck, freeing the little boy's hands. Only then did he open a magazine to find an appropriate picture.

But Boffo never did glimpse the vision of Valentine's Day. He cut out a truck; he cut out a toilet; he cut out three cows and a whole herd of chickens.

"THOSE AREN'T CATS," Jessie yelled helpfully.

"I don't *like* cats," Boffo said. "I'm going to put cows and a potty on *my* Valentine."

Sticking his tongue firmly between his teeth, Boffo created the ugliest Valentine that Kate had ever seen. He used black and orange sheets of construction paper, leaving the red and pink to Jessie and R.J. He also used doilies. Liberally. He surrounded the toilet with a doily and put doily collars on all the cows. He took a black marking pen and drew crude black hearts in the middle of the toilet and on the faces of two of the cows. At least he left a big blank space in the middle of the card, where Kate could print Boffo's birthday sentiments to Phideaux.

"Now, what words do you want to put in the middle?" she asked. "What about, 'Happy Birthday, Phideaux!'"

"Nope," Boffo said.

"What about, 'Happy Valentine's Day, Phideaux!'"

"Not that, either. I'm not gonna give this to no cat."

"Oh? Then what *do* you want me to put on it?"

Boffo blushed. "Not in front of *R.J.*," he said.

"Then whisper it to me."

Boffo climbed up on his knees and stuck his mouth directly into Kate's ear. Then, in a voice as loud as the regular Boffo voice, he said, "Put, 'I love you, Sister Carbine.'"

Jessie giggled. R.J. laughed. Boffo scowled at both of them. Picking up his woolen blanket, he put it over his head like a tablecloth.

Kate was touched. Despite the fact that calamity always seemed to follow in Boffo's wake, Fangs was lucky to have such a loving child. But then, Boffo had a mother like Fangs. If Kate were a good mother, Angela would be as loving as Boffo.

Pulling the blanket aside, she kissed Boffo on the forehead. Then she stuck the Valentine to the refrigerator, at child's eye level. Only then did she rub her ear. She didn't *think* Boffo's whisper had broken her eardrum, but she couldn't quite be sure.

Jessie got so excited thinking about the party that she threw up all over her party dress. Off came her clothes, and everyone waited as Kate hurriedly bathed Jessie and dressed her again. Then the whole family got halfway to Lissa's house before Jessie remembered she hadn't worn her new Chip 'n' Dale Rescue Rangers panties. Jessie didn't make many demands, but she insisted on returning home to change into her new underwear. The rest of the family had no choice but to follow her back to the house and watch impatiently as she decided between the red pair and the blue one. She never could choose. Finally she pulled the red pair over the blue ones, going for the layered effect.

The unexpected bath and two changes of clothes made the Carbines a half hour late — still within the bounds of Mormon Standard Time, if barely.

Phideaux's birthday party was already in full swing when they arrived. The men were off in the corner, eating cocktail cashews and discussing sports. If it hadn't been a Mormon party, they would have been getting plastered. Instead, they were staining their mouths with red punch. Martin joined the group, nodding intently as Arthur Aylworth offered his opinions on the chances of next year's BYU football team winning the national championship.

Sam and Jessie melted into the crowd. Sam and Jessie melted into any crowd where food was present. They were always on the lookout for it. Eventually, they always found it.

Angela discovered Fangs, who was wearing a tight black dress that was more appropriate for the opera than a cat's birthday party. Before Kate could stop her, she sidled over to the group of women who were clustered around Fangs. Kate was tempted to shoo Angela away from the adults, but she resisted. Maybe she should let Angela spend as much time as possible around Fangs. Angela could learn to be a better mother than Kate by emulating a perfect one.

Once her family had deserted her, Kate was absolutely alone. Unwilling to look as lonely as she felt, she wandered from one room to the next in the white house, nodding at people as she passed them and pretending to admire the Valentine decorations. Everything was done in red puffy hearts. There were hundreds of hearts — perhaps thousands of them. The artist in Lissa had forbidden her to use decorations made of construction paper or felt. These hearts were velvet, and satin, and brocade. Many of them were ringed with lace. Hundreds of dollars had been spent on decorations, and somehow Kate knew that these decorations would only be used this one time.

What space had not been filled by fabric hearts was packed with red heart balloons, both regular balloons and mylar ones. Every balloon had been inflated with helium, and curly ribbon streamers marked the place where every balloon floated overhead. Every time Kate took a step, she had to push balloons away from her face.

The streamer ribbons hung low enough that children could reach them with only a little bit of effort. Kate watched momentarily as R.J. opened a balloon, inhaled the helium, and showed Sam and Jessie how to make their voices sound like Mickey Mouse. Then Kate continued her exploration of the house.

The guests, too, were decorated for the occasion. There were dozens of guests, all of whom were crowded into the living room and dining room and kitchen. Lissa's parents, the Nichollses, were there. Sister Nicholls looked pleased as punch, but Brother Nicholls looked as if the last thing in the world he wanted was to be grandfather to a cat.

All of the children and most of the women — but none of the men except for Gus and the disgruntled Brother Nicholls — wore shiny cardboard red hats with hearts on them. Kate was determined not to wear a cardboard hat. Even as she made up her mind, Lissa appeared and put a hat on Kate's head.

"My! Don't *we* look glum tonight!" she said. "This hat will cheer you *right* up. There! I knew it. All you needed was a little color in your face. You should never wear a gray dress, but this hat does wonders for you. Now you look fine."

If Gus Chrousos could hide his magnificent bald head underneath a tacky cardboard hat, Kate could certainly make the sacrifice. Besides, Kate had no idea she had looked so colorless. She bit her lip and wore the hat.

As Kate toured the house, she found a running slide show in progress in the family room. The show had a single subject; pictures of Phideaux, sleeping as a kitten or snoring in the glory of full cathood, reflected off the stark white wall. Every twenty seconds or so, the projector clicked and the image changed. But always the subject was Phideaux, Lissa Chrousos's only child.

Kate watched the show in horror for nearly a minute. Then she realized that she was not alone in the darkened room. The guest of honor himself lay in a stupor on a table, facing the slide show as much as anyone whose eyes were glued shut could face anything.

Phideaux was not a party animal. He wore his perennial look of disgust, even as he snored in his place of honor. He looked so pathetic, with a cardboard Valentine hat affixed to his head by a tiny elastic strap, that Kate wanted to laugh. Then she thought how important this party was to Lissa, and she had to try hard to keep from crying.

Kate looked right, then left. No one was near. Then, carefully, she took Phideaux's left front paw and put it over his left eye. There it stayed. Good old Phideaux. She put Phideaux's right paw over his right eye and left it there, too. Now Phideaux offered a pertinent editorial opinion of the slide presentation. Kate thought that was appropriate.

She moved on quickly, unwilling for anyone to know that she had tampered with the guest of honor. Just as she arrived at the kitchen, Lissa rang a bell announcing dinner. The party had officially begun.

The refreshments were as spectacular as Fangs had promised. Dinner began with smoked salmon and paté with truffles, served by waiters who wore tuxedos and the now familiar red cardboard hats. The waiters buzzed from person to person, serving from silver trays as the guests stood in groups. Kate quickly tired of standing, but all the chairs had been removed to make way for the party guests. No bungalow was big enough to hold a sit-down dinner for Phideaux's most intimate friends.

As the waiters served platter after platter of exotic finger food, Kate smiled at the choice of menu. There were several varieties of caviar, all of which tasted like fish eggs to Kate's McDonald's palate. There were crab legs. There were triangles of shrimp toast. There were Buffalo wings, cooked in a mild garlic sauce and dipped in roquefort dressing. Lissa had planned her menu the way pet owners often do, choosing foods that would appeal to cats, but vainly assuming that Phideaux would want the food cooked and spiced the same way she would. After all, he was almost people.

Kate didn't think Phideaux would like roquefort on his chicken, but since Phideaux didn't appear, she didn't have the opportunity to ask him. Phideaux remained in the family room, unable or unwilling to tear himself away from the slide show long enough to share dinner with his guests.

As Kate was trying to swallow a mouthful of oysters Rockefeller, Lissa approached. Kate had never seen her look so radiant. Kate couldn't imagine that Lissa would have been any happier at her own wedding.

"Isn't it wonderful!" Lissa said. "All of Phideaux's dearest friends are here. We have all his favorite foods, and the presents are next. I can't wait till he sees his birthday cake!"

"Where *is* Phideaux?" Kate asked, even though she knew exactly where Phideaux was. Phideaux had organized a one-cat boycott of his own birthday party. "I can't imagine why he'd miss this great dinner."

Lissa sighed. "Phideaux doesn't like to eat in public," she said. "He'll have his dinner later, after all the commotion dies down. Right now, it's enough for him to know his friends are happy."

Lissa drifted away. Kate logged Lissa's comments in her memory, ready for retrieval when she and Martin discussed the evening. She found more shrimp toast, and some lobster eggrolls that she had somehow missed the first time around. She was glad her dress was loose around the waist.

Kate had just caught Fangs's attention across the room when, suddenly, a bell rang and the house fell dark. By the dim light of a street lamp, Kate saw a waiter standing at the light switch in the dining room. She assumed that waiters had been stationed at every light switch throughout the house, waiting for the bell to ring.

Then the birthday cake appeared, borne by two tuxedoed waiters. It was a huge cake, larger than Kate's wedding cake and decorated with hundreds of red and pink sugar hearts. Atop the cake, where the bride and groom would be, was a ceramic statuette of a flat-faced Persian cat. Kate blushed in mortification for Lissa, but she joined the other guests in the requisite gasp of delight.

After the cake was marched around the house and set down on the dining room table, Lissa appeared with the guest of honor. Both of Phideaux's eyes were securely closed, and Kate realized this caused more embarrassment to Lissa than the rest of the night's indignities combined. In fact, Lissa looked as though she were close to tears. Moments before, she had been radiant. Now she looked as though she were in agony.

Everyone sang an off-key rendition of "Happy Birthday to Phideaux". Kate couldn't believe she was singing happy birthday to a cat. Phideaux's eyes remained glued shut throughout the festivities.

"Take a look, Sweetheart," Lissa coaxed. "Open your little eyes. Look at all your guests, just waiting to eat your birthday cake. Does Phideaux want the first piece?"

Phideaux didn't ask for the first piece, but Lissa persisted.

"I just *know* how happy you are, Sweetheart. It *has* been an exciting evening, though. You just rest for a few minutes, and I'm sure you'll be ready to visit all your friends."

Lissa stretched Phideaux out on the dining room table, unappetizingly close to the cake. Phideaux didn't move, although he did snort just a little when Gus started taking flash photos — obviously ammunition for next year's slide extravaganza.

The evening ended with the opening of presents — an activity that aroused no more interest in Phideaux than the dinner or the guests or the red cardboard hats. Although Lissa was obviously upset, she oohed and aahed as she opened one gift after another on Phideaux's behalf. There were satin pillows. There were kitty pajamas, size extra large. Fangs even presented Phideaux with a velour-lined cat bed. Every guest seemed to know Phideaux's torpid disposition, and all the gifts had been purchased accordingly.

All of them except for one. Kate had bought the one thing in the world that might put a little animation in Phideaux's eyes — a mouse that was so heavily laced with catnip that it could arouse the drawing on a sack of Johnny Cat.

As the gift was unwrapped, Phideaux slowly opened one eye. The cat *is* alive, Kate thought, pleased that her birthday gift had gotten the only response out of Phideaux all night.

But Lissa's eyes widened in alarm. "Oh, he couldn't possibly have that," she said. "The excitement would be too much for him. But Phideaux thanks you *so* much for thinking of him — don't you, Sweetheart?"

To the surprise of nobody in the room but Lissa, Phideaux didn't bother to answer.

As everyone stood motionless, pretending to wait for some reaction out of Phideaux, Jessie took center stage. She elbowed her way through the crowd until she was standing next to Lissa and the cat. Throwing her dress over the top of her head, she snapped the elastic on her panties.

"LOOK, PHIDEAUX!" she yelled. "DAD GOT ME SOME CHIP 'N' DALES FOR VALENTINE'S. HE GOT ME *TWO* CHIP 'N' DALES, AND I GOT *BOTH* PAIRS ON. SEE? *BOTH* OF US GOT PRESENTS TODAY!"

Holding her dress up with one hand, Jessie reached down to reveal the blue pair of Chip 'n' Dales underneath the red one. Kate elbowed her way through half the civilized world. Moving as fast as Thompson's gazelle, she tugged Jessie's skirt down over her panties and pulled her into the crowd. All the guests laughed, but Lissa looked decidedly upset.

When the party was over, Kate took Lissa aside to apologize for the embarrassment that Jessie had caused. "I could see how unhappy you were," she said. "Jessie didn't mean anything, though. All little girls are fascinated with new panties. Wait till you have a little girl of your own."

"I wasn't worried about Jessie," Lissa said. "It's *Phideaux*. He's been acting so *strange* lately. I must have done something to hurt his feelings, but I can't imagine what I did."

"Phideaux couldn't possibly be upset with you," Kate said. "There isn't a cat in the world who's loved more than Phideaux."

"I *know* that. Then why is he so *upset*? He isn't acting like Phideaux at all. Just tonight, when I went to the family room to get him for the birthday cake, he had his little paws over his eyes. Kate, Phideaux *hated* his birthday party. I don't know what in the world I did wrong."

Kate almost didn't say anything. The last thing she wanted was to make Lissa angry with her. But Lissa needed help. She was already near tears. Kate knew that Lissa would cry herself to sleep unless Kate said something to comfort her.

"Lissa," she said, "Phideaux didn't cover his eyes. I did. He was squirming in his sleep, and I thought the bright light from the slides was bothering him. I didn't want to turn off the slides, so I covered his eyes with his paws. He stopped squirming right away. It made him feel a lot better."

Lissa hugged Kate so hard that it knocked her cardboard cap askew. "Thank you," she said. "Thank you. I should have known someone was only looking out for Phideaux. My little sweetheart didn't hate his birthday at all. My sweetheart *loves* me."

As Lissa hurried back to caress her beloved Phideaux, Kate finally removed the loathsome cardboard party hat. Somehow, just this once, Phideaux would forgive her for telling such an outrageous lie.

Chapter 15

W week was a milestone week for two reasons. Kate finally surprised Boffo in an act of mayhem, and at last she met the elusive Joanna Fries. Kate always expected trouble out of Boffo, and she wasn't shocked when she finally caught him in the act. Joanna was another story altogether. Nobody could have prepared Kate for her.

Tuesday of *W* week was Wild West day. Kate was a cowboy; R.J. was a cowboy. Jessie and Boffo were Indians. Boffo *had* to be an Indian; it was the only way Kate could get him to wear a blanket around his naked body in the chilly house. Because he and Jessie always played together, Kate and R.J. were left with the less romantic but less strenuous job of driving imaginary cattle around the living room floor.

Before the morning was half over, the Indians ambushed the cowboys and tied them up, using ribbon from Kate's giftwrap supply to bind their captives in shades of red and purple and green. Leaving Kate and R.J. tied together, the Indians disappeared into the bowels of the house.

R.J., ever cheerful, was a child who could be tied up forever. As he and Kate sat on the floor, waiting for their captors to return, he told Kate exactly how televisions worked. R.J. was looking at more than the pictures in his new set of Encyclopedias Britannica, Kate could tell. Nevertheless, he bored her silly with the intricacies of the cathode ray tube. Minutes of captivity seemed to last for hours.

Then Kate realized that Boffo and Jessie had been gone for a long time. She knew they were in the house; she could hear whispers and giggles. But she didn't know what they were actually doing, and as the minutes passed she got progressively more nervous.

Finally her curiosity won out. Slipping the ribbon bonds from her wrists, she instructed R.J. to keep watch for the Indians. R.J. cooperatively stood guard behind the living room sofa, and Kate hunted for Jessie and Boffo.

She found them in the bathroom, where Jessie was sitting on the toilet with her hands plastered to her eyes, protecting herself from the view in front of her even as she peeked through the cracks between her fingers. Boffo, brandishing Kate's pinking shears and standing on tiptoe on the rim of the bathtub, had almost finished cutting the shower curtain liner off below the curtain rod.

Kate snatched the scissors from Boffo before she yelled at him. "Boffo! What the *hell* are you doing?"

"Making a tepee," Boffo said cheerfully. "Indians always have tepees. It says so right on TV."

For once, Boffo couldn't blame his mischief on his older brother. But Kate realized that Boffo had no intention of blaming R.J. He seemed proud of what he had done. His expression revealed not a trace of guilt. In fact, Kate thought he was waiting for a compliment. He wouldn't get one.

Setting the pinking shears aside, Kate pulled Boffo down from the rim of the bathtub and swatted him on the fanny. He smiled at her forgivingly, apparently still waiting for the compliment. Kate sighed.

"Indians do live in tepees," she said, "but they don't make them out of shower curtains. And they almost never make them out of *my* shower curtains. Boffo, what am I going to do with you?"

"Tie me up?" Boffo asked hopefully. "Feed me to the bears?"

"I could feed you to your mother," Kate said, but she knew she wouldn't do it. Shower curtain liners only cost a few dollars at Kmart. Getting reimbursed by Fangs wouldn't be worth the embarrassment of telling Fangs that she couldn't control Boffo.

As far as Kate was concerned, *W* week was just another failure. Abandoning the Wild West, she removed her cowboy hat and herded R.J. and Boffo and Jessie into the station wagon, taking them to the Kmart on Parleys Way. There, for less than five dollars on sale, they replaced the shower curtain liner. Then they came home and drank hot chocolate with marshmallows — neither of which had any conceivable connection with the letter *W*.

On Wednesday, Kate was happy to relinquish the co-op children to Fangs. She looked forward to visiting Clarabell, and she wanted to look for a job. She had also set up the most recent in a series of appointments with Joanna Fries. In fact, Joanna called before Kate even got out of bed to confirm the appointment, saying she needed Kate to visit promptly so she could attend some Cleanway business. The long awaited meeting was underway.

As usual, Kate's plans were thwarted. When she woke Sam and Angela to go to school, Angela stayed in bed. It was allergy season for Angela; every season was allergy season for Angela. Today, even Kate could tell that Angela was too sick to go to school. Today Kate would be the one to break the appointment with Joanna Fries.

But Fangs offered a solution. "Bring Angela over here," she said when Kate took Jessie over to the co-op. "I'm already watching three little beasts. One more won't hurt."

Kate thought Fangs had a marvelous sense of humor. When Kate called children little beasts, she wasn't kidding. Taking one extra child for the day would be a sacrifice on Fangs's part; offering to take Angela was a heroic gesture.

Before Fangs could change her mind, Kate sprinted home to pick up Angela. Predictably, Angela was delighted at the invitation. She packed up her Sudafed and her Kleenex and the Afrin nose spray and three boxes of cough drops, apparently planning to spend the rest of the winter with Fangs. Kate bundled her up and took her over to Fangs's house, where she smiled so happily that Kate felt the familiar pangs of misery and guilt.

Breathless from three hurried trips through the snow, Kate settled on Fangs's living room sofa. Angela companionably sat on the adjacent love seat.

"I need to talk to Fangs," Kate said. Kate needed a refresher course on Joanna Fries, just in case Joanna really did keep her appointment.

Angela nodded agreeably, but she didn't budge from the love seat.

"This is old-person talk," Kate persisted. "You have to have wrinkles to sit here."

"Mo-ther." Angela hated being treated like an eight-year old. "I won't make any noise."

Fangs appeared with two cups of hot chocolate. She handed one to Kate and put the other on the coffee table next to her own seat. Looking at Angela, Fangs held her index finger in the air. "It's not the words you'll say, but the words you'll hear, young one. Cartoons are on in the family room. Vamoose."

Angela giggled and disappeared. Fangs had a wonderful touch with children.

"It's zero hour," Kate said. "I need to know about Joanna Fries. I've been in the ward months now, and I've never even seen her. Does she have a job in the Primary?"

"No." Fangs blew on her hot chocolate to cool it off before she took a sip. Then she set the cup aside.

"She's inactive, then."

Fangs laughed shortly. "Don't say that to *her*. *She* thinks she's the stalwart of the ward. As far as I'm concerned, though, she's inactive. She doesn't do her church job; she doesn't go to church meetings; she's never on hand to help when there's a funeral or a new baby or a problem in the ward. That spells inactive to me."

"What does she do with her life?" Kate asked. "Why is she falling through the cracks?"

"You already know all you need to know," Fangs said. "Joanna sells Cleanway soap."

"You've already told me that, and if you hadn't, I would have figured it out on Halloween night. But that's *all* I know about her. What *else* does she do?"

"I already told you — she sells Cleanway soap." Fangs shrugged, as if selling Cleanway products was the only thing a person could do with her life. "Joanna's sure she's going to get rich. It's worth it to sluff church for a few months while she gets the business off the ground."

"How long has this been going on?"

"Four years. Maybe five. If she's not rich now, she's not going to *get* rich. But don't say that to *her*. She has two teenagers she's ignored since they were in elementary school. They'll do anything to get attention — smoke cigarettes, take drugs, pick up boys — anything. Joanna doesn't even notice."

"That's sad," Kate said. "It would be terrible to go to those lengths to be noticed, and then fail."

Fangs nodded. "It's pathetic. She's traded her children's souls for laundry soap."

"What about Joanna's husband?" Kate asked. "Does he take up the slack?"

"Conrad? He's as obsessed as Joanna is. He's been our home teacher for three years, and he's never so much as called us on the telephone. At least, not on home teaching business. Once or twice a year, he calls everyone on the ward list and asks if they need any Cleanway products."

Kate took another sip of hot chocolate. It was laced with cinnamon, something that Kate had never thought to do with the hot chocolate she made at home. Fangs always did everything just a little better than everyone else.

"I can see why the Fries need help," Kate said, "but I can't understand why they need *me*. I don't even *like* cleaning products. What excuse will I use for going over there?"

Fangs picked up her cup and wrapped her fingers around it as if warming them on the stoneware.

"Does she have any talents?" Kate asked hopefully.

"Not that I recall. Joanna isn't even good at selling soap, or she would have made a go of it by now. When I think of Joanna Fries, it's in one of two contexts — either the soap or her kids."

"What's her ward job? Maybe I can talk to her about that."

"She's *supposed* to be a Relief Society teacher. She hasn't taught a class since August. The last time she taught a lesson, she got off on a tangent about black and white."

"I remember," Kate said. The lesson was suddenly clear. "She's the one who said there aren't any gray areas. Either you're good, or you're evil. That lesson depressed me for a week. I don't think of myself as a good person. If there aren't any gray areas, I'm on a fast train to hell."

"Me, too. It's funny, but people like Joanna should be hoping there are lots of gray areas. If *I* were doing the judging, she'd be on the train with us."

Fangs looked at her watch. "Didn't you say your appointment was at nine? It's nearly that now. You'd better run."

"I can't run," Kate said. "You still haven't given me a hook. What excuse can I use for going over there?"

"I'd tell you to buy soap, but you'd only be feeding the obsession."

"If you can't think of anything else, write a newspaper article about her," Angela said. "You did that with Lizbet Appleton."

Kate turned to see Angela sitting cross-legged on the floor of the entrance hall. She reddened with embarrassment.

"What are *you* doing here?" she asked. "You're not supposed to be listening to this."

Angela smiled smugly. Then she sneezed three times in a row. She had apparently been suppressing her sneezes and coughs the whole time Kate and Fangs had been discussing Joanna Fries.

"Angela's right," Fangs said. "You can always fall back on the newsletter. Now *you* vamoose. Joanna probably won't even be home. If she is, you'll be able to handle her just fine."

Kate stepped over Angela and escaped. She only wished she had as much confidence in herself as Fangs always had in her. It was futile, however. The closer she got to Joanna's house, the less confidence she felt.

By the time Joanna actually opened the door, Kate felt so inept that she almost forgot Joanna's name. Joanna did the talking for her.

"So you're Kate Carbine," she said. "I'm sorry I haven't been able to see you before now, but my life is so busy. *You* understand. Come on in and find a seat. Sorry about the house; it's a little cluttered. We run a business in here — I guess you know that. The living room is our office."

Joanna's living room was no mere office. It had been given over to cleaning supplies. Cartons of Cleanway inventory were stacked along the walls, obscuring the lower panes of most of the windows.

Papers were stacked on every flat surface. Kate found a path to the sofa and moved a sheaf of papers aside to find a seat. They were Cleanway order forms. This woman does a lot of business, Kate thought. Then she saw that the forms she held were nearly six months old.

Joanna perched on a swivel chair. She sat on a stack of papers, and they crinkled as she settled her weight on them. "I've been awfully curious about you," she said. "You must be my new visiting teacher. I'll bet we've missed each other half a dozen times."

"Eight times." At least, that was how many times Joanna had actually stood Kate up. But Kate had contacted her far more often than that; she had called Joanna or stopped by to visit at least twice a week since October. "I'm not your visiting teacher, though. I only want to write an article about you for the Relief Society newsletter."

"You've been that tenacious about a Relief Society newsletter article? I'm impressed."

Joanna didn't believe Kate's story for a minute, but Kate was locked in to her excuse. "Sorry I don't have anything more exotic in mind," she said. "Fangs asked me to write about you. She was quite persistent."

"That sounds like Fangs. There *is* a lot going on in my life, though. In fact, Conrad and I got a write-up in the Cleanway dealers' newspaper last month. I'll give you a copy."

Joanna sprang up and waded through stacks of papers until she reached a file cabinet. She pulled out a file that was full of Cleanway newspaper articles, each one of them neatly clipped and carefully tucked away. If Joanna were as meticulous about filing her business papers as she was about her newspaper article, she would have made her fortune long ago.

"There!" Joanna proudly shoved an article into Kate's hand. "That will tell you all you need to know. But I have a feeling you have another reason for being here. You do, don't you?"

Kate reddened. Frantically she tried to invent another excuse, but an excuse wasn't needed.

"You want to sell Cleanway," Joanna said. "You want to know if I'll sponsor you. Don't deny it — I have a feeling about these things. You don't need to be embarrassed. Multi-level marketing is the wave of the future."

Kate laughed. "I don't think I'd be a good Cleanway person. I've got my hands full with three children. You have children, don't you? How do you do it?"

Joanna looked puzzled. She stared at Kate's lap until Kate wondered what was wrong. Then she said, "I can't help but notice your hands are chapped. We have a great hand lotion that goes for $5.95. Would you like to try some?"

"I have lots of hand lotion," Kate said. "I just forget to use it."

"Oh." Joanna looked bewildered. "Don't your hands *bother* you?"

Kate looked down at her hands, which were just a little dry and pink from the winter air. They didn't hurt, and she didn't think they looked particularly ugly. But as Joanna stared at her hands in dismay, Kate thought perhaps they *should* hurt. Maybe she was underestimating the ugliness of her hands.

Embarrassed, she turned her hands palms up in her lap. Now none of the pinkness was visible. Remembering to smile at Joanna, she said, "My hands don't bother me nearly as much as other things. I'm not a very good mother, and *that* bothers me a lot. Your children are teenagers, aren't they? Maybe you can give me some advice."

"Advice? Who needs advice? Children raise themselves. I watched mine while they were little to make sure they didn't burn the house down. After that, I used television. My kids turned out fine. Are you *sure* your hands don't bother you?"

Kate said, "Absolutely. Tell me about your kids. What are their names?"

The telephone rang, and Joanna sprang from the swivel chair.

"Yes? I see. We have two sizes — you'll want to get the larger one. It's only $69.95. Of *course* it's a lot of money, but you get what you pay for. You don't want to buy that garbage they sell at the grocery store, do you? Your floors are worth more than that."

Joanna paused, and an expression of annoyance settled over her features. Then she added, "Are you *sure* you won't take the gallon size? Well, it's your money. I'll call you when it comes in."

Still looking annoyed, she hung up the telephone and went to a desk in the corner, where she pulled out an order form and meticulously filled it out.

"I hate cheapskates," she said. "Some people have no concept of unit pricing. Well, you're not interested in that. Where were we? Oh yes — you were asking me about a Cleanway dealership. I'd be glad to sponsor you."

Again Kate laughed. "I don't think I'd be good at that. I *am* looking for a part-time job, but it's probably too late in the year. After all, I can't leave the kids home alone during the summer."

Joanna arched her eyebrows. Her face was well-scrubbed and fresh looking, probably the result of one of the Cleanway beauty products. Joanna's hands weren't red and chapped. "That's the beauty of Cleanway," she said. "Cleanway soap is a family thing. We're all in it together. When I'm away from my children, they understand."

Kate bet they didn't.

"Why don't I sign you up for a new dealers' seminar?" Joanna continued. "Within a year, you can be making more money than your husband. In fact, I wouldn't be surprised if he quit his job and went to work with you, just the way Conrad did with me."

"I'm really not interested," Kate said. "All I wanted was to talk to you about the newsletter article."

Joanna frowned. Lines radiated from the corners of her mouth. Joanna needed some face cream; Kate bet that one of the boxes in the living room contained just what the doctor ordered.

"Well, I'm awfully busy," she said. "I need to meet with some people who *are* interested in the business. I'm glad you stopped by, but that article I gave you has all the information you'll need."

Waving goodbye at the doorway, Kate let herself out. Fangs had been wrong about Joanna. Joanna wasn't slipping through the cracks; Joanna was making cracks and purposely hiding herself inside them. Saddest of all, she was taking her whole family with her.

Chapter 16

By Z week, Kate was burned out on the alphabet. Alphabet week had been a stupid idea from the beginning. She was glad to be at the end of the letters.

It didn't help that Z week began with a Z. Of course there was the zoo, but zoo was the only practical Z word Kate knew. She couldn't build a whole day around zippers, and a zodiac day would be entirely inappropriate for Mormon children.

Kate hadn't been so lost since *Q* week, which she had salvaged by taking the kids to the copper mine quarry and playing Cleopatra, Queen of the Nile. Even *U* week was easy in Utah, and *X* had been redeemed when she and the children made homemade xylophones on Tuesday and had learned to play "Twinkle, Twinkle Little Star" on Thursday. Z week was another problem altogether.

March wasn't zoo month. It was kite month. Woefully, kite still began with a *K*. St. Patrick's Day was next week, but not a single St. Patrick-related word began with the offending letter. Despite the winter chill, Kate would have to take the children to the zoo at least one day of Z week. She hoped the other day would take care of itself.

Tuesday of Z week was colder than a day at the zoo had any right to be, but Kate didn't have any choice — snow was predicted for Thursday. She bundled Jessie in her mittens and her parka, ready to leave as soon as R.J. and Boffo arrived.

R.J. came dressed for the occasion, suitably tucked inside his own winter coat. Boffo arrived in tennis shoes, his naked body wrapped in a tattered green blanket.

"*Boffo*," Kate said, fully exasperated with Boffo's nakedness.

Boffo beamed up at her. He had such an angelic face.

"Boffo, you know it's zoo day. Why aren't you wearing clothes?"

Boffo shrugged.

"Boffo, it's winter. We can't go to the zoo unless you're wearing clothes. Don't you have any clothes you can wear?"

Boffo's face fell.

"You can be Superman," R.J. said helpfully.

"Yep," Boffo agreed.

"Boffo *likes* to be Superman," R.J. said. "I'll go home for the Superman suit."

R.J. was gone a long time. He finally returned with a filthy pair of Superman pajamas.

"I'm sorry I'm late, Sister Carbine," he said. "They were in the dirty clothes. We had spaghetti last night."

"So I see." The pajamas were encrusted with spaghetti sauce. Here and there, a drying strand of spaghetti clung to the fabric. Even nakedness would be better than the Superman pajamas.

"I think you'd better wash these," R.J. suggested.

"Nope," said Boffo. He drew the pants up over his bottom, fully ready to protect the zoo in any way that Superman knew how. Kate pulled the pajama bottoms back down, and Boffo reluctantly stepped out.

"That's Kryptonite on that suit," she said. "We'd better wash it off, don't you think?"

"Yep." Boffo relinquished the pajamas without further protest.

After throwing the filthy pajamas in the washer, Kate unbundled Jessie from her coat and her mittens. R.J. followed suit, carefully removing his own coat and hanging it over the back of a chair. Then Kate found some paper and crayons. She and the children drew pictures of zoo animals while the pajamas washed and dried.

Once Boffo was wearing a clean Superman suit, Kate was contented. Boffo wasn't. He refused to leave the house until R.J. returned home for a Superman cape. R.J. cooperatively went home for a red towel, which Kate tied around Boffo's shoulders. The outfit was complete.

Boffo claimed he didn't need a coat. Indeed, Boffo couldn't wear a coat without removing the red towel from his shoulders, but Kate took an old one of Sam's for him anyway. She had to carry it with her throughout the zoo visit, because Boffo never did admit to being cold.

The zoo trip began with disaster and never did improve. As soon as he was inside the gate, Boffo demanded popcorn. "Superman always eats popcorn at the zoo," he said, while R.J. nodded in agreement. Popcorn was an extra expense for Kate, but she paid it gladly. A satisfied Boffo was marginally easier to handle than an unsatisfied one.

Almost the first animals they encountered were the zebras. Other than camels, zebras were Kate's favorite animals. They were horses gone awry. As a child, she had colored all the horses in her coloring books to be zebras. The stripes appealed to her.

Zebras' personalities didn't warrant the fandom. They had nasty dispositions, as the warning signs on the fence testified. Boffo immediately grabbed a handful of popcorn and pushed it through the chain-link fence. A zebra trotted up to the fence, and Kate pulled Boffo's hand to safety.

"Zebras bite," she said. "You're not supposed to feed them."

Boffo glared at Kate. "I'm Superman," he said.

"MOM!" Jessie yelled. "COME SEE THE ZEBRA POTTY!"

"Even Superman doesn't feed zebras," Kate said. Turning her back on Superman, she pretended to admire a large pile of zebra excrement. Jessie clapped her hands in delight.

Suddenly, Boffo yelped. "Ouch, damn you!"

Kate turned around to see Boffo facing an irate zebra. He had dropped his popcorn to the ground, and he cradled one hand in the other. Kate trotted over to inspect the damage and saw that the zebra had broken the skin of two fingers.

"Boffo, I *told* you zebras bite," she said disgustedly. "Why did you put your hand in there?"

Boffo's lip trembled, but his voice was defiant. "I'm Superman," he said. That explained everything.

"There must be Kryptonite somewhere," said R.J. Jessie furrowed her brow and inspected Boffo's pajamas, apparently looking for an errant strand of spaghetti.

Kate gathered all three children and marched them to the infirmary, where Superman's injuries were bathed and he was wrapped in flesh-colored bandages. Only when Boffo's wounds had been treated and he had received a stern lecture at the hands of the zoo nurse did Kate allow herself to feel a perverse pleasure. After all, Boffo had been bitten by the major Z animal in Hogle Zoo.

R.J. and Boffo, who had visited Hogle Zoo many times before, led Kate and Jessie on a helter-skelter route through the zoo. They dashed from the pygmy hippos to the monkeys to the tropical rain forest, with no sense of orderly progression and no concern for the extra mileage their itinerary added to Kate's Reeboks. They never stayed in any place long enough for Kate to catch her breath; they darted from one display to another like insects flying around a room.

Jessie, unlike Kate, was only too happy to follow wherever Boffo and R.J. led. She had been to the Oakland Zoo, but because she couldn't remember it, zoos were new to her. Hogle Zoo was a big hit with Jessie, who was fascinated by animal poop. She was captivated by the different shapes and sizes, as well as the varying degrees of pungency.

"ELEPHANT POOP STINKS THE WORST," she announced, after Kate finished explaining the differences between African and Indian elephants.

"That's because there's so much of it," R.J. pointed out.

Jessie nodded wisely.

She was even more enchanted by the sea lions. As she watched a sea lion glide through icy water on its back, she giggled in delight.

R.J. tapped her on the shoulder. "Sea lions go to the bathroom right in the water," he said helpfully.

"DO THEY, MOM?"

Kate said, "I guess they do."

Jessie shook her head admiringly. "WOW," she yelled. "THESE ANIMALS IS SWIMMING IN THEIR OWN POOP."

"I'm glad to hear that, Jessie," Kate said. "I just can't wait to go to the beach again."

"WHY, MOM?" Jessie asked, puzzled.

"Never mind."

The zoo visit ended abruptly. After watching the sea lions, the next stop was the tiger house. The tiger house was indoors, away from the March wind. Kate liked that.

She leaned against the railing and watched a huge Siberian tiger, who paced his cage restlessly. His coat was thick and beautiful, thanks to the winter weather. Leaning against the railing, sheltered from the wind, Kate knew she could watch the tiger all day.

Just as Kate opened her mouth to yawn, the tiger turned its tail to her and squirted musk on her forehead.

Jessie giggled. Boffo wrinkled his nose. R.J. pulled on Kate's coat sleeve.

"Sister Carbine," he said. "That tiger tinkled on you."

"So I noticed." Shutting her eyes to keep the musk out, Kate wiped her forehead with the back of her hand. She fled to the water fountain, but the fountain was shut off for the winter. Then Kate hurried to the rest room. For once, she was yards ahead of R.J. and Boffo.

Kate learned an important thing about tiger musk: It doesn't wash off. As soon as she and the children got home, she turned on cartoons and let them watch television. As far as she was concerned, their minds could turn to Jell-o. She scrubbed. She bathed. She even scoured her forehead and her hands with Comet. Nothing helped.

"YOU STILL STINK, MOM," Jessie announced when Kate reappeared from the bathroom. "When are we gonna eat lunch?"

"Are you sure you *want* lunch?" Tiger musk was more than mildly nauseating.

"'COURSE. CAN WE GO BACK TO THE ZOO AFTER WE EAT?"

"Not today," Kate said. Not ever, she thought. Kate didn't like the zoo much any more.

The odor of tiger musk was a pungent reminder that Kate had failed in all twenty-six of her alphabet weeks. She hoped Martin would at least be sympathetic; she needed someone to tell her what a hero she had been, and that she couldn't help the tiger's rudeness. She waited for Martin to arrive home, so she could tell him the whole sordid story.

She got Martin's attention before she ever told him she had been to the zoo.

"What's that perfume?" he asked. "You smell *great*."

Kate got no sympathy from Martin, but she did get attention. In fact, Martin gave Kate lots of attention for several days after her trip to the zoo.

When Thursday arrived, Kate awoke with a headache. She still smelled of tiger musk, and she was tired of the heavy smell. But she was even tireder of the babysitting co-op, and of alphabet weeks. In particular, she was sick to death of the letter Z.

Having been to the zoo, she didn't know how to entertain the co-op children. Z stood for zebra, which had been pretty well covered on Tuesday. It also stood for zither, but Kate wouldn't recognize a zither if one bit her on the ankle.

"What's on the agenda for today?" Martin asked at breakfast. "Did you think of a Z word?"

"Only for lunch. We're having Screaming Yellow Zonkers and Zingers for dessert."

"Health food," said Martin, putting a tablespoon of bacon grease on his cream of wheat.

"You're one to talk. You're the one who came up with Vienna sausages on *V* week."

"It was a great success, if I remember. *I* know what begins with Z. Zygote!"

"What's zygote?" Angela asked.

Kate filled Angela's glass with orange juice. "Your father's just being rude," she said. Then, under her breath, she added, "I've *got* to get this tiger musk off me."

But Z week didn't go away. As soon as R.J. and Boffo arrived, before R.J. even took off his coat, he asked, "What's our Z thing for today?"

Kate held her hands to her temples. Even the sound of R.J.'s voice made her head pound. "That's a good question. There aren't a whole lot of things that begin with Z."

"Zoology," R.J. said. "Zuyder-Zee. Zinc."

"Those are all good words," Kate agreed, "but I'm not sure what we can do with them. Why don't we play zoo?"

Boffo wrinkled his nose. He was wearing his Superman costume again. In fact, the Superman pajamas were so dirty that he was probably *still* wearing the Superman costume. "We went to a real zoo *Tuesday*," he said. "Don't you remember? I got bit by a horse."

"It was a zebra," said Kate. "I certainly remember we went to the zoo. There just aren't that many other words that begin with Z."

"Zenith," R.J. said. "Zombie. Zanzibar."

"That's true," Kate admitted, "but I didn't know how to plan a day around those words."

"Zany."

"We have *lots* of days that are zany," Kate said. "I need to think about Zs. Why don't you kids go watch TV for a few minutes. I'll bet you can find some cartoons."

R.J. frowned. "You didn't used to let us watch cartoons. Don't you like us anymore?"

"Of *course* I like you," Kate snapped. She didn't mean to snap at R.J.; it was just that her head hurt so much. She needed a whole handful of Excedrin. "I only need a few minutes to think."

"Oh." R.J. kept his lips tightened in a little O for several seconds after he said the word. Then he disappeared into the family room. Jessie and Boffo followed, with Boffo's Superman cape trailing behind him. Soon the sound of cartoons buffeted Kate's ears. Her head throbbed along with Daffy Duck.

But Zs eluded her. Thursday's snow hadn't materialized, and it was perfect kite weather. Next week, once the stupid alphabet was behind her, it would probably rain till the end of kite season.

In desperation, Kate called Lissa. "My brain is melting down," she said. "I have to find something for the kids to do that begins with Z, and all I can think of is kites."

"So what's the problem?" asked Lissa.

"Kite doesn't begin with Z."

"Of course it doesn't. Kite begins with a K."

Lissa was so dense.

Then she continued, "Make a kite and decorate it with Zs. Put zigzags on it. Then you can go kite-flying and have your Zs, too."

Lissa wasn't the dense one; it was Kate who was stupid. If she hadn't had a headache, or hadn't been in a foul mood, or hadn't been so infernally tired of the alphabet, she would have thought of Zs all by herself. Now she looked like an idiot in front of Lissa.

Lissa twisted the knife. "I've got a few strips of balsa wood and a whole bunch of tissue paper. I always have stuff like that on hand for craft projects. That's everything you'll need except for string and glue, and I've got that, too. Why don't you send R.J. over and I'll load him up."

Kate smiled. Maybe the Excedrins were starting to work. "Lissa, you're a hero. I'll remember you in my will."

She summoned R.J., who was more than happy to run the errand. He ran haphazardly to Lissa's house and walked back almost on tiptoe, carrying the craft supplies as gingerly as nitroglycerine. R.J. was a lifesaver. He was almost as perfect as his mother.

Boffo turned off the cartoons, and all three children gathered around the table while Kate made the kite. She lashed two strips of balsa wood together to make the T-frame for the kite, connecting the corners with string. She used green tissue paper for the body of the kite, gluing plum-colored tissue paper zigzags to the front of it after wrapping the edges of the paper around the string border. Then she twisted pink tissue paper into bows to give weight to the tail.

The kite was finished. Kate looked at each of the children in turn to see their reactions.

"Wow," said Boffo.

"It's perfect," said R.J.

For once in her life, Jessie didn't say anything at all.

Kate slipped the short stick of balsa wood from its mooring and started to roll the kite on its long stick.

"Let me do that!" Boffo said.

Boffo's voice made Kate wince. The headache wasn't completely gone. But Boffo was so earnest that she relented. "Be *careful*, Boffo," she said. She guided his hands, and Boffo rolled the kite with the grace of a professional.

Kate stood the kite in the corner of the entrance hall. "Don't even *look* at this kite," she said. "It's fragile. I'm going to make lunch, and then we'll go to Sugarhouse Park and see if we can get the kite to fly."

Sending the children back to watch cartoons, Kate made a lunch of peanut butter and jelly sandwiches — the same lunch she had made every day since the fiasco at the Great Salt Lake. Today, though, she supplemented the sandwiches with Zingers and Screaming Yellow Zonkers instead of fruit. The sugar would probably have all three children climbing the walls, but R.J. and Boffo would be going home in just a few hours. Adhering to Z week was more important than sending placid children home to Fangs.

"Who wants to say the prayer?" she asked, when the children were once again gathered around the table.

She looked at Boffo. Now that he was wearing his Superman suit, Boffo was a little more presentable for saying the prayer. But Boffo was staring so intently at the Screaming Yellow Zonkers that he missed his cue.

"I'll say the prayer, Sister Carbine," said R.J. Without waiting for a response, he folded his arms and shut his eyes. "Heavenly Father, help us not to be squirmy and make Sister Carbine's headache worse. Help her not to be grouchy with us.

Bless our mothers and our fathers and our Primary teachers and our peanut butter and jelly sandwiches. Bless the prophet and the president and help us to be at peace."

Kate, who stood with her eyes squeezed shut, had to smile at R.J.'s prayer. R.J. was always practicing to be president of the church. His prayers could continue for several minutes.

All of a sudden, Boffo screamed, "I'm *Super*man!" Kate opened her eyes just in time to catch Boffo as he dove head-first from the kitchen counter. She had no idea how he'd crawled up there. She should have known better than to close her eyes during the prayer.

After picking at their sandwiches and consuming their Zingers and devouring the whole box of Screaming Yellow Zonkers, three screaming children ran for the car. Kate got the ball of string and the kite, carefully loading the kite in the back of the station wagon. Then she took a last Excedrin tablet. She suspected she'd need it; the sugar she had fed the children for lunch was already taking effect.

They drove to the park and walked to the top of the highest hill. The weather was perfect for kite-flying, and two or three kites already dotted the sky above the park. None of the other kites were homemade, and Kate was proud of her work.

She sat on the ground and carefully unrolled the kite, and her pleasure evaporated. The kite was ruined. There, in the middle of the kite, was a large hole.

"*Boffo!*," she cried. "Why did you do this? Why do you always ruin everything?"

"I didn't do it," Boffo protested. "I didn't *touch* the kite."

"You're the *only* one who touched it besides me," Kate said bitterly, "and *I* didn't put a hole in it."

Seeing Boffo's crestfallen face, Kate stroked the top of Boffo's head. "It's my fault," she said. "I never should have let you roll it. You must have put your finger through the paper by accident."

If Boffo had accepted the explanation, Kate might not have lost her temper. But Boffo shook his head, stubbornly refusing to accept the blame. "No I didn't! Honest! I didn't hurt your kite! R.J. must have did it."

Suddenly, Kate's headache returned with hurricane force. "All you ever do is blame your brother," she said angrily. "I'm fed up with it."

"But he *did* it," Boffo cried. "He *always* does it."

Before Kate could stop him, Boffo made a fist and punched R.J. squarely in the stomach. R.J. didn't defend himself, and he didn't strike back. He only looked up at Kate, appealing to her for justice.

"Don't lie to me. You'll only make things worse." Kate crumpled up the ruined kite. One of the cross-pieces of balsa wood snapped, cutting Kate on the palm of the hand and drawing blood. Somehow, this was Boffo's fault, too.

"Go to the car, Boffo," she said. "*All* of you, go to the car. As far as I'm concerned, Z week is over."

Boffo looked at Kate reproachfully. Tears streamed from his eyes, and he wiped them away with grubby fists. "Superman doesn't *like* you anymore," he said.

"Let me tell you something," Kate said. "Right now, I don't like Superman very much, either."

Somehow, Kate refrained from killing Boffo. She turned on the television and let the children watch cartoons until Fangs got home. As soon as Fangs's car turned into the driveway, she opened the door and let R.J. and Boffo escape. Boffo gave her a last angry look as he marched out the door.

There were eight more weeks of the co-op before school let out. That was sixteen more days of Kate and Boffo together. Kate sighed. At least the alphabet weeks were over. Kate could do whatever she wanted to do with the children, without worrying about Q or X or the infernal Z.

The following Tuesday, Kate learned differently.

"What letter is it today?" Boffo asked, when he and R.J. marched across the threshold.

Kate smiled. "We finished the alphabet, Boffo. The alphabet begins with A and ends with Z. Now the alphabet's all gone."

"I know that, but what letter is it?"

"There isn't a letter."

"I *want* a letter," Boffo persisted. "Make up a new one."

"I WANT A LETTER, TOO," Jessie yelled. "LET'S HAVE PURPLE."

"That's not a letter, Jessie," Kate said. "That's a color. The letters are all gone."

"THEN LET'S START 'EM UP AGAIN!"

When R.J. and Boffo nodded enthusiastically, Kate knew she was inextricably bound to the alphabet. As three round faces looked expectantly up at her, she racked her brain for A words. Surely there was something she hadn't already done that began with the letter A.

Chapter 17

Phideaux Revolts

Jessie's fourth birthday fell on a co-op day. It was *B* week again, which was awfully cooperative of Jessie. Kate planned a party for all Jessie's Primary friends, as well as Sam and Angela and Phideaux. The head count came to seventeen humans and one torpid cat.

Martin came home after lunch on party day. On Angela's fourth birthday, he had dressed up in a clown suit to entertain Angela's party guests. The children had been enthralled by his antics, and now Rollo the Birthday Clown was a fourth birthday tradition. Today was Jessie's turn. Excitement shone in Martin's face.

Jessie was sitting on the living room floor when he appeared. She looked way up at him, exaggerating the movement until she fell backwards onto the carpet. "WHAT ARE *YOU* DOING HERE?" she asked. "YOU'RE SPOSED TO BE AT WORK."

"I came home for your birthday party, Pumpkin," Martin said. "Wouldn't miss it for the world."

Jessie furrowed her brow. "IS HE INVITED, MOM?"

"I think so. You wouldn't want to have a birthday party without your dad, would you?"

Jessie thought about it for a minute. "YOU CAN COME," she said finally. Then, "ARE YOU GONNA GET ME A PRESENT, OR ARE YOU JUST GOING IN WITH MOM?"

Martin smiled weakly. "I'm just going in with Mom this time, if that's okay. I think you'll like what we got you."

School let out, and Sam and Angela came home. They joined Jessie, R.J., and Boffo in the living room, where they stayed out of harm's way by blowing up balloons for the party. They popped more balloons than they blew up, and one of the children was constantly appealing to Martin or Kate to start a balloon or to tie it, but the balloon blowing was great entertainment. If only the party would go as well.

Martin disappeared downstairs shortly before party time. When he reappeared, he was dressed in a baggy polka-dot jumpsuit and floppy red shoes. He had pulled a blue fright wig over his hair and had slathered greasepaint all over his face and neck. He wore a rubber nose the size of a tennis ball, too. Despite the costume, Martin didn't look at all like a clown. He looked exactly like Martin, pretending to look like a clown.

"YOUR FEET ARE FAT," Jessie announced. She poked Martin's oversized red shoe and giggled when it gave under the pressure. "DADDIES DON'T HAVE FAT FEET."

Martin picked up Jessie and tossed her in the air, straining under her weight. Then he gave her a hug. "I'm not a daddy," he said seriously. "I'm Rollo the Birthday Clown, here to do tricks for your birthday."

"NO YOU'RE NOT. YOU'RE MY DAD. YOU HAVE FUNNY BREATH JUST LIKE MY DAD."

Rollo's eyes widened. Setting Jessie on her feet, he blew a puff of air into his hand and sniffed it. His tennis ball nose fell to the floor and rolled across the room. Kate fetched the nose and returned it to Martin.

"Do I have bad breath?" he asked.

"Not necessarily *bad* breath. Just *distinctive* breath."

"Thanks. You've made me feel a whole lot better." As haughtily as his oversized shoes would allow, he stalked to the bathroom for Listerine.

One by one, the guests arrived. The Matthews twins appeared first, bearing one present between them.

Jessie frowned. "WHAT HAPPENED TO THE OTHER PRESENT?" she asked.

"Just one present," said Sally.

"BUT THERE'S TWO TWINS."

"There's only one Jessie," Rachel pointed out.

"OH. WHAT IS IT?"

"It's a toy dinosaur — the kind you blow up," Rachel said. Sarah gave Rachel a withering look.

"OKAY." Satisfied, Jessie put the wrapped gift in the corner.

R.J. and Boffo ran home and returned with a metal cage wrapped in a bow.

"WOW!" Jessie yelled. She pushed the bow aside and stared at the animal inside the cage. "WHAT'S THAT?"

"It's a rat," said Sam. "Neato!"

R.J. corrected, "It's a hamster. His name's Hamlet."

Angela stuck a finger between the bars of the cage and stroked Hamlet's brown fur. Hamlet nibbled her fingertip, and she giggled. "Hamlet means little ham," she said, exuding all the authority of a second grader.

R.J. sighed, obviously disgusted. "Hamlet was the name of a Danish king. Shakespeare wrote about him."

Angela scowled. She didn't like to be corrected by anyone, much less a child who was so much younger than she was.

"Is Hamlet a boy hamster or a girl hamster?" Kate asked.

"Doesn't matter," Rollo the Birthday Clown said pointedly. "There's only *one* of him."

When all the human guests had arrived, Rollo the Birthday Clown made his formal appearance. Kate drummed spoons on a pot to approximate a drum-roll, and Rollo burst upon the unsuspecting guests. Jessie giggled. Angela rolled her eyes. The rest of the children sat stone-faced. It was going to be a long afternoon.

Ignoring the hatchet faces on the children, Kate sang bravely:

This is Jolly Rollo, the Birthday Clown.
You'll never catch him in a frown.
Now here's a special birthday treat —
Something good for you to eat!

Martin dug down into a voluminous pocket and pulled out a handful of Snickers bars, which he passed to each of the children in turn.

"Thank you, Brother Carbine," said Anthony Young.

Rollo pantomimed his surprise. "Who is Brother Carbine?" his gestures said.

Penny Cannon tugged on the leg of Rollo's polka-dot jumpsuit. "I'm lergic to peanuts. What else do you got?"

Rollo turned his pocket inside out. Empty. He pantomimed a long face. Penny Cannon took the Snickers bar and proceeded to devour it, peanuts and all.

"When do we get to play games?" Boffo asked.

Kate laughed a deep, Santa Claus laugh. "You don't *need* games!" she said, speaking for Martin. "You've got Rollo the Birthday Clown."

Angela yawned.

Martin held up a finger for attention. Then he dug into another deep pocket and produced a banana and three multicolored balls. Rolling his hands with a flourish, he threw the balls and then the banana into the air one by one, juggling them as deftly as any circus clown. Martin's make-up was atrocious, but he had juggling down pat. It was one of his fraternity tricks, and he could juggle alarm clocks or dishes or trout without ever dropping a thing.

Kate waited for cheers from the children, but none came. When Angela had been four, clowns were still a big deal. But Jessie's generation was even more immersed in television and video games than Angela's had been. They were too blasé to want anything from a clown but a double cheeseburger and an order of fries. Martin progressed to more skillful tricks, but Kate knew it was futile. She scoured her imagination for something to play with seventeen bored children.

The doorbell rang. The children gratefully stared at the doorway, and Martin stopped his performance in mid-juggle. Lissa pushed the door open, carrying a big, professionally wrapped box in front of her like a shield. She held the box in both hands, and all eyes in the room were riveted to the gift. Phideaux was nowhere to be seen.

"Phideaux can't come today," Lissa said to Jessie. "It's his naptime."

Jessie was concentrating so hard on the box that she didn't even look at Lissa. "OKAY," she shouted agreeably. "CAN I HAVE MY PRESENT NOW?"

"What do you say?" asked Rollo the Birthday Clown. When he broke pantomime, the children laughed for the first time since he had appeared.

"THANK YOU, PLEASE!" Jessie grabbed the present and trotted over to the present pile, where she put Lissa's gift in the place of honor. Nobody could tell Kate that the size of a gift and the beauty of the wrapping paper didn't make a difference.

"WHAT DID YOU GIVE ME?" Jessie yelled.

"You'll see later," Martin said. He took a sandal off Jessie, and a tennis shoe off Larry Kringle. Then he spied an oversized clip-on bow atop Allison Regan's red hair. He pulled that out, too — a third item for him to juggle. Allison screwed up her face, ready to bawl. Quickly, Kate exchanged the bow for a ceramic owl she got off the coffee table. Allison sniffed and her lip quivered, but she decided not to cry.

The children watched Martin obediently, but they were obviously unimpressed. Kate hoped Martin wouldn't get so desperate that he'd try to juggle the hamster.

Lissa edged out of the group and found Kate in the corner. "I need to talk to you," she hissed. "Now."

Kate pointed her chin at the restless children. "Now isn't exactly a good time."

"Sure it is. Martin can take care of the party."

Lissa grabbed Kate by the arm and pulled her into the kitchen. "Something terrible has come up," she said. "The bishop called me last night. He wants me to be in charge of the Mother's Day program in Sunday School."

"Lucky you," said Kate. "Do we really have to talk about this now? I need to save Martin."

"Martin can wait. I can't do a Mother's Day program. I don't even *like* Mother's Day. I'm not a mother, you know."

"I don't like Mother's Day, and I *am* a mother. Mother's Day depresses me. It reminds me of the kind of mother I'm supposed to be, but I'm not. I'm sorry you got stuck with the program, but I really have to get back to the party."

Lissa tightened her grip on Kate's arm. "But he wants *children* in the program," she wailed. "I can't deal with children."

"You've been dealing with children all year," Kate said.

"No, I haven't. Not like this. Are there more kids like Boffo in the Primary?"

"Only a few dozen. I'll admit Boffo's a handful, but that's the way hyperactive kids are. Lots of them are troublemakers. I'll bet some of them are even worse than Boffo. You'll see."

Lissa moaned.

Kate pulled away from Lissa's grasp. She took cartons of chocolate and vanilla ice cream out of the freezer to soften. Kids liked their ice cream sloppy. "I can't talk to you now, Lissa. I have seventeen children in the living room. Tell you what — I'll come over early Friday afternoon, and we can talk all you want."

Lissa opened her mouth as if to protest. Then she shut it again. Finally she said, "Well, all right. But will you help me with the Mother's Day program?"

"Why me? I can't help you with the music. I can't even *read* music."

"I don't care about the stupid music," Lissa said. "*I* can read music. I need you for the children. Children love you. They'll listen to you. Will you help me?"

It was a rotten lie, Kate knew. But unless she promised to help, she never would get back to the party.

"All right," she said. "I'll help you with the program."

Lissa smiled her gratitude, and Kate hurried back to the living room. Martin was still juggling heroically, but the children were drifting away. Angela was shaking birthday presents. Several little girls were gathered around the hamster cage. Boffo and Sam were playing tag with most of the boys. R.J. was sitting in the corner, eating a banana that had probably been purloined from Martin's juggling inventory.

Only Jessie was engrossed in Martin's act. She sat cross-legged in front of him, fascinated by everything he did. As far as Jessie was concerned, Rollo the Birthday Clown was the only person in the room.

Jessie had just learned that her father had a useful skill.

Kate forgot all about visiting Lissa on Friday afternoon. Clarabell wanted Kate to do some shopping for her, and Kate had to make a trip to the candy store to buy about thirty-two pounds of Easter candy for Martin and the kids. The safety inspection sticker on the car was about to expire, and Kate needed a nap. Lissa and the Mother's Day program slipped her mind.

She had finished her errands and was working on her nap when the telephone rang. "Where are you?" Lissa asked. "You *said* you'd come over."

"I was just on my way." Kate yawned. "It's still only March, you know. You don't need to worry. Mother's Day is more than six weeks away."

Lissa paused for a moment. Then she said, "Mother's Day is the farthest thing from my mind. This is *important*, Kate. *Please* come over."

Kate shook her head to chase the sleep away. She yawned again, and the exhaustion returned. She pulled on her loafers and rebelliously ate an Easter egg before she left the house. Nobody ever asked Kate what Kate wanted to do.

When Lissa answered the door, she threw her arms around Kate's shoulders. "Thank *goodness* you're here," she said.

Kate repented her feelings of resentment. "It was a busy day. I came as soon as I could. What's wrong?"

Lissa pulled away. She took a deep breath, but she didn't say anything. Then she smiled half-heartedly. "Come to the kitchen. I'll fix you something to drink."

As Lissa went to the kitchen, Kate looked in on the children. They were watching *Bambi* on the video player, and they looked so peaceful that Kate felt a twinge of jealousy. For once, Boffo wasn't squirming and R.J. wasn't engrossed in a book. In fact, R.J. was as naked as Boffo was. He and Boffo shared a blanket in front of the television. It was the first evidence Kate had seen that R.J. and Boffo were genetically related.

"I'm in here," Lissa called. "I've poured you some grape juice."

Kate left the children and went to the kitchen. On the way, she saw Phideaux lurking under a dining room chair. Both of Phideaux's eyes were open, and he stared suspiciously at Kate. Kate reached down to pet him, and he shrank from her touch. Kate had never seen a spontaneous movement out of Phideaux, and she pulled her hand away. If Phideaux didn't want to be petted, Kate certainly didn't have to pet him.

Lissa thrust a glass of grape juice at Kate. There was no corresponding glass for Lissa.

"Aren't you drinking?" Kate asked. "I hate to drink alone."

"I can't have a thing. I'm too upset. My whole life is falling apart, and you want me to drink *grape* juice?"

Kate put her own full glass down on the counter. "Why is your whole life falling apart?" she asked. "Everything looks fine here, except for Phideaux. Speaking of Phideaux, Phideaux's hiding under a dining room chair. He looks a little nervous."

"Nervous isn't the half of it. I wish I'd never gotten involved with the co-op. I just can't deal with children. Phideaux can't, either. I've never been so unhappy."

"I don't understand. You've been dealing with these kids all year."

"I've *had* them, but I haven't *dealt* with them. The co-op has ruined my life. I can't control children. I'm not talking about Jessie," she added hastily. "*Never* Jessie. Specifically, I can't control Boffo."

"That's doesn't mean you're a failure," Kate said. "Nobody can control Boffo. But if the co-op is too much for you, just quit. I'll watch the kids on Fridays, and everything will be back to normal."

"No, it won't," Lissa said quietly. "Everything has gone to pot. I can't even enjoy Gus anymore. Every time he tries to touch me, I freeze up. I'm afraid I'll get pregnant. I couldn't handle being a mother."

"Neither can I, and I have three children. You'd adapt."

"I don't *want* to adapt. I don't want children, and I know I shouldn't feel that way."

"I've felt that way, too," said Kate, but Lissa ignored her.

"I've thrown away my fertility pills. Gus doesn't know that. He still keeps coming home for nooners, for what good that will do, but I can tell he isn't having fun anymore. I'm so afraid of losing him."

As she leaned against the counter for support, she knocked over Kate's glass of grape juice. The glass shattered, and grape juice splattered all over the counter-top. She stared at the mess and broke into tears.

Kate was glad that Lissa had poured her only a small glass of juice. "I'll clean it up," she said. "You just sit down."

Lissa sat down. She forlornly watched Kate wipe up the glass shards and the grape juice spill.

"I'm sorry," she said, when Kate had thrown the last paper towel in the trash. "It's been a terrible year, and today was the last straw. First I couldn't find my India ink. You just don't *lose* a bottle of India ink, but I can't find it anywhere. Then R.J.'s clothes got messed up. They're in the dryer now."

"So *that's* why R.J.'s naked. I thought he was just keeping Boffo company."

"Why would he want to do that? He's naked because his clothes are in the wash. His clothes are in the wash because Phideaux had diarrhea all over him. And Phideaux had diarrhea all over him because he was marching around the living room with Phideaux on his head. Phideaux must have gotten dizzy, and his bowels just let go. Poor Phideaux was devastated."

"I'll bet R.J. was even more devastated. Phideaux had diarrhea right on his *head*? That's disgusting."

"Why did it happen to R.J.?" Lissa asked woefully. "After all the times Boffo has tortured poor Phideaux, why couldn't Phideaux do that on *Boffo's* head? Boffo's the one who deserved it."

"Boffo?" Kate was lost. "What did Boffo do?"

Tears rolled afresh down Lissa's cheek. "What *didn't* Boffo do, is more like it. I told you about the refrigerator and the dryer. It's been one thing after another ever since. He dressed Phideaux in doll clothes. They were too small for Phideaux, and they constricted him something terrible. Then he rubbed tuna salad in Phideaux's fur."

Kate nodded. "Boffo never did like tunafish."

"He locked Phideaux in the closet, *with the light off*. Phideaux was there all morning long. Now Phideaux's afraid of the dark." Lissa lowered her voice. "Phideaux is afraid of lots of things now. Boffo has ruined our lives."

"As soon as you get out of the co-op, I'm sure Phideaux will forget all about Boffo," said Kate. "Cats don't remember things like that."

"Phideaux does. He's been acting strange for months. At first I thought he was angry with me. I was beside myself. You can imagine. Then I noticed how upset Phideaux gets on Fridays. Every Friday, Phideaux falls apart."

"That's one thing Phideaux and I have in common," Kate said. "I fall apart on co-op days, too."

Lissa glared. "This is not a laughing matter. Phideaux's analyst says he's been negatively imprinted in his mundane environment."

"His analyst? They have psychiatrists for *cats?*"

"Of course they do. Phideaux has been in analysis ever since his birthday party. That's when I really noticed how bad things were getting."

Kate was sorry she'd ever put that stupid cat's paws in front of its eyes. It was only a joke. Even Jessie would know that a cat wouldn't cover its eyes like that, but Lissa had forgotten that Phideaux was only a cat. As far as Lissa was concerned, Phideaux could fly if he put his mind to it. And in Lissa's paranoid state, anything Phideaux did reflected on herself.

She put her hand on Lissa's arm. "I told you at the birthday party that I'd put Phideaux's paws over his eyes. He wasn't criticizing you."

"I know that," Lissa said. "It wasn't just the paws over his eyes. Phideaux didn't enjoy his birthday at all. The morning after the party, I called the analyst.

"I want to tell you something," she continued. "I've always had the feeling that people laugh at me behind my back. When you helped Phideaux at the birthday party, it told me that at least *you* don't laugh at me. You love Phideaux, too. That was why I knew I could confide in you now."

Kate's guilt blossomed. Lissa didn't blame her. Far from it: Lissa trusted Kate because she believed Kate's lie. All Kate could do was be a friend to Lissa now, even if she hadn't been a friend before.

"Let me take the co-op for you on Fridays," she said. "It's only a few more weeks. I wouldn't mind a bit."

"I can't do that. I'd have to tell Fangs I've failed, and I can't bear to do that."

"Then let me take Phideaux on Fridays. I'll take him home with me when I drop off Jessie. I'll stay home with him all day and keep him company. We'll have a great time together, just Phideaux and I."

"Would you? You'd do that for me?"

"You said it yourself — I love Phideaux, too. To tell you the truth, the house gets a little quiet on Fridays. I'd be glad for the company."

Lissa's eyes shone. "I can't *wait* to tell Phideaux," she said. "Kate, I'll never be able to repay you."

"You already have. You've taken care of Jessie for a whole year. Speaking of Jessie, co-op time's over for the day. I'll take R.J. and Boffo, too. Fangs should be home in a few minutes."

"You're an angel," Lissa said. "Phideaux! The children are going home now! Come help Mommy look for her India ink."

Kate gave R.J. his clothes and watched him dress. Then she and the three children walked home together, where Jessie and R.J. and Boffo watched the end of *Bambi* on the Carbines' video player. Kate couldn't wait for the movie to end and the boys to go home. She sorely needed a rest.

At bedtime, Martin put his arm around her. "You've been preoccupied tonight. Did anything happen today?"

Kate put her head on Martin's shoulder. "Phideaux is revolting," she said.

"I've always thought that cat was revolting. I think Phideaux's *owners* are even more revolting."

"I meant rebelling," Kate said. "Phideaux is rebelling against Boffo."

"What did Boffo do to the cat?" Martin asked. "The kid seems pretty harmless to me."

"That's because you don't spend any time with him. If Boffo put *you* in the refrigerator, I think you'd rebel, too."

Martin scratched Kate's shoulder. Kate raised her shoulder to give him better leverage. Kate was drifting into sleep when Martin asked, "How in the world do you know he's rebelling? Did he open both eyes at once?"

"It's not funny, Martin. Even I can see the change. When Phideaux sees the children, he cringes. He doesn't sleep. He keeps one eye open all the time, staring at the children. Lissa has that cat going to a shrink."

Martin whooped with laughter, and Kate lifted her head from his shoulder to give him an irritated look. "I *told* you — it's not funny. Well, maybe it *would* be funny, if Lissa didn't live her whole life around Phideaux. If you'd seen her today, you wouldn't be laughing so hard."

Martin covered his mouth with a hand. At least he was trying to hide the smile.

"The analyst says that Phideaux has been negatively imprinted in his mundane environment. What does that mean? I didn't want to ask Lissa. She was already in tears."

"It means Phideaux doesn't like to be put in a refrigerator," Martin said. "I wonder how much money cat psychiatrists make. That would be a great job — pretending to listen to a cat's problems. 'Mrs. Chrousos, I have some bad news for you. This is no cat. It's a bag of peat moss.'"

Kate gave Martin a feeble smile. Then, settling back on his shoulder, she pretended to fall asleep. That ended the conversation.

Martin refused to understand how serious things were getting. Thanks to Boffo, the whole co-op was falling apart. The time was coming when somebody had to talk to Fangs.

That somebody would have to be Kate. Lissa could never confront Fangs about Boffo's sins — not even to get out of the co-op. Kate suspected that the responsibility would fall to her, the way unpleasant jobs always seemed to do. Kate always got to pick up the pieces that everyone else had dropped.

She sighed. After the way she had lied to Lissa, picking up the pieces was the least she could do. Besides, as painful as it was going to be, the time had come for Fangs to learn the truth about Boffo.

Chapter 18

Despite Kate's resolve to talk to Fangs, the opportunity didn't present itself right away. Fangs and her family went out of town for Easter weekend. By the time they returned, a ward member had died and Fangs had to supervise the funeral. On Wednesday, Fangs's co-op day, Fangs was tied up on the telephone when Kate dropped Jessie off for the co-op. The timing just wasn't right.

Kate spent that morning cleaning closets. She got so involved in her work that she ignored the telephone and the doorbell, trying to finish the job before the children came home. It was exhausting work, and by lunchtime she was ready for a nap. She was just settling down in bed with a book when the telephone rang. She gave the telephone an evil look and picked up the receiver.

"It's me," Fangs said. "I'm glad you're home. Lissa said you were out. Listen — I've got a baby on the way, and Lissa has a family emergency. Can you take over the co-op?"

Kate yawned. She had already had a long day. "I guess so," she said, feeling a little resentful. Lately, Fangs's babies always seemed to be born during Fangs's co-op hours.

"You're a lifesaver." Fangs's voice was effusive. "Don't worry about dinner for you and Martin. I'm coming home with a gift certificate for dinner for two. I'll feed your kids while you go out to eat."

That was the thing about Fangs. She took shameless advantage of people; then she was so nice to them that they thought they were taking advantage of *her*. Kate's mood brightened.

"That sounds fun," she said. "Are you sending the troops over here?"

"Not unless you want them. It's not fair having them mess up your house on my co-op day. Come as soon as you can. Ten minutes ago, if you can get here. I *do* appreciate it."

"You always do." Kate hoped her voice didn't sound bitter. After all, she was getting a dinner out of this. "What do you have lined up to occupy the kids?"

"Nothing. They're just going to play. I'll see you in a minute. By the way, this should be a fast baby. It's the patient's eleventh." Fangs put the receiver back in its cradle.

When Kate got to Fangs's house, Lissa was standing on the front step with Phideaux. She turned around to Kate and gave a mighty sneeze, a sneeze that was unmuffled because both of Lissa's hands were occupied in holding her cat.

"Excuse me," Lissa apologized. "I have the flu. Where have you *been*, anyway? I've been trying to call you *all day long*. Gus's father had a heart attack. We've got to go to Provo *right now*, and Phideaux won't get in the car. Fangs was the only person I could find at home to watch him, but I don't want to leave him here. *You* know what I mean."

She thrust Phideaux into Kate's reluctant grasp. "I've got to go," she said. "Fangs has the key to my house. Phideaux's food and his menu are in the kitchen. Please take care of him. And if you're taking Phideaux inside, *please* watch out for him around Boffo. I'm scared to death to have Phideaux in this house."

Lissa put her hands on each side of Phideaux's flat little face. "I'm leaving you now," she said mournfully. "I'll be back as soon as I can. I'll miss you *so much*. I'd kiss you if I didn't have the flu, but we don't want you to get sick."

As Lissa backed down the steps she cast a few baleful glances at Phideaux, as if expecting the cat to protest. Phideaux bravely held his peace.

Kate rang the doorbell, and Fangs thrust the door open. "*You're* a welcome sight," she said. "I see you even have Phideaux. That's *one* worry out of the way. Lissa made me promise to lock him in a bedroom by himself, but none of these old houses have room keys. Just put him in my bedroom and shut the door. He won't get out. Thanks again for bailing me out. Remember the dinner!" And she was off.

Kate didn't get nervous until Fangs had driven away and she was alone with the children and the cat. She held Phideaux firmly against her body while she said hello to the children. Phideaux stared down at them warily.

"WHY'S PHIDEAUX HERE?" Jessie asked. "THIS ISN'T *PHIDEAUX'S* HOUSE."

"I know that," Kate said. She stroked Phideaux, who bristled under her touch. "Lissa had to go out of town, and I'm taking care of Phideaux. He's not going to play with you. I'm going to shut him up in the bedroom so he can sleep."

"OH," Jessie yelled, mollified. "THEN WHAT ARE *WE* GOING TO DO? WHAT'S THE C THING FOR TODAY?"

Kate didn't have anything planned to entertain the children. If only Fangs had given her some notice. C stood for a whole lot of things. Kate could have found something for R.J. and Boffo and Jessie to do.

"I don't know," she admitted. She had already taken the kids to the Children's Museum and fed them at Crown Burgers and played cockroach with them on her own co-op days. This being the second C week, her creative juices were running thin. "Go watch cartoons for a few minutes and let me think. Cartoons begin with C, you know."

All three children disappeared, and Phideaux actually let his eyes slide shut. As if on cue, the neighborhood dogs started barking. For once, Fangs hadn't left her ocean waves tape playing to drown out the noise. Still carrying Phideaux, Kate went to the stereo to turn on the tape. She got the Beach Boys instead. The ocean waves were nowhere to be found.

"R.J.!"

R.J. appeared instantly, as if he had been waiting in the hall for Kate to call him.

"R.J., where is that neat tape your mom uses to drown out the dog barks?"

"What tape?" R.J. asked.

"The ocean wave tape. *You* know; it's always on the tape player."

"I know, Sister Carbine," R.J. agreed. "But *what* tape? Do you want a mom ocean tape, or a kid ocean tape?"

"I don't know," Kate said, puzzled. "Just give me *both* the tapes, and I'll pick what I want."

The ever helpful R.J. ran to a cabinet on the far side of the room and slid open a drawer in the bookcase. "Here they are," he said. "May I go watch TV now?"

"Go ahead. Thanks for finding the tapes for me."

As soon as R.J. ran from the room, Kate put Phideaux on Fangs's bed and shut the door behind him. At least Phideaux would get a nap. But Kate couldn't sleep anyway — not with the dogs barking. She went to the tape drawer and found a whole handful of tapes. She pulled them out, one by one.

Fangs's ocean waves weren't white noise at all. They were subliminal tapes with ominous titles. *Love Your Parents* was the name of one. Another gave equal time to the next generation: *Love Your Children*, it commanded. Other titles included *Parenting without Resentment*, *Controlling Anger*, *I am Honest*, *I am Helpful*, and a last, sad one, *I am Happy*.

Kate didn't know which tape to choose. All she wanted were ocean waves. She finally chose *Love Your Children*, but the tape made her uneasy. She wanted to love her children naturally. She didn't want to be brainwashed into it.

The ocean waves filled the living room, but Kate didn't find them as comforting as they used to be. Then the telephone rang, and Kate forgot the subliminal tape.

The voice at the other end of the telephone sounded upset and close to tears. "Fangs? It's Lizbet Appleton. I need to talk to somebody. *Now*."

"It's just me, Lizbet — Kate Carbine. Fangs isn't here right now. I'm sorry. You can talk to me, though."

"I'd *rather* talk to you," Lizbet said, surprising Kate. "I called you first. You're the only one in the ward who knows the situation."

Lizbet's birthday was just last week. Kate had seen Lizbet's name on the list of Relief Society birthdays for the last week of March and had sent Lizbet a birthday card, reminding her that thirty-five wasn't the end of the world.

"You didn't do it?" she asked. "You didn't go out and sleep with someone the day you turned thirty-five?"

"Not that day," Lizbet said, "but I did last night. I don't know what I expected, but it didn't help anything. It made me feel rotten. I feel so guilty. It wasn't even fun."

"It usually isn't, the first time. Not to say you should try it again," Kate added hastily. "You'll just feel guiltier, and next time things will be worse."

She took the telephone over to the living room sofa and settled onto the cushions. She spent nearly a half hour on the telephone with Lizbet, finally convincing her that she needed to talk to the bishop. Lizbet seemed a little more optimistic by the end of the conversation, and Kate felt both relieved and pleased.

As she hung up the receiver, she remembered that Lizbet had called her before she even called Fangs. That meant a lot. Kate had her faults, but she seemed to be helping the people that Fangs had called her to help.

A muffled yowl brought Kate back to earth. She hurried to Fangs's bedroom and was puzzled to find the door ajar. The door *couldn't* be open. She distinctly remembered shutting it. Phideaux didn't have enough energy to open a door.

Phideaux wasn't on Fangs's bed. Nor was he under the bed or in the closet. Kate even checked a dresser drawer before she realized Phideaux couldn't possibly be in there.

"Phideaux! Phideaux!"

Another yowl.

She looked in the family room first. Jessie was asleep in front of the television, a rarity for her. Boffo was watching cartoons, and R.J. was deeply engrossed in a book. Phideaux was nowhere to be found.

"Phideaux!" Kate called, softly enough that she wouldn't wake Jessie.

Boffo's head whipped around. "He ain't here. He's in Mom's room — remember?"

"Not anymore. I can hear him crying."

"Well, he ain't here," Boffo repeated, immediately losing interest once he gave his information.

R.J. never did look up from his book.

Kate heard another strangled cry and followed the sound to the kitchen. There she found Phideaux, and she was immediately sorry she had ever found him.

An open bottle of India ink sat on the floor. Most of the ink had been poured over Phideaux's back, although the perpetrator had also used the ink dropper inside the bottle cap to draw a black face over Phideaux's own squashed features.

Phideaux had tried to shake the ink from his fur coat, and ink was splattered all over the lower half of the kitchen. Then he had rolled over on his back to try to rub the ink off, only to paint the tile of the kitchen floor. Now he was frantically licking the ink from his pelt. His tongue was black, but the ink was permanent ink. Kate knew immediately that the only way Phideaux would ever be white again was if Lissa shaved his whole body and allowed the fur to grow back.

Phideaux looked reproachfully at Kate. He yowled once; then he yowled again.

"BOFFO!" Kate screamed. "YOU COME HERE THIS INSTANT!"

Boffo appeared. Kate watched his eyes widen in horror as he beheld the mess in the kitchen. He was the soul of innocence. His performance only made Kate angrier.

"Boffo!" Fury prickled in Kate's voice. "Why did you do that?"

"*I* didn't do it," Boffo said. "I was watching Elmer Fudd."

Kate had heard enough. She was eternally tired of Boffo's mischief. Even more, she was sick to death of Boffo's lies. "Well, who do you think *did* it?" she thundered. "Do you think *I* did it?"

"Maybe," Boffo said in a little voice. Despite his smart answer, he sounded afraid.

Furious, Kate grasped Boffo's upper arms. Leaning close to him, she said, "Why won't you tell me the truth?"

"I do," said Boffo. "I always do. You just don't believe me."

His shoulders slumped, Boffo went to his room. Kate looked inside a few moments later to find him lying on his bed, tears streaming down his cheeks.

She almost went to Boffo to comfort him, but she withdrew. Boffo deserved his punishment. Now she knew why Fangs had resorted to subliminal tapes. Subliminal tapes were a last-ditch effort to discipline Boffo. The tapes obviously hadn't done their job.

Abandoning Boffo to his tears, Kate returned to the kitchen. Phideaux had given up any attempt to clean himself and had crawled under the kitchen desk, where he trembled miserably. Phideaux desperately needed a trip to his analyst. Kate only hoped the cat psychologist could treat a cat owner's hysteria as well.

She grabbed a green mesh sponge and found a bottle of 409 spray cleaner. Then she sat on the floor and wiped ink from every available surface. The pickled pine cabinets had a thick enough finishing coat that she was able to remove most of the ink splatters with a little 409 and a lot of elbow grease, but the floor was another matter. Enough ink had soaked into the semi-porous ceramic tile that despite all her scrubbing, she could still see a faint outline of gray. The grout between the tile was hopeless. At the very least, the floor would have to be regrouted.

Kate's anger at Boffo fueled her cleaning efforts. Her thoughts kept returning to the subliminal tapes that were designed to make Boffo happy, helpful and honest. The happy ones seemed to have worked; for the most part, Boffo seemed blissfully happy. But the honesty tape had been a dismal failure. Boffo was the Grand Champeen liar of Farley Street.

After she had worked for more than an hour, Kate was leaning against a cabinet to rest when the front door opened.

"I'm back!" Fangs called. "I *told* you it would be a fast baby. Wait till you see where you're going to dinner tonight!"

"I'm in the kitchen." Kate was too tired to even get up off the floor. She waited for Fangs to come to her. She wanted Fangs to see exactly what Boffo had wrought.

Fangs took in the scene in one horrified glance. She knelt to touch the gray patch on the floor. Looking up, she ran her hands along the base of the pickled pine cabinets. Until then, Kate hadn't noticed that her scouring had taken off the finish as well as the ink.

Then Phideaux mewed, and Fangs turned to see him cowering under the desk. When she beheld the ink-covered cat, she sank to the floor tiredly and leaned against a cabinet, just as Kate was doing.

"Lizbet Appleton called," Kate said. "I turned my back on the kids for a few minutes to try to help her. *This* happened while I was on the phone."

"You don't need to tell me any more," she said. "I know the whole story."

Kate nodded. "He must have stolen the India ink from Lissa last week. She was looking everywhere for it. It never occurred to her that Boffo had stolen it. He denies everything, as usual. I don't know why he does these things. He can be such a cute little kid."

Fangs looked as if she had been hit in the face by a bowling ball. "Boffo? You think *Boffo* did all this?"

"Well, I haven't seen Santa Claus. *I* didn't do it, and it certainly wasn't Jessie or R.J. Besides, Boffo hates Phideaux. He's spent the whole year torturing him. He put him in the refrigerator once, for a whole afternoon. Lissa was beside herself. She has that cat going to a shrink."

"Why didn't Lissa tell me? Why didn't *you* tell me?"

"Lissa only told me most of it last week. She didn't want us to know. She said if she couldn't learn to control Boffo, she could never have children of her own."

Fangs rubbed the bridge of her nose with her thumb and forefinger, as if she were warding off a headache. Then she asked, "Is it just Phideaux, or have things been happening at your house?"

"It's always something. I didn't say anything, because I didn't want you to think I was a failure. In that respect, I guess I was just like Lissa."

Fangs said nothing, so Kate continued. "The first week of the co-op, Boffo jumped in the duck pond and said R.J. pushed him in. He pulled up every bulb I planted last fall. He cut up the liner from our shower curtain to make an Indian tent during *W* week. Once he threw a roll of toilet paper in the toilet and flushed. We had to call a plumber. There's a new catastrophe every week. In every case except the shower curtain liner — he almost bragged about cutting that apart — Boffo has blamed R.J."

Fangs exhaled heavily. "Kate, Boffo never told a lie in his life. He does get into trouble, but when he does, he acts the same way he did when he cut your shower curtain to shreds. He waits for congratulations. Boffo's too proud of himself to hide anything he does."

Kate felt a knot in her stomach. The knot grew and blossomed. She swallowed hard, but the nausea surged upward again. "You *can't* tell me R.J. did this," she said. "I won't believe it. R.J. has been my salvation all year. I know you're partial to Boffo, just the way I'm partial to Jessie, but you have to look at the facts."

"I *am* looking at the facts," Fangs said. She got a fresh roll of paper towels from under the sink. Picking up the bottle of 409, she scrubbed the gray stains in the kitchen tile without success. The tile was permanently gray.

After scouring for several minutes, she said, "Have you ever wondered why R.J. wasn't in kindergarten already?"

"I guess I should have. I know he's the smartest kid I've ever seen. I assumed his birthday was late."

"It's not *that* late. R.J. isn't in school because he isn't ready for school. He can't get along with people. I'm only glad that nothing worse has happened. All year long, I've expected some kind of disaster."

Kate was aghast. "You've known this all along?" she asked.

"Of course I've known it — I gave birth to him. R.J. was born without a conscience. There's not a lesson I can teach him or a thing I can do for him. Believe me; I've tried."

"I think that's why I've let Boffo go naked," she added. "With Boffo, nothing's hidden. With R.J., everything is. I hate to say this about my own son, but I don't trust him. I *can't* trust him. Furthermore, I don't think I'll be able to trust him when he's twenty or thirty."

Slowly, Kate's shock evolved into anger. She was appalled that Fangs had left R.J. in her hands without warning her first.

"Why didn't you tell me?"

"Would you have done the co-op if I *had* told you?"

"Probably not. No, definitely not. What if R.J. had hurt *Jessie*? You used me, Fangs. I can't believe that going back to work was so important to you."

Fangs sprayed some 409 into the tile grout and scrubbed the grout with a paper towel. When the paper towel shredded, she pulled off a fresh paper towel and scrubbed some more. At last she spoke.

"I did use you," she admitted, "but I didn't endanger Jessie. R.J. doesn't hurt people, or he would have gotten rid of Boffo long ago. And I *didn't* do it just to get a job. Going back to work wasn't that important to me — at least, not at first. I didn't tell you about R.J. because he was the reason for the co-op. I thought if he spent some time with people who didn't expect him to act rotten, maybe he'd improve."

"You were wrong," Kate said.

"I know that now. But I didn't want to be wrong, if that makes any difference. All year, I've waited for you or Lissa to tell me he'd done something terrible. The moment you said a word, I would have told you everything. But you and Lissa both said things were fine. You don't know what that did to me. I was happy for R.J., but at the same time I felt so guilty. If you could make R.J. behave, that meant R.J.'s problems had been my fault all along."

Kate put a comforting arm around Fangs. Fangs tensed as if she were unused to being touched, and Kate withdrew her arm.

She tried to think of something to reassure Fangs, but words didn't come.

Fangs was R.J.'s mother; Kate, who had shouldered her own share of guilt, could imagine the pain she felt. But when Fangs spoke, she didn't talk about R.J. or her own suffering. Instead she said, "I guess this is the end of the co-op."

"The *co*-op?" Kate's voice was almost a screech. "The whole world has fallen apart, and you're worried about the *co-op*?"

Fangs shrugged. "I hate to be so practical, but I have to go to work tomorrow. Don't look at me like that, Kate. R.J. has been the way he is ever since he was born. The only thing that changed today was that you found out about him. *I'll* deal with R.J., somehow — I always do. But tomorrow is *your* co-op day. Sometime before tomorrow morning, you have to decide if we have a co-op or not."

"If I have to make up my mind now, my decision is no. I think I could hold out for the rest of the school year, as long as you knew I wouldn't let R.J. out of my sight. But Lissa's out of the question. Look at Phideaux! *I'm* not telling Lissa about all this, by the way; you'll have to do it. And you'd better make sure you tell her it wasn't *my* fault. I don't want Lissa to blame *me* for what happened to Phideaux. I only came here as a favor to you."

Kate glared at Fangs for a long moment. She felt sorry for Fangs, but she also felt angry and used and betrayed. Fangs had treated her so unjustly. Then she remembered that all the injustice hadn't been caused by Fangs.

"Excuse me," she said. "I have an apology to make." Leaving Fangs on the kitchen floor, she went to Boffo's room.

Boffo was sitting in the corner, facing the wall as if resigned to eternal condemnation. He didn't hear Kate enter the room. Kate sat on the floor behind Boffo and put her arms around his thin shoulders. A single tear fell on Kate's forearm, and Kate felt a surge of love for the little boy she had so unjustly accused.

"I'm sorry, Boffo."

"I didn't *do* it," Boffo persisted, as fervently as though Kate were blaming him again.

"I know you didn't do it, Boffo. I was wrong to think you did. Will you ever forgive me?"

Boffo turned to face Kate. His face was smeared with tears, and his nose was dripping. But the way he smiled, she realized that Boffo had forgiven every transgression. She only wished she were as Christian as Boffo.

She kissed Boffo on the forehead and said, "Your mom's in the kitchen. I'm going home. You can come visit me any time you want."

"Yep," Boffo said. Already, his equanimity was restored. He spied a truck underneath his bed and squirmed under the bed to reach it. He ran the truck up Kate's left arm. "I'll come visit you tomorrow. Tomorrow's Fursday, you know."

"Yep," said Kate, in a perfect imitation of Boffo. "Tomorrow *will* be Thursday. You can come play with Jessie, just the way you always do."

His faith in the world renewed, Boffo played with his truck as though Kate weren't even in the room. She glanced in the kitchen, where Fangs was doggedly scrubbing the kitchen floor. Then she went to the family room. It was time to take Jessie home.

Miraculously, Jessie had slept through the afternoon's crisis. Gently, Kate put her hands under Jessie and lifted her. She cradled Jessie like a baby. Asleep, Jessie nestled her head into Kate's neck. Fangs had jeopardized Jessie for seven months, just to put R.J. in a neutral environment. Kate didn't know if she could be as forgiving as Boffo.

R.J. watched silently as Kate cradled Jessie in her arms. When Kate turned to go, the ever helpful R.J. opened the front door to let her out. He smiled sweetly as Kate passed through the door. She looked back at R.J., still disbelieving that a child who looked so innocent could be so vile. Then she saw the proof. As R.J. gallantly held the door open, she saw a smudge of India ink on the heel of his right hand.

Kate took a long bath, but the India ink on her hands and under her fingernails was as indelible as the ink that stained

Phideaux. The bath did have a therapeutic benefit, though, because the hot water seemed to leech away some of Kate's anger. Kate knew how desperate a mother could be; she felt the same desperation about Angela that Fangs felt with R.J. She could justify almost anything if there was a chance it would help Angela.

She and Jessie watched cartoons until Sam and Angela came home from school. Then all four of them played Chutes & Ladders and Candyland. Kate noticed that Sam moved his playing piece backwards a couple of times, purposely losing a game so Angela could win. It saddened her to think that even the younger children deferred to Angela.

Kate watched as Angela intensely moved her playing piece, determined to reach the finish line before anybody else. There was so much hostility inside Angela, but there was nothing that Kate could do to heal Angela of her anger and frustration. Fangs must feel equally desperate about R.J. No wonder Fangs had deceived Kate and Lissa, just to get R.J. in the co-op.

The doorbell rang, and Kate pushed herself up from the living room floor to answer it. She looked outside the glass window in the door, but nobody stood on the front step. Then she looked down. There stood the last person she wanted to see — R.J. Stevenson, big as life.

Of course Fangs had sent him to apologize. If the culprit were Jessie, Kate would have sent Jessie over to Fangs's house with the same well-rehearsed apology that she was about to hear from R.J. The least she could do was listen.

When Kate opened the door, R.J. pulled a hand from behind his back and thrust a bouquet of daffodils into her hand. Instead of cutting the flowers, R.J. had obviously pulled them straight from the ground. Strands of roots and clumps of bulb clung to the soil at the base of the stems. The daffodils had given their all to make this bouquet. Somebody's garden had a bare spot that wasn't there a few moments ago.

R.J. smiled his sunniest smile. "Hi, Sister Carbine. These are for you."

"Thank you, R.J." Kate smiled encouragingly, waiting for the apology. Then, when R.J. stood silently on the porch, she added, "Didn't you have something you wanted to say?"

"Not particularly," said R.J. "I saw these flowers and thought of you."

"Then your mother didn't send you over here?"

"No. She isn't home. I'm supposed to be home with Boffo, but I knew you'd want these flowers. Aren't they pretty?"

"They are pretty," said Kate, "but there's something I'd rather have from you than flowers. I hoped you'd come to tell me you were sorry."

"Sorry for what?" R.J.'s voice was so cold that Kate shivered. "*I* didn't do anything to Phideaux. Boffo did it. You said it yourself: 'Boffo hates Phideaux. He's been torturing Phideaux all year long.'"

So R.J. was an eavesdropper, too. He had heard Fangs's kitchen confession, and still he expected Kate to believe his innocence. His brazenness infuriated Kate. She reached down and snatched R.J.'s right hand. She held it up to the light and pointed to the blotches of India ink. "I suppose Boffo put those ink stains there," she said.

"He must have done it somehow," R.J. agreed placidly. "*I* don't know how they got there."

Kate dropped R.J.'s hand. "That's a convenient lapse of memory. You know, R.J., you aren't as smart as you think you are. If you had pretended to be sorry, you might have taken me in."

R.J. squeezed tears from the corners of his eyes. They were real tears, but not tears of repentance. R.J. was angry that Kate had believed Fangs's story instead of his.

"I didn't do anything *wrong*," he said. "I'm not going to be sorry if I didn't do anything wrong. You're just like my mother. You'll believe anything bad about me. I don't like you anymore."

He turned on his heel and walked partway down the front steps before he stopped and turned back to Kate. "Anyway," he said, "they were *your* daffodils. I took 'em from your yard." He flashed a triumphant smile at Kate before turning toward home.

Kate shut the door behind her. She threw the daffodils in the trash and washed soil and chlorophyll stains from the palms of her hands. She played another game of Candyland with the children, viciously taking out her fury at R.J. on the Candyland board. She only realized how angry she was at game's end, when Jessie yelled, "WOW! MOM WON A GAME! MOM *NEVER* WINS." Sure enough, she had moved the full count on every spin of the spinner, leaving the children in the dust behind her.

Kate was starting dinner in the kitchen when Jessie shouted, "MOM! FANGS IS HERE!" Spatula in hand, she hurried to the living room. Fangs, who was always so composed, looked afraid to see Kate. Kate smiled, and Fangs relaxed.

"I needed to apologize, but I was afraid to come over here," she said. "I wouldn't have gotten the courage, but I had to give you your dinner certificate. Are you speaking to me?"

"As far as I know," Kate said. "To be honest, I'm still a little upset. But I had a long bath this afternoon, and it gave me time to think. I guess I'll survive."

"I'm glad somebody will. Lissa is already back from Provo. Gus's dad's heart attack was a false alarm."

"Does she know about Phideaux?"

Fangs nodded. "I spent the whole afternoon at her house. It was worse than I ever could have imagined."

Kate went to the refrigerator and pulled a Pepsi from the vegetable crisper. She poured it over ice and handed it to Fangs, who took it without comment.

"Martin keeps these on hand for emergencies," she said.

Fangs drained half the glass in one long swallow. "In that case, I might need two of them. Lissa was hysterical. I can't even talk about it, or I'll start crying all over again. She's threatening a lawsuit, and I know she's going to the bishop. If she has her way, I won't be Relief Society president a week from now."

Kate shook her head. "You're overreacting. As tragic as this is, Phideaux is only a cat."

"You're wrong about that. Phideaux was never 'only a cat.' Not to Lissa, at least. Besides, you know as well as I do that Phideaux isn't the issue. I deceived Lissa, and I deceived you."

"That's what hurt me the most — the deception. When I think of all the times I accused Boffo, and how much better I treated R.J., I get sick to my stomach."

Kate pulled a pound of ground beef from the refrigerator and put it in a frying pan to cook. The fat sizzled in the frying pan, and Kate stood back from the stove to keep from getting splattered.

"I do have your dinner certificate," Fangs said. "You earned it."

"Put it on the table. I don't feel like going out tonight. Maybe I'll use it another time."

She stirred the ground beef in silence. When it was evenly browned, she drained it in a colander in the sink. Finally she said, "What are you going to do about work tomorrow?"

"I'd forgotten all about going to work. I guess I'll call in sick. I'll have to find someone to take care of the boys three days a week, and I can't do that overnight."

"I'd be glad to watch Boffo, but you're on your own with R.J."

"He wouldn't hurt Jessie, you know." Fangs's voice was hopeful. "R.J. is a coward. He only hurts things that can't fight back."

Kate studied her thumb, following the line of India ink that made a moon-shaped mark under the nail. "I *know* he wouldn't hurt Jessie," she said quietly. "He couldn't hurt her if he wanted to: I wouldn't let him out of my sight long enough for him to touch her. But I'm so angry with R.J. that I want to tear him apart. I don't trust myself with him. You don't want him over here."

Fangs sighed. "I'll have the counseling center recommend someone," she said. "If you're serious about Boffo, though, I'd like to hire you to take care of him. Boffo's crazy about you. Sometimes I think you're a better mother to him than I am. He'd be crushed if he had to go anywhere else."

Kate got another Pepsi from the refrigerator and filled Fangs's empty glass. Then she pulled a fresh glass from the cupboard and poured a Pepsi for herself. She needed a Pepsi as much as Fangs did. It had been a terrible day. She still felt guilty for falsely accusing Boffo — not just today, but ever since things had started going wrong in September.

"I'll be glad to take care of Boffo," she said. "Don't worry about the money: I'm as crazy about him as he is about me."

Fangs smiled. It was her first real smile since the afternoon, and Kate's anger melted. Nevertheless, she couldn't forgive herself so easily. Her affection for Boffo wasn't the only reason she wanted to take care of him again. Somehow, Kate had to prove she was worthy of Boffo's love and his forgiveness. She could hardly wait to see Boffo tomorrow.

Kate made a casserole with the ground beef. Then she set the casserole aside and ordered pizza for Martin and the kids. When the pizza arrived, she put aluminum foil over the casserole dish and carried the casserole to Lissa's house. She had a condolence call to make.

She stood at the front door for a long time before Lissa answered. Lissa's cheeks were blotchy and red from crying. She looked ten years older than she had just a few hours ago. To Kate's relief, she opened the door instead of slamming it in her face.

"It's you," she said tonelessly. "I'm just glad it's not Fangs. I don't want to see her again — ever. I've never hated anybody as much as I hate Fangs right now."

"I brought you a casserole." Kate held out the casserole dish. "I'm not much of a cook, but you and Gus will need to eat."

"Gus isn't here," Lissa said. "He's still in Provo with his father. I was supposed to be there too, but I had the most terrible feeling. I knew something was wrong with Phideaux."

Kate took the casserole inside and put it on the kitchen counter. Lissa sank into a kitchen chair and put her head in her hands.

"Did you *see* Phideaux? Did you see what that little monster *did* to him?"

"I was there, Lissa. I left him on Fangs's bed while I answered the phone. I should have let the phone ring, but the kids were all the way across the house. I didn't know anything could happen in just a few minutes. It's partly my fault. I never should have turned my back."

"You didn't know. How could you? Fangs didn't tell us. I am so *angry*. See? My hands are trembling." Lissa held out her hand, and the fingers shook like autumn leaves.

"Where's Phideaux? I want to tell him how sorry I am."

"He's on my bed. I took him to the animal hospital, and they gave him a pill to calm him down. I took a pill, too. It didn't help."

Lissa led the way to Phideaux, tip-toeing all the way across the house. Kate tip-toed, too. It was an easy enough thing to do for Lissa.

Lissa pushed open the bedroom door. There, limned by the dim illumination of a night-light, lay Phideaux, fast asleep. His squashed face, outlined in black, looked wide awake even in slumber. Thanks to R.J.'s artwork, Phideaux looked animated at last.

"I'd like to pet him," Kate said.

"Phideaux would like that. He knows how much you love him. He knows you're his friend."

So Kate petted Phideaux — not for Phideaux's sake, but for Lissa's. She scratched Phideaux under his comatose chin and stroked his matted black fur. "Good Phideaux," she said, rubbing him behind the ears. "We'll take care of you. I know you'll get better real soon."

Phideaux didn't awaken from his drugged sleep, but when Kate straightened up to leave, she saw Lissa smile. Kate didn't say another word. Tip-toeing from the room, she left Lissa alone with her beloved cat.

Chapter 19

On a Sunday morning in April, Kate's relationship with Angela finally bottomed out. The catalyst was a pink striped dress, which Angela decided to wear to church. Correction: Angela *had* to wear her pink striped dress to church. The world would end if Angela went to church in anything but her pink striped dress.

Scarcely a half hour before Sacrament Meeting, Angela reached in her closet to get her pink striped dress, only to learn the dress wasn't in her closet. Angela dealt with the situation the same way she always faced a crisis. "Mom! MOM!"

Kate, who had half her hair wound up in electric rollers, made a face at the bathroom mirror. She desperately wanted to finish the job of curling her hair. Otherwise, half her hair would be four inches longer than the other half during church. She continued rolling her hair, waiting for Angela to come to her.

Then: "MOM!" It was a screech of the damned. Kate burned herself on a hot curler. She put the roller back on its metal frame and went next door to Angela's room, sucking her scorched fingertip.

"What's the problem, Angela?"

Angela glared at her accusingly. "Where's my pink striped dress?" she demanded. "I *need* my pink striped dress."

"You don't need it today," Kate said. "Your pink striped dress is stained with grape juice. Remember? Last Sunday you drank grape juice in your pink dress when you got home from church. I had to take the dress to the cleaner's. I haven't picked it up yet."

Angela howled.

"I'm sorry," Kate said, not sorry at all. "I told you to change your clothes before you ate anything. You didn't do it. Now the dress is at the cleaner's. You'll have to wear something else."

Angela sat on the floor. "I'm not going to church," she said. "I was going to wear my pink dress, and it isn't here. You should have picked it up."

"You *are* going to church. We're leaving in twenty minutes. I'm going to finish my hair. Find something else to wear."

Sucking her burned fingertip, Kate returned to the bathroom and the electric curlers. Immediately, she burned the finger even worse when she picked up another hot roller with wet skin. At this point, Kate didn't care if Angela stayed home from church. Angela could run away to Mongolia, and Kate would wave goodbye at the door.

Then the doorbell rang. Kate heard Jessie stampede to the door. "WHAT ARE YOU DOING HERE?" she yelled. "IT'S SUMDAY."

"*I* know that." The voice belonged to Boffo. "I've come to live here. I'm movin' in."

Kate unplugged the electric rollers and took the curlers from the curled half of her hair. She looked like half a Shirley Temple, but it couldn't be helped. Boffo needed her attention.

She went to the front door, holding her bathrobe shut with her uninjured hand. Feigning surprise, she said, "Well, Boffo? What brings you here?"

"I'm movin' in," said Boffo. "Where's my room?"

Martin appeared from the kitchen. He stood in the hallway, watching the scene. Angela, wearing her white slip but no dress, hid behind him. With Sam and Jessie and Kate at the door, Boffo had commandeered a full house.

Kate waited for Martin to say something, but he only grinned. Kate scowled at him. Kneeling down to Boffo's height, she put her hands on his shoulders. "We don't have a room for you," she said. "You live next door. Jessie and Angela and Sam live here."

"*I* know that," Boffo said patiently. "Now I'm going to live here. Where's my room?"

"You can have my room," said Angela. "I'll go live at your house."

Boffo shook loose from Kate's hold. He pushed Martin and Angela aside as he ran toward Angela's room to stake out his territory. Kate rose to her feet. She put two fingers in her mouth and whistled like a drill sergeant, stopping Boffo in his tracks. "Hold on there," she said. "You can't just trade houses."

"Why not?" said Angela.

"Why not?" said Martin. "Maybe the best thing all around would be for Boffo and Angela to trade for a few days."

"I want to trade *forever*," Angela said.

"Me, too." Boffo's agreement was whole-hearted.

"Maybe that can be arranged," Martin agreed. "Boffo, you go home and go to church with your family. Angela, here, will go to church with us. After meetings, we'll talk to your parents and see if they want to trade. If they agree, you can move in."

"IS BOFFO GONNA BE MY BROTHER?" Jessie shouted.

Martin shrugged. "Maybe so. Would you like that?"

"Neato!" said Sam. "Then we'll have *two* boys."

Boffo pushed his way past Angela and Martin and ran home. With another "Neato!" from Sam, all three children disappeared to get ready for church. Even Angela scurried down the hall to her closet, the pink dress forgotten. Kate was left alone in the living room, staring dumbfounded at Martin.

"What in the world were you saying?" she asked. "You don't just trade children."

"Angela and Boffo don't know that. I say, let them trade. After a few days, they'll be so homesick they'll plead to trade back again. This could be exactly what Angela needs."

Apparently, Angela thought so, too. She reappeared in a dress that was neither pink nor striped, as happy as Kate had ever seen her. "I'm going to live with Fangs," she announced.

"Maybe." Martin's shrug was non-committal.

"What makes you think Fangs wants to live with *you?*" asked Kate. "You aren't exactly fun to have around."

"I will be for Fangs. Fangs likes me, and I like her. She isn't grouchy like you are."

"Don't get your hopes up," said Martin. "Fangs hasn't agreed to this yet."

But Angela only smirked. She knew better. She kept smirking all during Sacrament Meeting and the opening exercises of Sunday School. As long as she was in the same chapel as Fangs, she sat up straight and smiled in Fangs's direction, trying hard to make a good impression. Fangs couldn't help but like Angela as much as Angela liked her.

As soon as meetings were over and everyone was home for the afternoon, Boffo appeared at the Carbines' house.

"Mom wants Angela to watch me while you go over there," he announced.

"Where's R.J.?" Angela asked.

Boffo shrugged. "He doesn't come here anymore. This is *my* house. Can you watch me?"

"Sure." Angela smiled cheerfully, almost as if Fangs could see her from next door. "Do you want to play Candyland? That's a fun game."

"If I can win," Boffo said.

"ME, TOO," yelled Jessie. "I WANNA WIN, TOO!"

"Okay." That cheerful voice *couldn't* be coming from Angela, but it was Angela who hopped right up and went to get the Candyland game. Kate and Martin watched until all four children were settled on the floor. Then they took the fateful walk next door to Fangs's house.

Fangs's husband Rob took charge of the meeting. That was odd because Rob was home so seldom that Kate thought of Fangs as unmarried. As often as Kate saw Fangs, their visits were always church-related, or co-op related, or neighbor-related. Martin and Kate weren't part of the Stevensons' social circuit, and Kate saw so little of Rob that she felt uncomfortable calling him by his first name.

"Boffo says you want to trade children with us," he said. "Is this an across-the-board trade, or is it just Boffo you want?"

"We don't *want* Boffo," Kate said. "We don't want either of your children."

"Boffo thinks otherwise. He seems to think he can move in this afternoon. He hasn't been so excited since Christmas."

"I don't know why he'd want to live with us," Kate persisted. "It's *your* home that's perfect."

"Obviously, Boffo doesn't agree," Martin said.

Kate nodded in puzzlement. Obviously, Boffo *didn't* think his home was as perfect as Kate did. Of course, it couldn't be easy living in the same house as R.J. *That* was it. Boffo didn't want to live with the Carbines as much as he wanted to escape his brother.

Martin continued, "On the other hand, Rob, Angela wants to live with Fangs and you. I think we should give Boffo *and* Angela exactly what they want."

"I see what you mean," Fangs said. "We'll make Angela's life so miserable that she'll want to go home."

Martin shook his head. "I don't think we'll even have to do it on purpose. Just treat her normally, and we'll do the same with Boffo. Homesickness will do the rest. Boffo and Angela have both been looking for greener pastures ever since Thanksgiving. If we don't let them cross the fence, they'll never see how green the grass is in their own yards."

"I agree," said Fangs.

"Let's do it," said Rob.

Everyone looked at Kate. It would be such a good idea, if R.J. weren't in the picture. R.J. changed the equation.

"What about R.J.?" she asked. "R.J. won't hurt Angela, will he?"

Fangs sighed. "Despite what you think, Kate, R.J. isn't a rattlesnake. He doesn't hurt people. He may cut holes in Angela's clothes or tear her doll apart, but so what? She'll get homesick all the faster. R.J. won't be a problem. In fact, without Boffo here to blame for his mischief, he might even behave. What do you think?"

"Are you *sure* this is going to work?"

"Frankly, no," said Martin. "It can't hurt, though. I'm willing to give it a try. Kate?"

Kate nodded. "Let's do it now. I've got Sunday dinner to cook. Besides, if we don't do it now, I'll change my mind."

With Martin and Fangs and Rob trailing behind her, she marched resolutely home. She threw open the door, and four pairs of eyes stared up at her from the Candyland board.

"We did it," she said. "We traded Angela for Boffo."

"Neato!" said Sam.

"WOW!" shouted Jessie.

"Hot dog!" cried Boffo.

"YAY!" screamed Angela. Jumping to her feet, she stepped over the Candyland board and tugged on Martin's sleeve. "Dad, help me take my stuff over. I want to move *right now.*"

"Don't you want a good-bye dinner with the family?" Kate asked.

Angela rolled her eyes. "Of *course* not. If I wanted to eat here, I wouldn't be moving next door."

Kate clenched her fists. An argument wouldn't help now. "Very well, then. It was nice knowing you. But you're talking to the wrong dad. Brother Stevenson is your father now. Your *old* Dad will help *Boffo* move."

"Okay." Angela accepted the correction placidly. She turned to Rob and gave him her friendliest smile. "New Dad," she asked, "will you help me take my things to our house?"

Boffo didn't even wait for Rob to answer. Without giving his parents a second glance, he tugged on Kate's skirt. "Sister Carbine?" he asked.

Kate looked directly at Angela. "You can call me Mom," she said. "You're my little boy now."

"Wow! Does that mean I can eat here?"

"*Eat* here? You *live* here. What would you like for dinner?"

"Bubspetti," Boffo said. "Do you got any of that?"

Kate looked skyward, pretending to consider. Spaghetti was Angela's favorite meal, too. She liked spaghetti with garlic bread, and chocolate chip cookies for dessert.

"Let's see," she said. "We were going to have pork chops, but we can have those tomorrow. I think we can arrange spaghetti and garlic bread. If you're real good, we could make some cookies later. How about chocolate chip?"

"Wow!"

Angela glared, and Kate smiled sweetly back at her. "I'd better get to work," she said to nobody in particular. "I don't want my three children getting hungry."

Leaving everyone else to move Angela out and Boffo in, she went to the kitchen and put the pork chops back in the refrigerator. The petty act of revenge felt good.

Dinner progressed normally. Boffo spilled spaghetti all down his front just as Angela would have done, but the advantage of Boffo was that Boffo was washable. Where Angela would have dropped spaghetti all over her clothes, Boffo dropped it all over his person. There were benefits to raising naked children.

When dinner was over, Boffo picked up his plate and silverware. "Where do you want these to go?" he asked.

"The kitchen counter will be fine." Kate suppressed a cheer. No Carbine child had ever taken a plate to the kitchen except under threat of death. Boffo was looking better all the time.

A few hours later, Kate felt a momentary twinge of regret. She was lying asleep on the sofa when she was awakened by shouting children.

"DON'T FLUSH! DON'T FLUSH!"

"But he ain't swimmin'!" That was Boffo.

"*Wait* a minute," Sam cried. "Maybe he'll come up on his own."

Boffo shouted, "DO somethin'! I think he's gonna drown."

Boffo was being Boffo, Kate thought. Catastrophe loomed. Groggily, she sat up on the sofa. Then she remembered Hamlet, Jessie's birthday hamster. She fervently hoped Boffo hadn't put Hamlet in the toilet.

Then she heard a flushing sound. Instantly awake, Kate bounded from the sofa and ran to the bathroom. Pushing all three children aside, she thrust her hand into the toilet — and retrieved the lavender love bug from Home Shopping Club, Clarabell's treasured Christmas present to Kate.

The love bug had seen better days. In fact, the fuzzy creature had probably hopped its last. The red satin heart bled dye onto Kate's hand. The crimson pigment ran down her arm and dripped off at the elbow like blood gushing from a mortal wound. As Kate held the love bug, its six churning legs ground to a halt.

"Who did this?" Kate thundered, knowing full well that Boffo was the culprit.

But it was Sam who hung his head. "I did," he said.

"He did!" Boffo agreed. "He put the bug in the potty. He wanted to watch it swim."

"IT DROWNDED," Jessie yelled, "BUT YOU SAVED HIM."

"I think the love bug is beyond saving," Kate said. "Step aside. I need to put him in the garbage can."

"Can't I keep him?" Boffo asked.

"Hardly. We don't keep things that swim in the toilet." She held the bug over the garbage can and let go. It fell into a bed of wadded Kleenexes and used toilet paper rolls, where it leeched dye onto the rest of the garbage.

"BYE, BUG!" Jessie yelled. "I'LL VISIT YOU LATER." Brushing her hands together as if to bid good riddance to the love bug, she led Boffo and Sam to different adventures.

Other than the death of the love bug, Sunday progressed smoothly. The children helped Kate make chocolate chip cookies after supper. Then everyone watched *Old Yeller* on videotape. All three children cried at the end, but Boffo sobbed uncontrollably. As Kate took him into her arms to comfort him, she marveled once again at how tender-hearted Boffo was. Angela never shed a tear in public, but Boffo cried openly. He was such a sensitive child that Kate couldn't help but love him.

When all three children were tucked into bed, she put dishes in the dishwasher and picked up toys from the carpets and the bathtub. She bent over to throw away the bathroom garbage, but it was gone. Monday was garbage day, and Martin had already bagged the upstairs trash. So much for bidding farewell to Clarabell's love bug. Yawning, Kate shuffled downstairs.

Martin was bagging the downstairs garbage when Kate climbed into bed. He gave her the thumbs-up sign. "Well, we survived Day One. How do you feel?"

"Miserable," said Kate.

Martin raised his eyebrows. "*That's* a surprise. I thought that not having Angela at your throat would make you feel great."

"That's the problem. I don't miss her at all. I'm *worried* about her, sure. But I should *miss* her, shouldn't I? I'm her *mother*."

"I didn't miss her, either, and I'm her father. It was peaceful around here today. Nobody fought. Nobody whined. Maybe we can make the trade permanent."

Kate glared.

"Relax. I was only kidding. Still, I've never seen one of *our* children take his plate to the kitchen after dinner the way Boffo did. Think of this as a vacation from Angela — and a vacation for her from you. Don't feel guilty. She'll be home soon enough. She may even be home tomorrow."

But she wasn't. Angela didn't even call on Monday, or on Tuesday or Wednesday, either. None of the children mentioned Angela's name, and that was disturbing. *Somebody* should have missed Angela. Somebody should have wanted her home.

If Angela was happy in her new environment, Boffo was ecstatic. He didn't even look out the window toward his old house. As far as Boffo was concerned, his former life had vanished.

As the days passed, Kate's guilt compounded. She called Fangs on Tuesday night, long after she knew Angela would be asleep. Fangs was less than reassuring.

"Things are *fine* here," she said. "We haven't had any problems. Of course, I *am* having to teach Angela to clean up after herself, but she'll catch on."

Kate ignored the reproach in Fangs's voice. "Is Angela homesick yet?" she asked hopefully.

Fangs paused. "She seems okay to me."

"That wasn't what I wanted to hear."

"I'm sorry to disappoint you," said Fangs. "Give her a little time."

Kate didn't have that much time. A million years wouldn't be long enough for Angela to like Kate better than she already liked Fangs.

On Thursday morning, Kate parked Jessie and Boffo in front of the television while she set up a fish pond in the kitchen. It was *F* week again. Kate had a sackful of trinkets to put on Jessie and Boffo's fishhooks when they dropped their lines behind a designated kitchen chair. Lunch would be Fritos and finger sandwiches, but not tunafish sandwiches. *F* week or not, no fish salad would pass Boffo's lips.

The phone rang. Kate, sprawled on the floor with the fish pond, glared evilly up at the ringing telephone. When it kept ringing despite her stare, she dusted herself off and picked up the receiver.

"Mom?"

Kate's heart jumped. "Angela? Why are you calling? You're supposed to be in school."

"I *am* in school," Angela said in a little voice. "I'm sick."

Kate's first impulse was to get in the car and bring Angela home, but she stopped before making the offer. One wrong move would ruin everything. Angela had chosen Fangs to be her mother; Fangs was the person Angela had to call. It took all the self-control she had, but she said, "I'm sorry to hear you're sick, but you're calling the wrong person. Fangs is your mother now. Do you want her phone number?"

"Fangs knows I'm sick," Angela protested. "She made me go to school anyway. She says she's too busy to have a sick kid at home. Will you pick me up?"

"I thought I wasn't your mother anymore," Kate said.

"Mom. Mommy. I need you."

Angela hadn't called Kate Mommy in five years. Kate's resolve crumbled. "I'll pick you up," she said. "Of course I'll pick you up."

Kate gathered up Boffo and Jessie and herded them into the station wagon. Ignoring the posted speed limits, she hurried to the school and parked illegally in front of the building. With Boffo and Jessie trailing behind her, she went to the nurse's station to find Angela.

As soon as Kate saw Angela, anger welled up within her. This wasn't just a case of the sniffles. Angela was red with fever, and her eyes were glazed. Fangs never should have let Angela get out of bed, much less go to school.

"You look barfy," Boffo said.

Angela groaned.

"Don't talk to her, Boffo. She doesn't feel good. Angela, can you walk out to the car?"

Angela nodded.

Putting her arm around Angela's shoulder, Kate half-carried her out to the car. She tucked all three children inside the station wagon, shooing Jessie and Boffo to the back seat so Angela could have the front. Angela drew up her legs into a fetal position and huddled against the car door.

Kate stopped at the supermarket on the way home and bought crackers and pineapple juice and lemon sherbet — Angela's sick foods. Angela waited patiently for Kate in the station wagon while Kate and the other two children did the shopping.

When Kate returned with the sackful of food, Angela said, "Will you be my mother again?"

Kate started the car and got the car on the road before she answered. Finally she said, "I thought you wanted Fangs to be your mother."

"Not anymore. She doesn't care about anything. She never even came to my room to visit me."

"If I remember, you don't like visitors. You keep your bedroom door shut to keep people out."

Angela looked away. "I used to. Maybe I don't anymore. Besides, Fangs is never home. She's always doing Relief Society things, or doctor things, or cleaning the house. She never has time for me. She acts like I'm her slave. I have to wash my own clothes and put all my dishes in the sink. I have to make my bed, too — every day. *Even* today. I want to come home now. I want to live with you."

As Kate pulled into the driveway, Boffo unlatched his seat belt and scampered to the front seat of the car. He lodged himself firmly between Kate and Angela. As soon as Kate turned off the ignition, he squirmed into Kate's lap.

"What about me?" he demanded.

"What *about* you?" Kate asked.

Boffo threw his arms around Kate's neck. "She can't come home," he cried. "She don't live here anymore. She goes to my *old* mom and dad."

Kate opened the door of the station wagon. She put her arms around Boffo and slid off the car seat. When she stood, she was carrying him next to her breast.

"I love you as much as if you were my own little boy," she said, "but Angela belongs here. You know that. If Angela wants to come home, you'll have to go to your other house to live."

Boffo slipped to the ground. "No fair!" he whimpered. "You said I could stay here. I don't wanna go home. Don't you want to keep me? I'll be good."

Boffo ran ahead of everyone else. He opened the front door and ran to Angela's room. Drawers slid open and slammed shut, and a chair fell over with a clatter. He appeared in the kitchen as Kate was setting the grocery sack on the counter. He was dressed in a pair of shorts, which he had pulled on backwards in his haste.

"See? If I wear clothes, can I stay here?"

Kate put her arms around Boffo. "I'm glad to see you're wearing clothes," she said. "You look so handsome in those shorts, and you put them on all by yourself. But don't you think your mom and dad will be sad if Angela comes home and you stay here too?"

"Don't care," Boffo said stubbornly. "I wanna stay *here*."

"Your mom will let you watch cartoons," Kate countered. *There* was a bargaining chip.

But again, Boffo surprised her. "That's okay," he said. "I don't hafta watch cartoons. I've seen 'em all anyway."

"I'll talk to your mom when she gets home," Kate said. "Until then, stay away from Angela. I'm going to put her in your room to sleep. She's sick, you know. She might be contagious."

"Okay," Boffo said forlornly. His shoulders slumped and he went back to the living room, where he stared sightlessly at the television. Kate had seen fear in his eyes — fear that Kate would send Boffo home.

Kate fed some children's Tylenol to Angela and tucked her in bed. Then she returned to Jessie and Boffo, trying to salvage *F* week. It was hopeless. The fish pond was a total disaster. Jessie fished enthusiastically, clapping her hands in delight at every treasure she hooked, but Boffo stoutly refused to touch his fishing pole. He had no interest in the trinkets Kate had carefully chosen at Pic 'n' Save. Instead he found a corner and sat there as if Kate had punished him. Faced with imminent doom, Boffo sat cross-legged for hours. His only movements were occasional tugs at the fabric of his shorts, as Boffo tried to make his body's confinement more bearable.

Boffo ate lunch in the corner, refusing to move from his self-imposed exile. Kate and Jessie made a picnic on the floor next to him, pretending that he wasn't eating his Fritos with his back to them. Jessie tried everything she could to cheer her friend. She finally put her arm around him and shouted, "POOOOOR BOFFO!" Boffo solemnly nodded his head in agreement, but he didn't move from the corner.

As vitality drained from Boffo, Angela slowly improved. She thanked Kate for every favor. She never complained that Kate had brought her crackers instead of sherbet, or that Kate used the flowered bowls instead of bowls with birds on them. She never blamed Kate for her illness or complained that Jessie was making too much noise in the living room. It was too early to tell for sure, but Kate's preliminary diagnosis was that flu had cured Angela of all her other ailments.

Everything would have been perfect, if it weren't for Boffo. Kate waited impatiently for Fangs to come home from work. She and Fangs needed to talk.

When Fangs's car drove into the driveway, Kate picked up Boffo from the corner and kissed him. "We're going to go downstairs and watch a movie," she said. "You can lie on my bed and watch the movie with Jessie. Doesn't that sound fun?"

"I dunno," Boffo said dully.

"Well, it *will* be fun. Don't you think so, Jessie?"

"YEAH! CAN WE WATCH *DUMBO?*"

"I think that can be arranged, if that's what Boffo wants to watch. Boffo?"

Boffo risked a half-hearted smile. "Can we go right to the part where he flies?" he asked. "*That's* the part I like."

"Yep," said Kate, in her best Boffo voice. Cradling Boffo with one arm, she pulled down the covers of her waterbed with her free hand and tossed Boffo on the mattress. Jessie jumped on the bed beside him, and Kate wrapped both children in the bedspread. She found the *Dumbo* tape and fast-forwarded it to the appropriate spot. Boffo watched the tape despite himself, and Kate retreated upstairs to call Fangs.

"I need to talk to you," she said.

"Now? I was just on my way to the French bakery. If I don't get there soon, they'll be out of the good stuff."

"Forget the French bakery," Kate said. "We have a problem. Angela got homesick."

"That's a problem? It's what we planned. Angela and Boffo would switch, they'd get homesick, and then they'd go home."

"You don't understand," said Kate. "Boffo doesn't want to go home." Quickly she amended, "That is, Boffo doesn't want to go home *yet*. The timing's wrong. We should have known that Angela would get homesick before Boffo. She's a girl."

Fangs sighed. "Being a girl has nothing to do with it, I'm afraid. Boffo will never want to come home. I should have known that from the start. We'll have to talk about it another time, though. I'm sorry, but I *have* to get to the French bakery."

"You don't *have* to go anywhere," Kate said, but she was speaking to a dead receiver. Fangs had already hung up the phone.

Angela coughed weakly from her bedroom, and Kate's anger overflowed. Kate had her own shortcomings, but at least she would never send a sick child to school. Angela should never have gotten out of bed this morning, but Fangs had pushed her out the door without a second thought. French bread was more important to Fangs than Angela was.

Slamming the door behind her, Kate ran outside and stood behind Fangs's car, blocking the driveway. Fangs, who had already started the engine, motioned Kate out of the way. Kate stood firm, and Fangs turned off the ignition and opened the car door.

"Do we have to talk about this *now?*"

"We sure do. *Forget* the French bakery. I want to know why you sent Angela to school today. You could see she was sick. That wasn't part of the deal. You weren't supposed to treat Angela any worse than you would have treated Boffo."

"I didn't." Fangs's eyes widened. "R.J.'s just as sick as Angela is, and he's at the counseling center. Don't *yell* at me. What *else* could I do? I had to go to work."

"Was it that important, Fangs?"

"There's nobody there to replace me."

"There's nobody to replace you at home, either."

Fangs slowly got out of the car. Leaving the door open and the ignition buzzer humming like an angry hornet, she leaned against the trunk of the car and folded her arms in front of her chest. She looked off in the distance, away from Kate. Then, quietly, she said, "Kate, when I told you about R.J., I only told you half the story. I told you about R.J., but I didn't tell you about me."

She rubbed her eyes with a hand and shook her head. Then she said, "The staff at R.J.'s counseling center do a better job of mothering him than I do, and Angela's teacher can take better care of her than I would. I don't have the genes to be a good mother. That's why I sent Angela to school."

"You're a horrible liar, Fangs. You know you're a better mother than I am. You just don't give a damn about any children but your own."

"That's not true!"

Kate saw the tears in Fangs's eyes, but she was unmoved. Fangs wasn't sorry she had abused Angela; she was only sorry she had been caught.

Fangs sniffed and rubbed her left eye with the back of her hand. "I'll tell you the truth, then," she said. "You're right — I *don't* give a damn about Angela. *But I don't care about my own children, either.*"

Kate sank against the car, dumbfounded. This *couldn't* be Fangs talking. Fangs was the perfect mother. *Kate* was the one who didn't care.

At last, that was what Kate said. "You're the perfect mother, Fangs. I've known that from the day I met you."

"I'm not a perfect mother. In fact, I'm not a mother at all."

"You have two children, Fangs. Of course you're a mother."

Fangs shook her head. "Giving birth doesn't make you a mother. Any adoptive parent can tell you that giving birth is the least of it. It's what you do after the children are here that matters. *That's* what I don't know how to do."

Fangs stood quietly for a moment, rocking the heels of her hands on the trunk of the car. Then she said, "Everyone is given certain gifts, whether they be gifts of healing or of prophecy or of motherhood. It's a gift, just like a gift for singing, to have the gift of motherhood — the ability to love children and communicate with them and be comfortable with them. I don't have that gift."

"It doesn't come naturally. You have to practice."

"As a matter of fact, a good part of it *does* come naturally to most women. There are bonding hormones released during childbirth. Some mothers don't get the hormones. No matter how hard they try, they never learn how to love their children. I'm one of those mothers.

"I didn't always understand that," Fangs continued. "At first I thought that once I had a child, I'd automatically know how to care for him. I didn't. When R.J. turned out the way he did, I was sure it was my fault. It's taken me a long time to see that R.J. was born the way he is, just as I was born the way I was. Both of us will be handicapped all our lives. But you'll never understand that. You were born to be a mother."

Kate opened her mouth to protest. Then she shut it again. It wasn't any use. Fangs didn't know her at all. Fangs didn't know that Kate struggled just as hard as Fangs did, and failed just as miserably. There was only one difference between the two of them

— as rotten a mother as Kate was, she would never send a sick child to school.

"I wish I'd never had children," Fangs said miserably.

"Then why did you do it?"

"Why does *anyone* do it? With some people, it's their passion. They think of themselves as mothers, not as people, and they reproduce like bunnies. You know women like that. Other women have children to strengthen their marriage, or to make a family like the one they grew up in. There are dozens of reasons. I did it for the church. I couldn't imagine being a Mormon and not having children."

"Lissa doesn't have children."

"Lissa didn't have a choice. In this culture, if you *can* have babies, you *do*. I was afraid there wouldn't be a place for me in the church if I didn't have children."

"That's nonsense," Kate said. "Everybody's different. There's a place for all of us."

"I know that now. In my own case, I was born to be a Relief Society president. I don't miss a birth or a death or a menstrual period of anyone in the ward. After I'm released as ward Relief Society president, I can see me serving as stake Relief Society president until I'm sixty. But I can't see myself going to my grandchildren's piano recitals, or their baseball games. It's not that those things aren't important; on the contrary, they're probably *more* important than being a good Relief Society president. It's just that being a mother or a grandmother isn't what I was put here to do."

"So you're just going to ignore your children and hope they raise themselves. Fangs, you've seen Joanna Fries and her family. They're a mess. Her kids haven't adjusted to Cleanway, and your kids aren't going to adjust to you. They need you, whether you want to be a mother or not."

"I know that," Fangs said. "And believe me, I do the best I can. But they can tell. Why do you suppose Boffo wanted to live with you? Despite what you may think, he wasn't just getting away from R.J. The greatest blessing of my life is that Rob was born to be a father. He isn't home very often, but my kids know he loves them more than anything else in the world. Rob is the glue that keeps our family together. I thank God for him every day of my life."

Kate laughed softly. "I envied you so much," she said.

"Why would you envy *me?*"

"I thought you'd done everything right. You're so beautiful. Your house is always clean. Everything is so *organized.* I thought you were the happiest person in the world. If I could have traded places with you, I would have done it without ever looking back."

Fangs only laughed. Kate politely waited for her to stop. Instead, the laughter turned to tears. Kate discreetly looked away while Fangs dried her eyes.

Still crying and laughing, Fangs said, "And all this time, I wanted to trade places with *you.* You and your alphabet weeks. Boffo never wanted to come home from your house. He asked me to do alphabet weeks, but I was too embarrassed that it was your idea and not mine.

"If you want to pattern your life after mine," she continued, "tell Martin to get a promotion. I spend more than two hundred dollars every week seeing a psychiatrist. I don't think Martin could swing it on his salary."

Kate swallowed. Fangs looked back at her. Then Fangs lowered her gaze. "Thanks for staring at me like that. You're making me feel *so* glad I confided in you."

"I'm sorry," Kate said. "I didn't mean to stare. It's just that I thought you were so well adjusted."

"I am — in every area of my life but motherhood. In that, I'm a colossal failure. It's never going to get better, Kate; I know that now. That's why I'm going back to work full-time."

Again Kate stared. Then, realizing she was staring, she looked away.

"Everyone says that mothers belong in the home," Fangs said. "Maybe we do. But some of us can stay home until our children are in college and still not do it right. I love my children enough to know I'm not the best person to take care of them."

Kate asked, "If you don't, who will?"

"I'm not going to leave them in the streets. R.J. will have to start school next year. Until then, I've arranged for him to be in a day care program through the counseling center. They know his problems, and they're qualified to help him if anyone can."

"And Boffo?"

"Boffo is special. The first time I held him in my arms, I could sense how different he was. Boffo was given the gift of loving. That gift is so strong that even being my child hasn't dulled it — yet. But I don't want to ruin him. I want him to spend his days with someone who's as loving as he is. I want him to stay here with you."

"With *me?*"

"Who could be better? You've been talking about getting a job all year, and this is the perfect job for you. I want you to take care of Boffo while I'm at work. I want you to keep love alive inside him."

"I'll do it," Kate said.

"Don't you want to think about it? I haven't even told you what I'm willing to pay."

"I don't care. Boffo's almost a part of the family. I wouldn't want him going anywhere else."

Fangs smiled. "That solves one problem, anyway. Now, all we have to do is get him to come back home with me. I don't know what to tell him. Rob could do this so easily, but I don't know what to say. Where *is* Boffo, anyway?"

"He's downstairs watching *Dumbo*. And believe it or not, last time I saw him, he was wearing clothes. Come inside the house with me. I think I can bring him up."

Leaving Fangs in the living room, Kate sprinted down the stairs to the basement. Jessie was absorbed in the movie, but Boffo sprang to attention as soon as she entered the room. She sat down on the edge of the bed and put her arm around Boffo's shoulder. Boffo looked up at her warily.

"Boffo, do you know what a compromise is?"

"Nope."

"I didn't think so. It's a pretty big word. In fact, it's a *grown-up* word. A compromise is when you do something to make everybody happy. You want everyone to be happy, don't you?"

Boffo hesitated for a moment. Then he nodded. "Yep."

"I'm glad you do," Kate said. "I want everybody to be happy, too. Now let's see — what would make you happy?"

Boffo got straight to the heart of the matter: "I wanna stay *here*."

"That's good," said Kate. "I want you to stay here, too, so we both want the same thing. But Angela wants to stay here, too."

Boffo's lower lip began to stick out.

"Hold on," Kate said. "You don't need to pout. I told you — we're going to try to make you happy. We've already talked about you and me and Angela. Let's think about your mom and dad for a minute. Now, what do you suppose would make your mom and dad happy?"

"I dunno." Boffo's voice was sullen.

"Well, I happen to know they'd be very sad if you weren't their little boy anymore."

Boffo's lower lip protruded even farther. "But I wanna stay *here*."

"I know you do," Kate said. "Now we get to the compromise. How about if you come over and play with me every day, and then go home to your house at night?"

"Not just Tuesdays and Fursdays?" Boffo asked.

"No. Mondays and Tuesdays and Wednesdays and Thursdays *and* Fridays. How would you like that?"

Boffo sucked in his lower lip. He bit on the flesh of his lip for a moment as if he were looking for a catch. Then he exhaled in a long breath, blowing the shaggy yellow hair from his eyes. "If I do it, will you do the letters?"

Kate sighed. She saw a succession of alphabet weeks that stretched forth until the moment Boffo entered first grade. "Aren't you *tired* of the alphabet weeks?" she asked hopefully.

"Nope."

"Then I'll do the letters. Do we have a deal?"

"Yep."

Kate held out her hand to shake, and Boffo slapped her fingertips with his own tiny hand. Then he held his own hand open while Kate slapped his fingertips in return.

"Boffo, you're a good compromiser, but now it's time for you to go home. Your mom's in the living room. She misses you a whole lot. Why don't we go upstairs together, and you can give her a big hug. Then she can take you home."

"Okay," said Boffo agreeably. He held out his hand to Kate. Pulling her behind him, he scampered the stairs to the living room. Then he dropped Kate's hand and ran to his mother. He threw his arms around Fangs's neck and hugged her. Fangs looked so surprised and pleased that Kate felt tears sting her eyes.

"I can go home now," Boffo said. "Cartoons are on at home."

"They sure are," said Fangs. She picked him up and tossed him in the air. She caught him in her arms and carried him to the front door.

Kate held the front door open when Fangs and Boffo left. Smiling, she shut the door behind them. Despite her misgivings, exchanging Angela for Boffo had been an inspired idea. Kate and Angela had wiped the slate clean between them. For the first time in years, Kate knew that she and Angela could one day be friends.

But there was an even greater blessing, Kate realized. Fangs was right — being a mother was what Kate had been born to do. Kate had been so anxious to find a career that she ignored the truth: For *her*, the career she was supposed to have was within the walls of her home. It had taken Fangs, who couldn't be a mother, to teach Kate what motherhood was all about.

Martin had been right about moving to Farley Street. There had been a purpose for coming here. As Kate went to the kitchen to pour Angela a glass of pineapple juice, she smiled. The bungalow had never looked so beautiful to her.

Chapter 20

Lissa planned the ward Mother's Day program with the same single-mindedness as when she had orchestrated Phideaux's birthday party. From the script to the announcements to the decorations in the chapel, everything was meticulously planned and replanned. If Lissa could have gotten away with it, she would have gone to each child's house and chosen an outfit from his or her closet. She compromised by taking a curling iron to church so she could groom the children whose hair had wilted during Sacrament meeting.

As Mother's Day approached, Lissa trekked to Kate's house several times a week, bearing a blanket-wrapped Phideaux to keep her company as she and Kate went over the details of the program. Phideaux's hair was slow growing back. He hadn't had a luxurious coat at all — only a thick one. The individual strands were wispy and weak, and the stubble of his pelt looked like a military haircut on a balding man.

Lissa always kept Phideaux with her when they came to visit. She set him in her lap, and he burrowed his face into her stomach. Phideaux evidently believed that if he couldn't see people, no one could see him. Thus, he hid. Every noise that Jessie and Boffo made caused his tail to twitch nervously until the commotion died down. Phideaux's nerves healed as slowly as his fur grew back.

On the Friday before Mother's Day, Lissa drove the short distance between her house and Kate's. Her car was packed with a picnic lunch and a checklist, as well as the ubiquitous blanket-wrapped Phideaux.

"I've brought a lunch to celebrate," she said, bringing in the picnic basket on her first trip inside Kate's house. "We're so close to the end now that I wanted to thank you for all you've done to help."

Kate took the picnic basket and peeked inside. There were ham salad sandwiches on croissants, purple grapes, and a plastic container of sesame noodles. There was also a bottle of carbonated apple juice — the Mormon equivalent of champagne. "This was worth the work," she said. "That is, it would have been if I'd *done* any work. You've done all the planning. All I've done is hold your hand."

"That's exactly what you're going to continue to do. On Sunday, when all those horrid little children are standing at the front of the church and there's nothing else I can do, your hand will be my life preserver."

Lissa returned to the car to fetch Phideaux. As she bore him inside she petted him atop his grizzled head, but she didn't croon at him the way she usually did. She wore a look of consternation.

Leaving Lissa to brood, Kate fixed plates for Jessie and Boffo and set out a towel in the living room, making a picnic for them in front of the television. Daffy Duck would keep the children occupied while she and Lissa talked about the Mother's Day program.

Only after Boffo and Jessie were settled did Kate set the table for herself and Lissa. Popping the plastic cork on the carbonated apple juice, she poured juice into two tall glasses. She put two cubes of ice in each glass to chill the drink. Lissa pulled the ice from her own glass with a thumb and forefinger and threw the ice in the sink. She settled back in her chair with a heavy sigh.

"I can have a baby if I want to," she said.

Kate pulled the grapes from the picnic basket and set them in a bowl on the table. Settling on a kitchen chair, she took a sip of apple juice and waited for Lissa to continue.

"We have an attorney friend, Christian Fordham. You may know him — he lives in the other ward. He called us on Tuesday and said he has a baby for us to adopt. He says it's a blue chip baby. The mother's a college student who wants her baby raised in the church."

Kate raised her glass. "That's wonderful!" she said. "I guess this *is* a celebration."

"Is it? Then why don't I feel right about it? I've been praying about this for three days, and all I get is confusion. I've been wanting a baby all my life. Now that I can have one, I don't know if I should take it."

Kate put a reassuring hand on Lissa's arm. "It's just pre-baby jitters. We all get them."

"Not like this. I've spent all my life preparing for motherhood. I've bought baby clothes ever since I was in high school. I have baby toys coming out my ears. I have a room all furnished as a nursery, and I have a whole library of 'name the baby' books. But now that I *can* be a mother, I don't know if I'm *supposed* to be one. The more I pray, the more I feel that adopting a baby is wrong for me. I never expected this reaction."

"What does Gus think?" Kate asked.

"He's the one who wanted to adopt in the first place, but now he's just as unsure as I am. He doesn't want us to be alone when we're old — I know that. But he doesn't *like* children. Ideally, he'd like the children to show up full-grown when we're sixty and thinking of retirement. Right now, he wants our life to be just the way it is."

Kate smiled. "You have time to decide, you know. Babies take nine months to be born."

"This baby's already *had* nine months. It's due next week. If we don't decide by tomorrow, Christian is going to give him to somebody else. He says he has a feeling that this baby belongs to us. If *he* does, why don't *we*?"

Kate squeezed Lissa's arm. "I'm sure he means well, but your lawyer isn't the head of your family. He isn't entitled to have inspiration for you. Don't adopt a baby because *he* has a feeling about it. Adopt a baby because *you* have a feeling, or *don't* adopt a baby if you don't get the feeling."

"It's not that easy," Lissa said. "You don't know what it's *like*, being childless in the church. People don't intend to hurt me, but they constantly point out that I'm different from them. Every time there's a church lesson or a talk on parenthood, some idiot takes a few minutes to tell everyone that the poor childless people will have their children in the next life. I feel like a German shepherd having a bone thrown at him. They make me feel as if the only reason I was born was to reproduce, and if I *can't* reproduce, I might as well jump off a bridge."

Kate furrowed her brow. That sounded like the kind of stupid remark that she herself would make. She hoped she had never done it.

"Is it true?" Lissa asked. "Am I going to have babies in the next life?"

"You're asking the wrong person, Lissa. I don't know any more about the next life than you do. I've heard a lot of people say it, but it isn't doctrine. Not that I know of, anyway."

"That's my point. Unless I adopt this baby, I may *never* have children — not in this life, and not in the next one. If I don't say yes now, I may never have another chance. Then I'll go childless throughout eternity."

As often as Kate herself had wished she weren't a mother, she should have been able to offer Lissa some words of comfort. Instead, she felt unbelievably sorry for Lissa, and the emotion surprised her. There were so many good things about being childless, and part of Kate still wished she had never had children. But she couldn't bring herself to say that to Lissa. Lissa would never believe it.

Finally she mustered the courage to ask, "Would it be so bad to never have children?"

Lissa's eyes widened. "I've been debating that ever since the co-op started. Maybe I'm defective, but I'm starting to think that I don't have a need for babies. Kids drive me crazy. I like them fine, for as long as an hour at a time. If it's more than that, they wear me out so much that it's not worth the effort."

Kate started to speak, but Lissa held up a hand for silence. "I know what you're going to tell me," she said. "'You'd feel different if they were yours.' I've heard *that* song and dance before. I even believed it, at first. It's taken me all year to accept that I may not have a talent for children. Not everybody does, you know."

Kate thought of Fangs and nodded.

"If God made me childless, He had a reason. I need to find out what that reason was."

"Maybe the only reason was that your plumbing doesn't work."

"I'm not ruling that out," Lissa agreed. "If that's the only thing standing in my way, maybe we *should* adopt. But what if there's *another* reason? Maybe there's something else I was put on earth to do. If I adopt this baby and I'm not supposed to, I could ruin everything."

Lissa picked a grape off its stem and actually peeled it, discarding the skin on her luncheon plate. She popped it in her mouth and sucked the juice from it before swallowing it whole.

"Can I ask you a question?" she said. "Do *you* think I should adopt this baby?"

Kate shrugged. "That's not for me to say. I know one thing, though: If you *are*, you'll get the first birth announcement. God will tell you directly, or tell Gus directly — *not* your attorney. He doesn't work through a middleman."

Lissa smiled briefly. Then she chewed the inside of her cheek for a moment, contemplating.

"It could be that your failure to get an answer is an answer in itself," Kate continued. "You could be right, after all; maybe you're not supposed to *have* children. Besides, even if you're supposed to adopt, this isn't the only baby in the world. If you don't take this one, there will be another baby you *do* feel good about adopting. You'll know when the time's right."

Lissa smiled. "I think I will. You've made sense about one thing: We can't adopt now just because Christian feels inspired. I guess I'll do some more praying and see if I can find an answer on my own."

She stroked Phideaux between the ears and leaned over, making kissing noises with her lips. Phideaux looked up for a moment before burrowing his face into Lissa's stomach again.

Lissa reached into the picnic basket. Drawing out a ham salad sandwich, she said, "I feel better than I have all week. I knew you'd help me. You always do. Now it's time to eat. I'm starving, and I *can tell* Phideaux's hungry, too. He's been waiting *so patiently* for his picnic, haven't you, Sweetheart? I made the croissants myself. I hope you like them. They're Phideaux's special favorites, and Phideaux has an excellent palate."

Kate meant to call Lissa on Saturday, but life intervened. Clarabell came down with a case of the shingles, and Kate spent the day at her bedside. She forgot all about Lissa and the adoption, and she put the Mother's Day program right out of her mind. She even forgot about Mother's Day, remembering only when she overheard whisperings between Martin and Angela at bedtime. Secrets were in the works. Kate smiled as she wondered how Martin and Angela planned to surprise her.

The surprise was that there was a surprise before the day even dawned. Mother's Day began with an unscheduled visit from Jessie, who crawled in bed with Martin and Kate shortly after two A.M.

"I'M SICK," she announced, sounding more proud of herself than ill. As Kate reached over to feel Jessie's forehead, Jessie threw up a puddle of fried chicken on the bed between Kate and Martin.

"Yech!" Martin leapt out of bed as though he had splattered by battery acid. "Jessie, why did you do that *here?*"

Kate peeled off Jessie's nightgown and thrust Jessie into Martin's arms. "You hold her." As Martin held Jessie at arm's length, Kate stripped the bed and put the soiled bedclothes in the washing machine. After washing her own hands, she found clean sheets and blankets and pillow cases for the bed.

Finally clean again, she took Jessie into bed with her. Jessie smiled cheerfully, and Kate felt her forehead. No fever. Jessie wasn't sick; she had only disagreed with her dinner. Things could have been worse.

"I FREW UP," Jessie chirped. Settling herself in the crook of Kate's arm, she almost immediately fell asleep.

Angela's Mother's Day contribution arrived less than six hours later. After a fitful night's rest, Kate finally fell into a deep slumber shortly after seven o'clock. She was sleeping dreamlessly when someone shook her shoulder.

"What?" She hoped Martin didn't want *that*. Not when Kate was so sound asleep.

"Happy Mother's Day," Angela said.

Kate, whose face was mashed into her pillow, opened one eye. The first thing she saw was Jessie, whose eyeball was less than three inches from her own.

"SHE'S AWAKE!" Jessie yelled. Then, to Kate, she added, "YOU SLEEP WITH YOUR TONGUE HANGING OUT. YOUR PILLOW'S ALL WET AND DROOLY."

"Thanks for the tip," Kate said. Pushing herself off the damp pillow, she struggled into a sitting position. It was then that she saw Angela, standing next to the bed with a breakfast tray. The aroma of breakfast filled the room. Kate smelled eggs, and her stomach knotted. Although Kate fed her family eggs all the time, she seldom ate them herself. Her stomach was never awake enough for eggs until it was too late in the day to eat them.

She yawned. Trying to look pleased, she said, "What a nice surprise! I was starving."

Angela beamed.

Angela's breakfast was a sumptuous one. There was orange juice, straight from the can. No one had told Angela that frozen orange juice had to be diluted with water. There was cold toast. Angela had obviously made the toast first and set it aside, buttering it only after all the heat had escaped. There was bacon, too — bacon so raw that it could have been slapped on a pig's backside for skin grafts. The fat in the bacon was still white, not having been cooked long enough to turn translucent.

"WOW!" yelled Jessie. "LOOK AT THE FOOD! CAN I HAVE SOME?"

"Sure," Kate said. If she shared the food with everyone, she wouldn't have to eat more than a bite or two.

Moving at the speed of light, Angela stuck a hand between Jessie and the breakfast tray. "Not today. This is Mother's Day. You'll have to get your own breakfast."

"OKAY," yelled Jessie companionably. She scooted off the bed and ran upstairs, leaving Kate to face breakfast on her own. Kate smiled broadly at Angela, who puffed out her chest and grinned. Still unable to face the bacon, Kate ate both slices of toast. Angela watched every bite, smiling proudly.

Then Kate had an idea. "This is so much food I'd like to share it with you. Let's have breakfast in bed together."

"Not today." Angela shook her head solemnly. "This is your Mother's Day breakfast. I made it all for you."

Kate smiled bravely. Ignoring the bacon, she inspected the scrambled eggs. They looked okay, as far as eggs were concerned. They were overdone rather than undercooked. She took a big bite.

And spit it out again. Angela's eyes widened in dismay.

"Are there shells?" Angela asked. "I *tried* to get the shells out."

"No shells. Angela, did you wash the pan before you cooked the eggs?"

Angela nodded. "It still had chicken grease in it from last night. I threw the grease down the sink and washed the pan with Comet."

"Did you rinse the pan out after you washed it?"

Angela shrugged miserably. "I think so. I don't remember."

Kate wadded up the paper towel that Angela had given her for a napkin. She moistened the towel with orange juice and used the wet wad to scrub off her tongue. She remembered to grimace dramatically as she cleaned the Comet from her mouth. Angela rewarded the theatrics with giggles, her disappointment forgotten.

A shout from the kitchen rescued Kate. It was Jessie.

"MOM! MOM! THE SINK'S OVERFLOWING! HELP!"

Angela's discarded chicken grease saved Kate's life. In the hubbub of running upstairs to bail out the sink, even Angela forgot the Mother's Day breakfast that she had so lovingly prepared.

The rest of Mother's Day was predictable. Martin gave her a bouquet of daisies; Sam gave her a miniature Tonka truck that he'd bought with his own allowance. Kate put the flowers on the dining room table, adding a few fronds of Boston fern from a plant in the kitchen to provide extra greenery to the bouquet. Then she admired the Tonka trunk just long enough to make Sam feel proud before she returned the truck to him for safekeeping.

After Sacrament Meeting, Kate stood in the Primary room and straightened little boys' ties while Lissa wielded the curling iron. Then they relinquished control over the program to the Primary workers who marched the children into the choir seats.

Kate and Lissa found seats on the first row of the chapel. Even though the program was completely out of Lissa's hands, she seemed to find some comfort in the idea of being at the forefront of things. If an earthquake swallowed the children before they said their appointed lines, Lissa could step right up to the podium and fill the gap.

"Who's the little boy in the *suit?*" she hissed, as Kate pulled her skirt down around her knees and settled down in the pew.

Half the little boys in the choir seats wore suits, but Kate looked obligingly in the direction Lissa indicated and immediately spotted the suit that had caught her attention. It was a child's suit, just like any other. Short pants. Jacket. But nobody's head peeked out of the collar, because the jacket had been pulled up and buttoned over the head of the wearer. All that was visible was a tuft of yellow hair — that and a fuzzy lavender football that the child carried in a hand that stuck out below the jacket.

If Kate hadn't recognized the yellow hair, she would have immediately known Boffo from the fuzzy lavender football. It was the Home Shopping Club love bug, which Boffo had apparently resurrected from its grave in the bathroom garbage can. Red dye from the satin "I Love You" heart had stained the lavender body of the love bug, and the orange feet hung limply from the torso. Boffo held it like a talisman.

Kate watched helplessly as a Primary teacher tried to pull the coat down over Boffo's shoulders. Boffo slugged her in midsection with the love bug, and the Primary teacher retreated.

After an opening prayer, the youngsters started singing. Kate saw Angela standing in the middle section, obediently following the chorister. Jessie was easy to spot, because she screeched louder than anyone else in the choir. Sam, however, had apparently reached the age where singing was no longer cool. Instead of singing, he and Stevie Fenton hopped from leg to leg, changing feet with every downbeat like hyperactive flamingoes. Kate tried to frown at Sam, and she pointed a stern finger at him. Sam was so busy watching the chorister for his signals to hop to the other foot that he didn't see Kate in the audience. She lowered her finger and enjoyed the show.

Before the song ended, loud sobs from the front row of children diverted the audience's attention from Stevie and Sam. One of the Sunbeams stopped her howling long enough to elbow the girl next to her and make *her* start crying.

"What started *that?*" Lissa hissed. A Primary teacher pulled the two girls apart, but their combined volume only increased.

"Who knows? Don't worry, Lissa. *All* Primary programs are like this. If the kids didn't act up, it wouldn't be fun."

"I just hope they follow the script."

"Don't worry. If they don't, nobody will care."

"*I'll* care," Lissa said indignantly. "I worked *hard* on this program."

Kate put her arm around Lissa. "Everyone knows that. Look at the parents smile! Everything is going fine."

Sure enough, the program calmed down after that. It was hard, of course, to smile benignly as R.J. narrated the program. The Primary president had picked him as the star of the show over Lissa's strenuous objections. He narrated the program clearly, not even missing a syllable.

"Isn't he a *precious* little boy?" Kate turned slowly to see that the speaker was a blue-haired grandmother in a huge orchid corsage.

"And he's so *young*," whispered the white-haired woman sitting next to her. "He's not even in school yet, you know. He's just as smart as a whip, and so *polite*. I wish *my* grandchildren were just like him."

Kate put her hand on Lissa's arm to keep herself from clenching her fists. She couldn't blame other people for failing to see what had taken her nearly a whole school year to understand. Instead she concentrated on her own children in the choir seats, hoping that the sheer force of her will would keep Sam's fingers away from his nose.

Sam recited the scripture he had rehearsed all week, saying the words flawlessly even if he did have a finger up one nostril at the time.

It was Jessie who stole the show, however. She was the fourth of six children whose task it was to tell the audience why she loved her mother. Like Sam, Jessie had rehearsed all week. Her chosen line was, "I LOVE MY MOTHER BECAUSE SHE LETS ME WATCH CARTOONS." They weren't the words Kate wanted on her tombstone, but they were good enough.

But Jessie was moved by inspiration. When she opened her mouth, she shouted, "I LOVE MY MOM BECAUSE HER TONGUE HANGS OUT WHEN SHE SLEEPS. SOMETIMES SHE DROOLS."

Kate sank into the bench, hoping the laughing audience couldn't spot her. Lissa patted her hand sympathetically.

Angela had only one line, "Mothers make our houses happy." She smiled as she said it, and Kate beamed.

Even though Lissa had written Angela's line, Kate knew that Angela's words were true. Kate's house *was* happy. Even more important, her *life* was happy. Suddenly Kate understood that motherhood was more than her career; it was her joy. Her life had been enriched by Jessie and Sam and even Angela. She couldn't imagine living without them. Wiping a tear from her cheek, she put her hand through Lissa's elbow and squeezed her arm gently.

Now, for the first time, she understood the agony that Lissa had suffered all these many years.

At last the program ended. The Young Women passed out African violets to the mothers, each plant in its own ceramic pot. Lissa had made all the pots herself, and Kate was glad to take a flower. When the flowers were passed out, however, Lissa only shook her head and refused to take one for herself.

"I take it you got your answer," Kate said.

"I never did get an answer," said Lissa. "Gus agreed with you, though — if you don't get an answer, that means no. I can't tell you how relieved I am."

Kate looked deep into Lissa's goldfish eyes. Lissa spoke the truth. She was at peace with her decision. Kate was at least happy for that.

"I've been so wrong," Lissa said. "I thought that we couldn't be a family without children. Now I see that Gus and I were a family all along. And Phideaux, of course. He's all the baby we need."

Kate fingered a fuzzy leaf of her Mother's Day violet. She needed more than that, she knew now, but there were different answers for different people. Lissa hadn't chosen her path, but she had finally accepted the role that life had chosen for her. God would find another way to give Lissa joy.

When the postlude music began, Kate saw someone making her way down the aisle toward her. It was Lizbet Appleton, who had been to church almost every week since the day she confessed to Kate over the telephone. Lizbet had her own pot of violets, and she thrust them into Kate's hand.

"I already got my flowers," Kate said, holding her violets aloft.

Lizbet shook her head. "Those violets came from the ward. *These* violets are from me. Happy Mother's Day, Kate. I hope you have a wonderful day."

Kate didn't even get a chance to answer before Lizbet was pushed aside by Jessie, who detoured down the aisle on her way to Primary.

"HI, MOM!" she screamed. "HOW DID I DO?"

"You did fine, Jessie. I was *so* proud of you."

Jessie climbed on the bench and leaned over to kiss Kate on the mouth. For the millionth time since Angela was born, Kate wondered what children did with their lips to make them so sticky all the time. Jessie kissed Kate a second time, and a third.

"HAPPY MOTHER'S DAY, MOM!" she yelled. She patted Kate over and over on the cheek.

"Yes," said Lissa. "I forgot. Happy Mother's Day."

"Thanks," Kate said. "It *is* a happy Mother's Day. It's the happiest Mother's Day ever."

Sitting on the front row of the chapel, with the members of her new ward around her, Kate forgot the messy sheets of last night and the miserable breakfast of this morning. She forgot that she had ever wanted to go back to San Francisco. This was home now, and the Church members in this chapel were family to her.

Putting her arms around Jessie, Kate realized she wouldn't trade places with Lissa or Fangs, or anyone who lived in California. All along, God had known Kate better than she knew herself. Despite all her protests and all her complaining, He had given her exactly the life she had always wanted.

— 7 March 1991
Sterling, Virginia

About the Author

Orson Scott Card made me write this "about the author" piece. He has a crazy idea that the people who read my books have a passionate craving to learn every nasty detail about me — what's my shoe size and how many fillings I have in my teeth. I think Scott's brain has been pickled from too many caffeine-free diet Cokes. The people who read my books barely have time to make it through the chapters. They're too busy living their own lives to read about mine.

But Scott pays the bills, so I'll answer his questions. In order, they are nine and one. My shoe size is nine, and I have one filling in my mouth. The one filling spans all my teeth, since my mouth is solid metal.

I am also larger than any of the continents except Asia.

I have a husband, Clark, who fantasizes about a telephone call from Ed McMahon. He already has the money spent.

There are no children, with the exception of Clark. It's just as well we don't have children, as I do not clean house.

I am a Relief Society spiritual living teacher in the Sterling North Ward in Sterling, Virginia, a calling I attained because everyone in the congregation sat in shock until it was too late to vote against me. I am also a visiting teacher, which I do poorly, and a home teacher, which I do infinitely better. I think husbands and wives should always home teach as couples. Clark and I do home teaching better than we do anything else.

As for hobbies, Clark does a great job with stained glass. My most outstanding talent is that I can write more legibly backward than forward. (On a chalkboard, I can write passably well upside-down.) I used to draw, and I used to do ceramics. Now I only write (and complain about having to write).

Our other hobby was watching *Twin Peaks* on television. The world ended the day *Twin Peaks* was canceled. It was a dream that Clark and I shared to write a book about the series. Judging by the number of people who watched *Twin Peaks* to the bitter end, the book would have sold thirteen copies.

Since the *Twin Peaks* book has been abandoned, other writing projects take precedence. I am writing a science fiction trilogy with Orson Scott Card, which is a lot of fun to create. I'm also writing a series of young adult novels based on the New Testament, called *Young Disciples*, which are being published by Hatrack River Publications. The New Testament series is causing me to study the life of Christ, and I'm glad for the opportunity.

Other books on the horizon for the Mormon audience include the *Paradise Vue* sequels *Paradise, Too* and *Return to Paradise*, and a book about singles in the church, *Spite and Malice*. I also spent seven miserable months of my life writing and rewriting another book, *Atlas Music*, which may never be published because it isn't funny. Mormons evidently don't buy depressing books.

For spending money, I write political fund-raising letters for various organizations. Recipients of my letters unkindly call my works of art "junk mail," and the odds are pretty good that you've thrown away a letter I have written.

People who have read *Paradise Vue* write to me with two questions. First, they want to know if I'm Amy. The answer is no. Even though Amy was a childless, artistic slob, we shared nothing else in common. Readers think I'm Amy because I wrote the book in first person, which I did because it was (and is) the easiest way for me to write. One reason I'm enjoying the science fiction trilogy so much is that it, too, is written in first person. When the first book of the trilogy, *Lovelock*, is published, people will undoubtedly ask if the narrator, who is a four-pound capuchin monkey, is supposed to be me.

The other thing *Paradise Vue* readers want to know is which ward was the *real* Paradise Vue. Dozens of people have told me they know exactly which ward I used as a pattern for the ward in my book. Then they go on to tell me the names of the people who were *really* Bess and Alex and Emma. The only problem is, they're all wrong. I've never even been to Alaska, I don't know anyone in Pennsylvania, and I've never been to church in Texas or Arizona or South Carolina. And if the Paradise Vue ward were based on the wards I allegedly inhabited in Salt Lake City, Clark and I would have had to move every two months during the eleven years we lived in Salt Lake to live in every ward. We couldn't sell *one* house in Salt Lake City, much less sixty-six of them.

So if anyone tells you they know exactly who is Emma or Alex or Bess, you have the author's permission to smirk. There are evidently hundreds of Besses and Alexes and Emmas facing their own personal crises all over the church. The *real* Alex or Emma or Bess is whichever one you visualized when you read *Paradise Vue*.

As for *The Alphabet Year*, I don't appear in that book, either. I'm not Lissa, and I don't know a Boffo or own a Phideaux. I wrote *The Alphabet Year* because, as a person who never reproduced, I decided I was the best qualified to write a book about what everyone but myself could do.

I do owe thanks to the friends and relatives who told me horror stories that happened to their own children. With their permission, I stole some of the things their children had said and put them in Jessie's ninety-decibel mouth.